T0246549

Praise for the Nora Barnes and Toby Sandler Mystery series

Murder in Lascaux

"A whodunit that nicely balances a breezily light travelogue with urgency and suspense. Readers will hope this is the first of a series."

—*Publishers Weekly*

"This densely written and marvelously detailed excursion through the Dordogne will leave you dreaming of castles, châteaus, and caves."

—*Library Journal*, Starred Review, "Mystery Debut of the Month"

"With a colorful mélange of art, French history, food, and a surprising perp, this tale will keep readers entertained (and entice them to visit southwestern France)."

—*Booklist*

"Some fascinating French history—and prehistory—is layered into the plot. . . . Skillfully blend[s] a travelogue with an intriguing mystery."

—*France Today*

The Body in Bodega Bay

"If you're a fan of Alfred Hitchcock's *The Birds*, you will thoroughly enjoy this murder mystery."

—*Mystery Scene*

"Nail[s] the vibe and history of . . . the Sonoma County coast. Antiques dealer Toby Sandler teams with his art historian wife, Nora Barnes, to help solve a murder and art theft."

—*Sacramento Bee*

"Betsy Draine and Michael Hinden must be having a wonderful time researching and writing their mystery series. It certainly is a lot of fun reading their books."

—*The Capital Times*

Death on a Starry Night

"Nora and Toby are utterly delightful. . . . Mystery devotees who want an atmospheric crime novel with an art history slant . . . will enjoy this series." —*Library Journal*

"Into the mix of personalities, the authors weave in tantalizing snippets of letters written by Isabelle's grandfather about his acquaintance with the extremely moody and vulnerable Van Gogh in 1890. The result is an entertaining whodunit." —*Alfred Hitchcock Mystery Magazine*

"A rich and colorful novel that sometimes seems almost as real as the history it's based upon. . . . Readers who cherish France, fine dining, classic art or simply a smart mystery will find plenty to enthrall them." —*Isthmus*

"Highly recommended." —*Midwest Book Review*

The Dead of Achill Island

"An engrossing mystery, all nicely wrapped in an Irish travelogue." —*Publishers Weekly*

"A compelling novel that should please fans of the series and attract a new legion of readers, really anyone who enjoys a charming, classical mystery novel well told with a droll wit, compulsive readability, intelligence, and charm. Nora and Toby's banter is delightful. I'd love to have this couple as friends!" —Michael Norman, author of *Haunted Heartland*

"I . . . savor[ed] the story and let my imagination walk the Achill hills and beach with Nora, Toby and the Barnes family." —*Mesabi Daily News*

"A mystery lover's treat from beginning to end." —Aaron Elkins, Edgar Award winner for lifetime achievement

The Bones of Bascom Hall

A Nora Barnes
and
Toby Sandler Mystery

Betsy Draine and Michael Hinden

The University of Wisconsin Press

The University of Wisconsin Press
728 State Street, Suite 443
Madison, Wisconsin 53706
uwpress.wisc.edu

Copyright © 2024
The Board of Regents of the University of Wisconsin System
All rights reserved. Except in the case of brief quotations embedded in critical articles and reviews, no part of this publication may be reproduced, stored in a retrieval system, transmitted in any format or by any means—digital, electronic, mechanical, photocopying, recording, or otherwise—or conveyed via the Internet or a website without written permission of the University of Wisconsin Press. Rights inquiries should be directed to rights@uwpress.wisc.edu.

Printed in the United States of America

Library of Congress Cataloging-in-Publication Data

Names: Draine, Betsy, 1945– author. | Hinden, Michael, author.
Title: The bones of Bascom Hall / Betsy Draine and Michael Hinden.
Description: Madison, Wisconsin : The University of Wisconsin Press, 2024. |
Series: A Nora Barnes and Toby Sandler mystery
Identifiers: LCCN 2024014091 | ISBN 9780299349745 (paperback)
Subjects: LCSH: Barnes, Nora (Fictitious character)—Fiction. | Sandler, Toby (Fictitious character)—
Fiction. | University of Wisconsin—Madison—Fiction. | LCGFT: Detective and mystery fiction. | Novels.
Classification: LCC PS3604.R343 B66 2024 | DDC 813/.6—dc23/eng/20240408
LC record available at https://lccn.loc.gov/2024014091

This is a work of fiction. All names, characters, and incidents are either products of
the authors' imagination or are used fictitiously.

To our colleagues in English, ILS, and
Women's Studies

And to the institution that put a roof
over all our heads.

The Bones of Bascom Hall

1

IT STARTED WITH A WHOOSH. One minute the speaker was nearing the climax of his remarks; the next, he was holding on to the lectern with white knuckles as a deluge of water slammed down from above, raining debris and almost sweeping him off the stage. He fell to one knee, then rolled over the edge and came to rest like a mendicant at the feet of the VIPs who were seated in the first row. Toby and I were sitting near the back, where visitors, staff, and latecomers clustered. All during the speech there had been hoots and catcalls from disgruntled faculty in rows ahead of us. University police lined the lecture hall, but no one had anticipated a finale like this. So much water! It continued to splash over the lip of the stage as people started for the exits, glancing up apprehensively.

It was the summer of 2018, and we were in the grand lecture hall next to the rotunda on the second floor of Bascom Hall at the University of

Wisconsin–Madison. The old building houses the chancellor's office, and, with its sandstone facade and white neoclassical columns framing the entrance, it serves as the campus icon. When the university is in the news, a photo of Bascom usually runs with the story. It was sure to make the TV news that night.

The speaker was J. Millard Reynolds, a fertilizer magnate and controversial member of the Board of Regents. Standing at the podium, Regent Reynolds was Wisconsin-stocky, gray-haired, and gifted with a booming voice. With a hand raised to heaven, he bellowed that the university must revise its curriculum to better serve the interests of the state. "In these uncertain economic times," he argued, "the liberal arts, especially the humanities, are luxuries the state cannot afford. Wisconsin parents want job training for their sons and daughters, not courses that stir up agitation or encourage navel-gazing."

His main gripe was against the humanities faculty: "Professors call it 'research' when what they do is sit at home all day, reading and looking out the window. They talk about 'the search for truth,' but what have they come up with? As far as I can tell, nothing but meaningless disputes. Why should the hardworking taxpayer be asked to fund the idle speculations of pampered professors?"

His voice rose, his fist shook the air. "Let those who wish to, donate to support the humanities, as they do with public television. But don't depend on funding from the state. What we need from the university is greater accountability—to the voters, to the taxpayers, and to the job creators!"

It was just then that the floodgates opened above the regent's head and a torrent of water knocked him off his feet. Now he lay on the floor, insensate, soaked and bedraggled. Several of the pampered professors rushed to his aid. One of them shouted for a doctor. Others who had been sitting up front swarmed the small stage, looking up into the darkness, trying to figure out what had happened.

This extraordinary event would trigger an investigation of a mystery that was decades old, an investigation in which I played a part. But at that moment, I was just an outside observer—Nora Barnes, an art history professor from a small liberal arts college in Northern California.

I was in Madison on a faculty exchange. Even so, I felt assailed by the speaker on a personal level. I didn't relish the idea of going from door to door, shaking a tin can in order to fund my art history department. I guess I'd do it if I had to. Thankfully, for all the crazy referendums that Californians are always voting on, the state has stood firm on the value of higher education. In comparison, Wisconsin was looking wobbly.

My best friend from graduate school, Eve Olson, teaches art history at Madison. Her specialty is medieval art; mine is nineteenth-century painting. With the consent of our deans, we had arranged an exchange for the summer session, each of us teaching a course at the other's institution. Eve went to the small school, I to the big one. We even swapped cars and houses, though we drew the line at husbands. Mine, Toby Sandler, was planning to take a short course on Frank Lloyd Wright while he was here and to scout the Wisconsin countryside for antiques. Toby runs an art and antiques gallery back home, in Sonoma County's Russian River Valley.

As soon as Eve suggested the idea, I was for it. It didn't take much to convince Toby, either. I'd been to Madison once before. That was in March at the tail end of winter, when it was still biting cold and walking a few blocks was an endurance test. In summer, though, Madison's a lovely city, surrounded by rich farmland and nestled between two sparkling lakes. The university campus, which lines the south side of the larger lake, is one of the prettiest I've seen. There's no more inviting spot in the academic world than the Union Terrace, where you can sip a local brew from a tall paper cup and watch the sailboats skimming by on Lake Mendota.

However, Eve had more in mind for me than a change of scene. She told me she was hoping to get me hired. There was going to be an opening in her department because of a retirement, and she was eager to bring in someone to direct graduate students with an interest in my field. I'd been noncommittal with her on the phone. I was perfectly content where I was, teaching undergraduates in classes small enough to get to know each student. I'd worked hard, had tenure, and recently had been promoted to full professor. Who could ask for more? Besides, Toby and I loved living by the port in Bodega Bay. Though an offer from a major research institution like Wisconsin would be flattering, I was in no hurry to upend our lives. Eve brushed aside my reservations. She scolded me for settling as a big frog in a small pond. She said I needed a new challenge. There might have been some truth in that. But from a frog's perspective, why risk leaping to a larger pond if you've already found a toasty place in the sun?

Regent Reynolds had stirred up waves in this big academic pond by attacking the university on its first principles. The title of his talk— "Can Wisconsin Really Afford the Search for Truth?"—was intended to provoke. Now the talk had been violently interrupted.

Toby nudged me toward the aisle. He coolly observed, "Telling a roomful of professors to forget about the search for truth was asking for trouble. Still, he had a right to be heard."

I worried that the man could be hurt.

"Oh, he's all right," said Toby, looking over at the speaker, who now was sitting up. "The cops will have their work cut out looking for who's responsible. There must be about two thousand suspects."

"You mean the entire faculty," I said.

"That's right. I don't see students pulling off a stunt like this. I can't figure out where all the water came from. I mean, a couple of angry professors hanging from the rafters dumping a few buckets, that I can imagine. But this is something else. I'm guessing hundreds of gallons pouring down. From where? And how did they get all that water up there? I'd say your new friend has her hands full."

He meant Diane Young, a detective with the UW–Madison Police. She and Eve are close friends. At Eve's request, Diane had picked us up at the airport when we arrived. Since then, she and I had lunched on campus and discovered we both liked to golf. We agreed to play soon. We'd have plenty to talk about now.

I kept my eye on Diane as she and the other officers checked the perimeter of the auditorium. Several were busy shooing away the Good Samaritans and gawkers huddled around the speaker. Then Diane climbed up on the stage, along with two male colleagues. Water dribbled from the ceiling, with much less force than before. The men held big, club-sized flashlights, which they aimed over their heads, scanning the flies. But Diane was staring at the floor, scrutinizing the rubble that littered the stage. Something caught her attention. She reached down and brought up an elongated object with a knobby end. From across the room, it looked like a splintered baseball bat, but Diane knew better. Then more officers started combing the floor. One found a fist-sized object of the same color. Another picked up a piece with a delicate curve.

"A rib," I heard Toby murmur. "Those are bones." And then everyone forgot about Regent Reynolds, who still sat on the floor, wearing a wet mop of gray hair and an expression of bafflement. Following Toby, I left our row and moved closer toward the stage to watch Diane and her team do their job.

That evening, one of the local TV news programs covered the event. A well-scrubbed, whey-faced reporter, who looked about twelve years old, described the scene and played a clip of an interview with the provost, who assumed the flood was some vicious prank. He apologized to the regent on behalf of the university and condemned the interruption of his speech. Nothing was said about who might have been responsible for the prank (if that's what it was) or about the discovery of any bones. The sportscaster bantered with the weatherwoman and closed by forecasting a sweep for the minor-league Madison Mallards.

The next morning, the student newspaper, the *Daily Cardinal*, crowed, "Regent Gets Drowned Out." A brief story followed. The *Wisconsin State Journal*, the city's daily newspaper, had more to say. The headline on the front page read, "Bones Found in Flood of Campus Building." The story was accompanied by a photo of the wet stage and another of the hapless regent looking shaken. The chief of campus police was quoted as saying that bones had been found in the debris, but it was not yet known if they were human. However, they had determined the source of the flood.

I summarized the story in the newspaper, while Toby clung to his second mug of coffee and tried to snap awake. He is not by any measure a morning person. His maxim in defense of sleeping late is that life is too short to keep getting out of bed. Not that he's a slacker. He manages a successful business, partners in a successful marriage, and has lots of interests. As he sees it, none of that requires his attention before 10:00 a.m. Toby slathered a soft pat of butter on an English muffin and slowly munched. "Say again?" he said.

"According to the article," I repeated, "the university police have a theory about the flood."

"Okay. I'm listening."

"It seems that Bascom Hall originally had a rooftop dome to match the one on the State Capitol."

"What happened to it?" asked Toby.

"I'm about to tell you."

Toby put down his cup and waited.

I read aloud: "In 1900, a cistern was installed under the dome to serve as a source of water in case of fire. Made of sheet iron, the storage tank was twenty feet in diameter and fifteen feet high, with a capacity of forty thousand gallons. In 1916, a fire broke out in the wooden dome and destroyed it, but the water in the storage tank saved the building. The burning timbers fell into the tank and were extinguished, preventing the flames from spreading."

"Ah, so there's a water tank in the picture," said Toby.

"And a big one," I said and continued reading: "The dome was never replaced, and the cistern was patched and left where it was, in the attic above the rotunda. The police theorize that over the years the cistern filled with rainwater from an opening in the roof. Then when the tank started to leak, the timber underneath it rotted bit by bit until Friday, when everything came crashing down." I put the paper aside. "So that's where the water came from."

"You mean the whole damn thing was an accident?" asked Toby, incredulous. "It just happened to come down during the regent's speech?"

"That's what it looks like, pure chance."

"Nothing is pure," said Toby. "Besides, the cause might well have been the opposite of chance."

"What's that?" I asked.

"Call it fate, for want of a better term," he said.

"Chance, fate, what's the difference?"

"The difference is that chance is indiscriminate. It can happen to anyone, like bad luck. Fate singles you out. It's when the powers that be have it in for you—you personally."

"I hate when that happens."

Toby refilled his cup. "Example: in Greek tragedy, the gods decree that for his arrogance, Oedipus will kill his father and marry his mother. That's fate. A random person walks under a window ledge on a windy day and gets hit by a flowerpot. That's chance. Instead of the gods, the powers that be are the wind and gravity."

"Well, who or what are the powers that be in this situation?"

Toby shrugged. "How about the Wisconsin League of Humanities Professors?"

"There's no such organization. You just made that up."

"I did, actually. But if we were still living in the classical age, I'd say the Muses. Clio for history. Calliope for poetry, and so forth. They were the goddesses of arts and letters, the humanities. Imagine them having to listen to that fertilizer pooh-bah going on about the liberal arts and spouting his militant ignorance—I should say they'd take offense."

"Militant ignorance?" I hadn't heard that term before.

"I made that one up, too," said Toby. "Because there are two types of ignorance in the world, natural and militant. Natural ignorance is nothing to be ashamed of. We're born to it, and the cure is education. Militant ignorance, on the other hand, is acquired. It's an attitude that says, 'I don't know, I don't care, and I don't want to know.' It's the enemy of education, and we just got a snootful of it."

Toby is a bit of an explainer, and he can turn a phrase. I sometimes think he should have been the academic in the family. Professors get to explain things every day, and by the end of the week, some of us are all talked out. Toby by the weekend has verbal energy to spare.

"'Militant ignorance,' that's good," I said. "You know, I'd like to challenge Regent Reynolds to a debate. I've been making a list of all the reasons why art history is important and worth teaching. Here's point twenty-two: Sometimes art is the only history that's left when a civilization dies, and it survives because the people treasured it. Would you like to hear point twenty-three?"

"Not right now."

"I could go on."

"I know you could." Toby paused. "But what do you suppose a future civilization will think of us? I doubt they'll know us by our art. By our junk is more like it, by the oceans we filled with plastic and the mountains we stuffed with garbage."

"That's a thoroughly depressing thought," I said. "And anyhow we've wandered far afield from the subject. We were talking about the cistern giving way. The consensus seems to be it was an accident."

Toby, who by now was rocking back on a rickety chair with his legs crossed at the ankles, replied, "All right. For argument's sake, let's accept that the flood was an accident. But an accident doesn't begin to explain the bones. Cisterns don't come loaded with them ready to spill out if there's a flood. There was a body in this one, and that means murder."

"Can you drown in a cistern by accident?" I wondered aloud.

"It's hard to see how. Not the way you can drown in a lake in a swimming accident. If you drown in a cistern, it's because somebody put you in it, somebody who wanted you dead."

The conversation left me with goosebumps and unanswered questions. Yet I realized I had to move on. Whether I was ready or not, classes began on Monday. As usual, I'd left much of my preparation to the last minute. I tried to work at the breakfast table but found it impossible to concentrate. The regent's speech kept ringing in my ears. I heard him asking skeptically, "What use are the humanities, art history in particular?" I pictured him sitting in the first row of my class, poisoning the atmosphere, and I wanted to blow him away with an answer.

"You're talking to yourself again," said Toby.

"Okay, you're right." I needed to put all that behind me. With determination, I tried again to review the notes and images for my first presentation. My imagination, though, insisted on revisiting the harrowing scene of the day before—the water crashing down onstage, the discombobulation of the speaker, the hail of bones, the brute fact of death. Annoyed with myself, I picked up my papers, moved to Eve's study, and spent the day working at the desk with only a short break for dinner (cheese omelets with salad and broiled potatoes), which Toby prepared. It was well after midnight by the time I crept into bed.

Toby had stayed up to give me a reassuring hug. "Are you ready for Monday?" he asked.

"I will be by Monday," I said with more hope than certainty.

I awoke on Sunday after a troubled sleep and went downstairs to make breakfast. Toby had left a note that he was out for a walk. It was unusual for him to be up this early. He hadn't slept well, either. I could see he had already made his coffee (there was a dirty mug in the sink), but the morning paper looked unopened. I put the kettle on for tea and glanced at the front page. Now I could tell that Toby had read the paper and carefully refolded it, smoothing out the creases for me. That was thoughtful of him—no one likes to handle a mangled newspaper. This edition carried a follow-up on the incident in Bascom, which I was eager to read. The story reported that the bones discovered onstage were definitely human. A search of the cistern had turned up other bones, almost enough for a complete skeleton. All the bones had been collected and sent to the State Crime Lab for analysis, and the inevitable speculations had begun. Whose bones were these? How had the victim died? How long ago? By whose hand?

The university police were investigating. That was all that was known so far. It was little enough, yet the story was on the front page, and predictably, a photo of the attractive nineteenth-century building, with its serene white columns, was displayed above the fold. The caption read, "The Bones of Bascom Hall."

2

MY CLASSROOM IN THE EDUCATION BUILDING, halfway down Bascom Hill, was pleasant and old-fashioned. The chairs were the kind I like: movable, so they could be arranged in a circle for discussion or in rows for visual presentations. There was a pull-down screen behind the teacher's desk and room-darkening shades for the windows. A projector with a link for my laptop was the extent of available technology, but that was all I needed.

The course, "French Painting in the Nineteenth Century," was one I had taught before, but it took some doing to adapt it to fit the six-week summer session. It was a popular course back home because it included the impressionists—Claude Monet, Edgar Degas, Mary Cassatt, Berthe Morisot, and other favorites. The class met in the morning, as did Toby's three-week course on Frank Lloyd Wright in Wisconsin, leaving us both free in the afternoon.

That morning a roster had appeared in my faculty mail slot listing twenty-two students. Only twenty showed up, which was fine with me. However, two older women (I guessed they were of retirement age) were standing by my desk, waiting for me before class began. Would I mind if they just sat in? My course was exactly what they were looking for, claimed one. I wouldn't have to grade their work, said the other, and they promised to stay mum in class or join in the discussions, whichever I preferred. I couldn't think of a reason to say no, so I said yes.

The first day of class is always a little awkward. I feel stiff standing before a new group of students. They're stiff too, casting sideways glances, sizing up their classmates and me. I suggested we begin with a round of self-introductions to break the ice, and it worked. When the turn of the older women came, I could sense some discomfort in the room. After they spoke, the young woman whose turn it was next said, "Welcome to our class," and after that we were fine.

My first class was an introduction to the course in the form of a dialogue. I set up the terms for a debate between the Paris Salon and a band of young outsider artists. The Salon was a state-sponsored annual exhibition that followed a strict set of academic rules. Studio art was the norm, and the acceptable subjects were limited to religious, mythological, and historical scenes. The rebel artists scorned those traditions. They painted outdoors, *en plein air*, in the fresh air. They painted nature using natural light and celebrated scenes of everyday life. Religious subjects were replaced by leisure activities—café life, the opera, the ballet, horse racing, boating parties, picnics. The rebels invented a style of their own, using broken, fluttery brushstrokes, even dots, as a way to define forms. A hostile critic dismissed their work with an insult. He called them "impressionists," and the name stuck.

My plan was to end the class on an expectant note, and the strategy was successful. People were chatty as they filed out, always a good sign. At least we were over the first day jitters. It always helps, I've discovered, to turn out the lights and show a few pictures. There's something amiable about sitting together in the dark. You feel closer to the person next to you. It happens too in the theater when the lights go down and you become a member of the audience. It's a social experience.

After class, I took the time to pack up properly and return the classroom to its previous order. While fussing about, I thought about lunch. The Union Terrace beckoned. I shouldered my backpack and followed the river of students down the pathway toward Library Mall and the Memorial Union. In contrast to the simple sandstone buildings on the hill, the architecture of the Union goes all out, with a frontal display of flourishes, columns, balustrades, and carvings. Hardly anyone is aware of the simple back of the building, though, because it faces the lake, and so does everyone who steps outside. The view from there is stunning.

Inside the building, I found a jumble of spaces—all a little hard to see because of the number of students. I took the direct way forward, under modern signs that said Terrace and Food Court. I passed up my first food choices because of long lines and had to settle for a packaged salad and canned soda. But my spirits picked up when I stepped into the eating area, a cavern of glass, with an unrestricted view of Lake Mendota. I made for one of the tables by the windows, but the flow of traffic showed that the seats of choice were on the outside, through the door marked Terrace.

I stepped out into a noontime bacchanalia—a throng of students in shorts and T-shirts, eating, drinking, playing, singing—arranged in three sweeping tiers, the last of which reached the lake. All three levels were crowded with round metal tables and chairs painted green, yellow, or orange. The palette was joyful, sun-drenched Cézanne. This vibrant panorama was set against a vista of blue lake waters.

I stood for a while considering whether to take the one empty table in the center of the patio, but it was exposed to the sun and abutting the trash can. I could just make out the attendant wasps.

"Professor Barnes," a voice called from behind me. I turned and recognized one of my two senior auditors approaching with a welcoming smile. "Come join us," she said, pointing back to a table on the first level. "There's a seat in the shade for you."

"Thank you," I said. "I'd be delighted." I turned and followed her, careful to keep my tray level as I fought the direction of traffic. She led me up a few stairs to a table deep in the shadow of the largest oak. Her friend was watching our progress and arranging things on the table so there'd be room for my tray.

"This is the sweet spot!" said my guide, pulling back a chair for me. I dropped into it, grateful for the seat, the shade, and the company. "You remember Maureen from class. Maureen Day from Philadelphia. And I'm Helen Foreman from Chicago." Tall and slim, Helen sat straight-backed, with her chest high. She was dressed to be noticed, in a fire-engine-red T-shirt with the university logo in white. Heavily applied lipstick matched the T-shirt, and her abundant white hair waved to the world.

"Thank you so much," Maureen said warmly. "We really wanted to get into your class. We're both art lovers."

Helen added, "I used to be a teacher, so I know that every little detail of setting up a class has consequences. We'll do everything we can to make sure you're not sorry you let us in."

I flipped open the lid of my plastic salad container and asked Helen, "Did you teach art?"

"Oh, no, not me. I taught social studies in middle school. It's Maureen who's the artist." She turned her snowy head toward her friend.

Maureen hunched her shoulders in a self-deprecating shrug but admitted, "At last, I am. I had a career as a lawyer, but I've been an artist full-time now for ten years. It's a return to my Madison self. I was an art major here."

I asked, "What kind of work do you do?" as I attacked my salad. It was crisp and fresh.

Uncomfortable with the attention, Maureen flushed, pink rising from her neck. Though aging, she was still an Irish beauty, with milky skin, deep-blue eyes, and auburn hair that retained its natural color. She looked at my tray rather than at me, and she took her time before answering. Helen stayed silent, waiting.

"I draw in charcoal." Her voice was low, confiding. "Then I color. I'm using chalk now, but I've used other media—crayons, oils, colored paper." She glanced at me, as if to judge whether my interest was sincere enough for further disclosure. Then she lowered her eyes and said, "My subject is inequality, in the city. In Philadelphia."

Helen said to me: "I was saying before you joined us, you can take the girl out of the sixties, but you can't take the sixties out of the girl." She looked at her friend with pride and then explained to me. "Back in the day, Maureen was our best artist during the demonstrations against the Vietnam War. She did murals and signs and drawings for our newsletters. And now she's back at it." She pointed her long finger at her friend, as if signaling her to expand.

"Really?" I said. "I'd love to see some of your work." Turning toward Helen, I asked, "When you say 'our' artist, were you part of a movement?" I was thinking of SDS, Students for a Democratic Society.

Maureen looked to Helen for an answer.

"Yes and no," Helen said. "We were friends and roommates. We didn't belong to any organization. But we went to the same protests, and we each contributed. I got people out on the street, and Maureen did the visuals. We just did what needed to be done, on the spur of the moment."

"So, would you call yourselves flesh-and-blood sixties radicals?" I asked.

"I suppose. We were here in the late sixties," said Helen. "The days of mace and glory!" She lifted her water cup.

"The days of blood and truncheons," Maureen countered. "It wasn't so glorious getting beaten to the ground." Her cup stayed on the table. She wasn't toasting.

Helen was fast to backtrack. "Sorry, hon. I know I promised you a break from political talk." She waited a moment for a reply that didn't come and then turned to me and explained, "We just ended a long weekend of discussing our time here during the Vietnam era. We've been at a conference celebrating the sixties in Madison, and we've been reliving the Dow demonstration and all the protests that came before and after. It's been our version of an alumni reunion, the reason we're here."

"And since we were here for the conference," Maureen said, "we decided to stay on for the summer, to enjoy Madison again." She waved a graceful hand, palm up, in the direction of the lake.

"And now we'll have the benefit of your course as well," said Helen.

"I'm flattered. This conference of yours sounds interesting. Was it run by the university?"

"No," Helen replied with excitement. "It was put together by an alumni couple who are longtime Madison residents, two of our class-mates, Ben and Judy Sidran. He's a jazz musician. She's a community volunteer and big supporter of the arts. Their idea was to bring back people who lived in Madison during the sixties and get them talking. There were panel discussions, some academic, some personal, really heart-wrenching, looking back at the choices we struggled with. There was a terrific concert, too, that brought back the joy of it all. 'A party with a purpose'—that's what Ben and Judy called it."

"I'm sorry I didn't get to hear any of it," I said. "I've been pre-occupied with the incident in Bascom Hall over the weekend, not to mention getting ready to teach. We were there when the stage flooded and they found those bones."

"We heard about that," said Maureen. She resettled herself in her chair, her head lowered. "Do they know any more about it?"

"The campus police are looking into it. That's all I really know." I turned to Helen. "But to get back to what you were just talking about, what was the Dow demonstration you mentioned?" The term seemed familiar, but it could have referred to the stock market, or even a calcu-lus proof, for all I knew.

The question took my listeners aback. Helen attempted diplomacy. "I'm surprised you've never heard of it. How long have you been teach-ing at Wisconsin?"

"This is my first day." I laughed. "I'm from California." I explained the faculty exchange.

"I guess that excuses you," said Maureen, smiling. Quickly turning serious, she added in a husky voice. "We're talking 1967 and the biggest campus demonstration ever against the war. We wanted to denounce the partnership between the university, the military, and the Dow Chemical Company for making and using napalm against civilians in Vietnam."

Helen jumped in. "Dow was funding research on napalm here on campus. And then the company scheduled job interviews for seniors. The way we saw it, the university was feeding its graduates into the war machine." She sat up straight and said with a proud nod, "We decided to put our bodies between the students and the machine."

"Were you both seniors?" I asked. Finished with my salad, I tidied my tray and took a sip from my can of soda.

"No," Helen answered. "It was our sophomore year. October '67. We had a pretty ordinary September, but in October we got fired up."

"Or more accurately," Maureen said, "you got gassed."

"That was the second day," Helen insisted. "The first day went just as planned, with pickets and speeches, and the police staying on the sidelines. But the next day, when we occupied the Commerce Building and shut down the interviews, the cops started clubbing us. It got bad very fast. What I remember best is being trampled over and jammed in with other bodies, while the clubs kept coming down with a thwomp, thwomp." She crunched her eyes shut. "When we finally found our way out of the building, there was tear gas to get through. I was close to collapsing, but somebody propped me up and walked me to the University Hospital. Some of us had injuries that never fully healed. We talked about that after the session Friday on 'The Day of Dow.' I've had hearing loss ever since from the blow to my head."

Maureen took up the story. "The thing is, I had a problem with blocking students from going to job interviews they wanted to have. I came to the first day for the rally, but I didn't go to the second day, because the plan was to occupy the building and block the interviews."

"That was the main goal of the demonstration, Maureen."

Maureen's headshake cut across Helen's statement, and she spoke more forcefully than before but with a rasp. "I'm sorry, Helen. Blocking the students who wanted interviews was a mistake. It gave the police just the excuse they needed to come into the building and pull people out. They were brutal in the way they did it, but that's not what the public remembered. People heard 'student riot' and 'violence' and stopped listening right there. We lost our moral standing for opposing the war."

"That's what the media said, but it was a load of bull," Helen blurted, then immediately apologized.

Maureen looked at her tray and shuffled things around. "I admit I was naive then. And I didn't have any skin in the game. The guys did, because they were draftable into that vicious war, and they were thinking about that all the time." She stared out at the lake.

Helen sighed. "I promised we wouldn't talk about politics all day. We have six weeks to work this out."

I thought I'd help change the subject by asking, "Are you here for the summer by yourselves?"

"I'm here with my boyfriend," said Helen.

"My husband is with me," said Maureen.

"Maybe they can help as referees," I suggested.

"Are you kidding?" Maureen scoffed. "They're more polarized than we are. Jimmy still calls himself a radical, while Alan's as much of a pacifist as the day he burned his draft card."

Helen explained: "Jimmy is Maureen's husband. We've all known each other since college. The same for Alan. After graduation, he stayed in Madison. I got married and divorced. Then he and I rediscovered each other a few years ago and we've been seeing each other. The four of us are having a mini reunion this summer."

"What are the men going to do while you're in class?" I asked.

Helen replied, "They're taking a three-week course on Frank Lloyd Wright."

"That must be the same course my husband's in," I said, pleasantly surprised. Summer school is a small world.

Helen explained, "They're taking that one because Alan lives down the street from an important Wright building, the First Unitarian Meeting House at the west end of campus. He's part of a preservation group for Wright's Madison buildings. And Jimmy's interested in Wright too, as any artist would be."

"Give me their names again, and I'll let Toby know to look for them," I said, while rummaging in my backpack for a pen.

"Jimmy Montana and Alan Knight," said Helen. "And your husband?"

"Toby Sandler. He'd introduce himself as an antiques dealer from Northern California. And speaking of Toby, I'd better get going. We agreed to meet at the art library after lunch."

We said goodbyes and headed out, stopping for a moment at the center of the Terrace, where we could see the full sweep of the lake, blossoming with white sails that billowed in the wind. I looked forward to getting to know this beautiful place. For the afternoon, however, I had to find Toby, go back home, and prepare a class for twenty undergraduates and two senior auditors who came with an intriguing past.

I knew that Wisconsin, along with Berkeley and Columbia, had been an important hub of the student protest movements of the sixties. It must have been tremendously exciting to be on campus at that time, but also stressful and intense. By comparison, my own college years had been quiet. And working fifteen hours a week in a campus dining hall while taking a full load of classes left me little time for politics or much of a social life. I found it intriguing talking to these two women, who were participants in the dramatic events of a different era. I knew, of course, that the Vietnam War had a traumatizing impact on many students of their generation. Yet these women had weathered the storm, and now, with their youth and middle years behind them, appeared to be thriving at the gates of old age. Helen had a gruff vitality and seemed to be comfortable in her skin. Maureen had her art and was back to doing what she loved, though I sensed an underlying sadness. For both women the sixties reunion seemed to have rekindled memories of a fiery era. As it turned out, the past wasn't finished with them yet.

I spent the afternoon at my laptop in the art library preparing for my next two classes, while Toby browsed in the reading room. On the way home we stopped at a market and Toby picked up fresh Wisconsin brats, with potato salad and greens for sides. Lately I've increased my share of meal preparation, but Toby's still the chef in the family. He does most of the marketing and is fearless when it comes to trying out new recipes. However, tonight's meal was simple. Toby unwrapped the brats and took them out to our small backyard, where Eve had left us a grill. Because of the bugs, though, we ate inside. As one local wag put it, Wisconsin's state bird should be the mosquito. They are big, mean, and relentless, and when they are out, you'd better be in, unless you've slathered your entire body with DEET.

The bratwursts, thick and juicy, with a dollop of German mustard, were delicious. We washed them down with Spotted Cow beer for Toby and artisan ginger ale for me and shared our experiences of the first day of class. I went first. I described my two veterans of the campus protest era and mentioned that the husband of one and boyfriend of the other were in Toby's class. He dutifully took down their names and promised he'd introduce himself.

"It would be really nice if you did that. Thanks. How did your class go?"

"It certainly won't be dull," Toby began. "We're going to cover most of the houses Wright designed and built in Wisconsin, and we'll visit some of the public buildings together. That's fine. That's what I want. The prof seems to know his stuff. That's good, too. *But . . .*" Having scarfed down his brat, Toby tore off the end of an uneaten bun and swirled it around his plate, sopping up the remaining juices.

"But what?"

"There's something off about the guy—he's a bit of a wacko."

"How do you mean, a wacko?" I batted the phrase back, waiting for him to elaborate. Toby likes an audience, even if it's only me.

"Listen," he said. "He gave a perfectly sane introduction and then spent the second half of the class venting about how the campus police are interfering with his research project."

"Hmm. What's his name?"

"Magnus Arp. He's got a theory that Frank Lloyd Wright, who studied here for a semester in the 1880s, admired the old dome on Bascom Hall before it burned down. He claims Wright even designed a replacement for it. One of his apprentices mentioned in a letter that Wright was working on the project, but somehow the plans were lost. Arp's been conducting a one-man search party for them and working in the Bascom attic. But now the police are tramping all over the place and moving things around, and the site has been taped off as a crime scene, so he can't get up there to complete his measurements."

He paused, sipped his beer, and continued. "Whether Arp has anything to do with the bones is a legitimate question. He's already been interviewed by the police, he says. He was seen lurking around the roof where the old dome used to be, which is right above the cistern where they found the bones. He claims he's being treated like a criminal while he's just trying to do his research." Toby paused to take a breath.

"Well—"

Toby put up his hand to stop me. "All the while," he continued, "Arp was prancing around the room like an imp, waving his arms and punching the air. Then he opened a window, stuck out his head, and shouted at the top of his lungs to nobody in particular, 'Ahoy! Have you seen the white whale?'"

"Wait. Isn't that a line from *Moby-Dick*?"

"Spot-on. It's what Ahab shouts whenever they encounter another ship at sea. I think Arp was asserting a kinship with him by play-acting. They're both on a quest. The thing is, Melville describes how the quest for Moby Dick has twisted Ahab's mind. I wonder if Arp sees the parallel?"

"What happened after he yelled out the window?"

"Nothing. He repeated the performance, slammed the window shut, and ran out the door before anyone could ask a question. How's that for a first day of class?"

"Bizarre," I said.

"He's going to be trouble," said Toby.

3

ON TUESDAY AFTERNOON, I transferred Eve's red bag of clubs from her garage to her car. This was the day Diane and I had set for a round of golf, and I was hoping for an update on the investigation. I arrived early at the course so I could spend a half hour on the putting green getting used to Eve's clubs. Glenway is a nine-hole city golf course that is short enough to play in an hour and a half on foot. Eve had warned me that the greens were small and I'd better practice my short game. First, I had to check in at the clubhouse.

"My tee time's 4:08. Nora Barnes," I reported. The young man squinted at his computer screen and then at me.

"With Diane Young," I added.

"Ah. Welcome to Glenway. She'll give you a good game. Good luck." He rung me up at an astonishingly cheap rate of twelve dollars and promised to let Diane know I could be found on the putting green.

I needed every minute I had there. My putts kept slipping by the hole, denying me the satisfying thunk I was waiting for. At least my percentage of success was better at the end than at the beginning. Diane arrived just in time to see my ball teeter, then halt on the edge of the cup. She wasted no time commiserating; instead, she waved me toward her.

Diane is hard to miss. She stands straight and tall, gracefully carrying an attractive amount of weight in the chest and hips. Here on the golf course, a plain white polo shirt contrasted with her rich brown skin, and a pink visor kept Afro-style curls away from her eyes. Her handsome face was lit by a wide smile that made me feel welcome.

We were up next, so we hustled to the first tee, only to find that the group ahead of us had been slow to launch. One of four young men was thanking his partners for granting a mulligan, as he took his sweet time setting up his second drive. A loud whack that did not sound correct sent his ball far to the left and into the wrong fairway. As the unfortunate driver threw up his hands and begged for "just one more try," his friends laughed and set off walking. He packed up his clubs, breezily calling over, "Sorry, ladies."

It was a short enough hole that we couldn't tee off until the foursome was off the green. To my relief, Diane declared herself patient. "If they invite us to play through, we'll take them up on it, but otherwise let's chat and enjoy our downtime." That was fine with me. "So, how's the teaching going?" she asked.

"So far, so good. It's an interesting group. We'll see what they say in the evaluations at the end of the course."

"I bet they'll be great."

"Thanks, I'll shoot for that."

Small talk led us to our mutual friend, Eve, who had called both of us over the weekend. To me she'd said she was comfortable in our house, liked the students at my college, and had played a round of golf with my weekly group. "Tell me," I asked, "how did you and Eve become friends?"

"We met in our first week here. Women's Studies throws a party to welcome the new women hires on campus, and it's a great place to make connections. We traded cards and said we'd get together soon. Well, 'soon' came that very night. At 9:00 p.m. her name came up on my cell, and she was whispering, 'Help me, I need help here, oh my God.' I pictured her bloodied and wounded, but then my assessment changed when she said, 'This is humiliating!'"

"I never heard about this. What did she do—lock herself out of her car?"

Diane shook her head and suppressed a smile. "She was at her office when she called me, and she was having trouble leaving. Because down the hall, between her and the elevator, was a teenage boy in a Dracula cape. When she approached, the boy spread the cape wide to reveal a very nude, very adult-sized member, at attention."

"Yikes! What did she do?"

"The normal things. First, she froze. Then she fled. She ran back to her office and locked the door and waited."

"Waited? Why didn't she call campus police?"

"She did eventually, but not the emergency number. She called me, on my work number. She had my card sitting on her desk."

"So, what did you do?"

"I had to talk her down, so she'd feel okay if I came with a patrol officer. I promised to keep her anonymous. The kid was gone by the time we got there, but my people caught him the next night."

"And that's how you became friends?"

"That's how we began. Later she helped me with a campaign for women's safety on campus, and then we started golfing. And here we are. Time to tee off!"

We dropped the chat and each succeeded in placing our first shot ten or so yards in front of the empty green. Good start. Then Diane shone, and I flubbed. An elegant chip put her hot-pink ball within three inches of the hole. One below par. My overpowered chip sent my ball soaring over the green and down a hidden slope. After walking around a bunker and behind the green, I rescued the ball with two choppy shots and three putts to get into the hole. This fiasco took so much time that I expected the guys would be clearing their green as we reached the next tees. Not so. Forced into waiting again, we stepped into the shade.

25

"Eve tells me you've worked with law enforcement on a few big cases," Diane said as we waited for the guys to navigate the fairway. "She says you and your husband are indispensable to law and order on the Sonoma coast." Her cheeks crinkled a little toward a smile.

"In a limited way," I conceded. "Sometimes our experience with art or antiques can be useful."

"Don't be modest." She gave me a joshing tap to the elbow. "Eve found a box of calling cards in your desk, and they list you as investigative consultant for the Sonoma County Sheriff's Office."

I had to smile, remembering how our friend Dan, the deputy sheriff for Bodega Bay, had enlisted me to help him solve a murder case and thwart a thief. In thanks, he had the official-looking cards made for me. They had since come in handy when art fraud or theft hit the county. And somehow on vacation I've managed to get mixed up with murder investigations in France and Ireland.

"Well, I'm at your service, if ever I can be of help," I said with a mock salute. Then I thought of the probe she had in process. "Can you tell me anything more about your investigation of the bones? We were in the audience in Bascom when the flood happened, saw the whole thing."

"Astounding, wasn't it? The bones are in the hands of the medical examiner at the State Crime Lab. In fact, I've got my phone on buzz because I'm expecting a preliminary report today from the forensic anthropologist." She patted her back pocket.

"Is the case being handled by the city police or the university police?" I asked, unsure of the boundaries in local law enforcement.

"By us. We're a full-service police department with investigative powers. If a crime occurs on university property, it's in our jurisdiction. We call on the city police if we need them, or the FBI, but it's our call and our case. And right now I'm the lead detective working it."

"Wow. I didn't realize the university police had those responsibilities."

"We sure do. With forty thousand students on campus, a lot can happen. We have eight detectives working for the department. I've worked John Doe cases before, and I've been attached to the FBI's Joint Terrorism Task Force, so I know the drill."

"Diane, I am impressed."

She bent to plant a tee. "Here we go. The boys are out of sight."

The short fairway begged for a hole in one, but we were quite happy to land near the green. Once we were both on, Diane picked up our conversation exactly where she'd left off.

"We've started checking names of everyone who's ever gone up to the attic. We've talked to the custodians, staff from Buildings and Grounds, and the guy who yanks some pulleys when the flag on the roof needs to be lowered to half-mast."

I steadied myself and tapped my ball gently to the hole. Plop. I was thrilled to have parred the hole and tried to act as if that happened for me every day.

"Did you get up there yourself?" I asked. I picked up my ball and walked well away from the potential path of Diane's.

"Shush," she said with a finger to her lips. "No exciting talk till I sink this baby." She did, reset the pin, called her par, and resumed talking as we headed for the next tees.

"I sure did get up to that attic, and it's the spookiest place on campus. Hottest place, too, in the summer, like any old attic. We went early in the morning. You open a door marked Utility Room, and you're suddenly in a witch's warren. It's dark, because there are no windows, and the electric switch turns on a bulb that's far up and doesn't provide much light. There's only one way to go, straight ahead to a beaten-up ladder. When you reach the top, you're practically hanging over the cistern. It was a mess from the collapse, and we had to wait until the engineers got in there to check the structure and shore it up."

I had to ask. "Did the collapse of the cistern look like an accident? That's what the papers called it."

"The papers can say what they want until there's real information available. There's a thorough investigation going on right now to determine how the tank filled and emptied. But yes, a spontaneous collapse is the working hypothesis. Rain came in through the roof and filled it over time. The support beams below it rotted away. No one remembers the last time the cistern was inspected. People just forgot about it."

"My husband's taking a summer course, and his art history professor has been up there exploring the space for a research project on Frank Lloyd Wright. You know about that, right?"

Diane has a good poker face, but I thought I saw a tinge of exasperation before she said, "Oh, yes, we know about Professor Arp's trips to the attic and the roof. Every time he goes up there now, he has to have one of us unlock the door and stay there till he's finished with his measuring and sketching or whatever the hell he's doing. Have you met him?"

"Not yet," I said.

"He's a piece of work. You'll see what I mean if you meet him." Diane's face lit up with an idea. "Say, you're the art consultant. Maybe you can tell me what Frank Lloyd Wright has to do with the attic."

Architecture isn't my field, but like Toby, I'm a fan of Frank Lloyd Wright and consider him an important artist. One attraction for us of being in Madison that summer was the opportunity to see some of his famous buildings. Wright considered Madison his hometown, and there's no better place than Wisconsin to sample the variety of his work.

I told Diane it would be an interesting discovery if Wright had designed a dome for the university, particularly if he had done so early in his career. It certainly would be of interest to the university and to a scholar like Arp, who could publish his find. Publications are the currency of the academic world and the surest path to advancement.

"All I ever heard about Frank Lloyd Wright," Diane admitted, "was that for all his genius, the roofs leaked."

"I've heard that too," I conceded. The Prairie-style homes that Wright designed were low to the ground, with flat roofs and cantilevered extensions. "His defenders say his vision was years ahead of the building materials available in his day."

Diane looked doubtful.

"Anyhow," I said, "getting back to Arp, I wonder if you think he could have any connection to the bones."

"He's on my list. In the meantime, our first priority is to identify the victim. Somebody died up there. We don't know who or when or how. It's my job to find out."

Even with all this on her mind, Diane managed to par the eighth hole and bogey the ninth, for a game score of forty-five. She's got skill, experience, strength, and great nerves. My score was way higher, but I resolved to shave off strokes in future weeks as I got to know the course better. I offered to get drinks and chips, and I took her order.

When I brought our tray to the flagstone patio, I found Diane seated at a metal table under an umbrella, reading a message on her phone. There were several other tables on the patio, but they were empty.

"The report's in," she said, looking up as I sat down. "When they laid out the bones, they had a nearly complete skeleton. I'm going to skip to the bottom line. The preliminary finding is that the remains are those of 'a white male between the ages of twenty and twenty-five, about six feet tall, with a robust athletic build.' That description could fit a lot of the population. Given the age range, I'm thinking a student, because the remains were found on campus. But that could be jumping to a conclusion. You get transients in a university town. I'll ask the Dean of Students Office to begin a search of their records over the years for any reports of missing male students, and I'll get the Madison police to search the city records. It's a beginning."

"I'm impressed they can tell that much just by looking at the bones," I said.

"You'd be surprised what a good forensic anthropologist can do. I've taken a couple of courses in the subject, so I think I understand the basics. That doesn't mean I'm a professional. That takes years of training and experience and developing a skill set you can't get from a course."

"It's the same with detective work on art," I said. "You can take a course in how to spot a fake, but it takes years of looking, and knowing what to look for based on experience, to develop what they call 'an eye.'"

Diane nodded in agreement. "Some of it is straightforward, though. Take height. You don't even need a complete skeleton. You can measure the thigh bone, if you have it, then apply a mathematical formula, and you end up with a fairly accurate estimate.

"Determining age takes more knowledge and skill," she went on. "There are cartilage caps at the ends of the long bones that fuse with the bones at different ages. Most of them are fused by the age of twenty.

There's one on the clavicle that fuses around the age of thirty. Now, it's one thing for me to say that and another thing to recognize it. And that's just one of the criteria they use. The teeth tell a lot about age, too."

"What about sex?" I asked, taking a sip of my Diet Coke.

"I'm all for it. If you know any good-looking men of color, let me know," she deadpanned.

It took me a second to get it, and when I did, I sprayed a mouthful of drink all over the table.

Diane flashed a smile. "You sure walked into that one."

"I sure did."

She resumed her explanatory tone: "Well, for obvious reasons, the pelvis can help you determine sex. In females, the pubic bone has to allow for the birth canal. The skull, too, can tell you a lot. Men tend to have more prominent brows and jaws, and bigger heads in general."

"Fatheads. I've met my share," I said.

"Now, as to race—don't get me started." Diane narrowed her eyes.

"Let me guess. It's complicated?"

"Tell me about it. What discussion about race in America isn't complicated? So much of what we mean by race is cultural rather than biological. And some of the assumptions that have been made about race in the name of science don't pass the smell test." She downed her drink and shook the ice left in the paper cup. We sat in silence for a while. "I'd leave race out of it, if it were up to me," she said. "But it's not. The report will include the complete analysis from the State Crime Lab."

I finished my drink too and asked, "Do they give any indication of how long the body was in the cistern?"

"That's the first question I had for the medical examiner," replied Diane. "And the answer was, they can't say. At least six or seven years at a minimum, since all the soft tissue is gone and traces of clothing as well. But the timespan could be longer. Even a lot longer. With bones in water, there's no easy way to tell how long they've been there without external clues, like objects found at the scene, but there weren't any."

"What about DNA evidence? Can they get DNA from bones?"

"Yes. The problem is how long it takes to get results. The average wait time in Wisconsin right now is eighty days."

"Why so long?" I asked.

Diane sighed. "It's not just the extraction and preparation of the samples but a backlog of cases at the State Crime Lab. There are thousands of rape kits that never were processed. Some of them date back to 2014."

That was shocking. "How come?"

"The lab claims lack of resources, which is one reason, but a lot of those kits were warehoused because the police didn't believe the victims. It's a real scandal. The media are putting pressure on the lab to speed things up. They'll fit us in, just not as soon as we'd like. For now, we'll have to rely on the forensic anthropologist. He's promised a more detailed analysis in a couple of days."

"How accurate is he usually? Do you know him?"

"Not personally. The State Crime Lab uses outside consultants. But to give you an idea of the level of information they can provide, I'll tell you about a famous case. This isn't the first time an unidentified skeleton has turned up in Madison."

"Really?"

"It happened in 1989, before my time. They call it 'the skeleton in the chimney case.' A maintenance worker was cleaning out the flue of a boiler in the basement of a store when he found a pile of bones scrunched in the bottom of the chimney. The opening was less than a foot wide, but the victim was petite, and the police theorized she had been murdered on the roof and her body stuffed down the chimney. They recovered a complete skeleton and clothing, too. I said 'she,' because the victim was wearing a dress, no underwear, and pointed shoes. But the forensic anthropologist discovered that the skeleton wasn't a woman at all. It was that of a slim man dressed in women's clothing. It came as quite a surprise."

"I'll bet."

"That wasn't the end of the mystery. The victim was carrying a German iron cross, a comb, and a butter knife."

"A butter knife?"

"Correct. The police speculated that the victim was a cross-dresser or transgender prostitute who lured a customer up to the roof to have sex, and when the john discovered what was what, he flew into a rage, committed murder, and stuffed the body down the chimney." Diane raised her finely arched eyebrows, inviting a different explanation.

I didn't have one. "Why a butter knife?" Somehow that detail seemed the weirdest part of all.

Diane shrugged. "I'll take a pass on that one."

"And the German medallion?"

"Could be a fashion accessary. Or maybe the victim was a neo-Nazi cross-dresser. Who knows?"

"You mean the case was never solved?"

"Nope, it's still on the books as an ongoing investigation. It's not that easy to identify unknown remains. They tried matching dental records with those of missing persons from three states. They checked abandoned-car reports and records of arrests for prostitution. They reconstructed the face and broadcast photos of it, but no one came forward to identify the victim."

She pushed back her chair, saying, "I'd better get going. But if you have any ideas about the skeleton in the cistern, please let me know. Or for that matter, the skeleton in the chimney."

We said goodbye. I felt ill at ease as I wheeled my clubs back to the car. It was sad to think that, with all the tools available to modern investigators, a person could disappear from the face of the earth and never be traced—or even missed.

4

2:27 A.M. *Bobby is perfect but I miss home*
2:34 A.M. *I can't sleep*
6:01 A.M. *I feel lonely*
Is that normal?

MY PHONE IS SET TO STAY SILENT between midnight and morning, but after six it's free to ping. Toby moaned in protest. He knew what that meant—news flash from my younger sister, Angie, who was six time zones away, in the west of Ireland, testing her devotion to her latest love, Bobby Colman, sheepman and musician.

It was a year since they'd met, during the Barnes family's summer vacation on Achill Island. Angie had now lived through the four seasons of an Irish sheep farm, at Bobby's side, learning the business and testing her new life. She was so sure of her future with Bobby that she applied for Irish citizenship on the basis of having a grandparent born in Ireland—and got it; yet, suddenly, she sounded homesick.

I didn't like this development. I'd been hoping that Angie's Irish romance would break the chain of her bad luck with boyfriends. Throughout her life, her good looks have been a curse, drawing the attention of inappropriate men. Her dating history consists of a series of painful disillusionments. She deserves better, and she seemed to have found it in Bobby, an honest, hardworking sheep rancher, who was handsome, too. The only trouble was location. His sheep farm on Achill Island, just off the coast of Galway, was a long way from home on the north shore of Boston.

The big sister in me wanted to call and offer comfort, but I had counted on the next several hours for preparing class. If I got into a crisis call with Angie, I'd use up more than time; I'd lose my focus. I texted: *Hang in there. Big hug.*

As soon as class was over, I checked my texts, and, sure enough, Angie had written. *Please call.* I didn't want to. Toby was waiting for me at the Union for lunch. I didn't have time right then to help Angie sort out her feelings, or maybe I was afraid of getting in the middle between her and Bobby. I texted back that we'd catch up on the weekend, then headed for the Union to meet Toby.

The weather had changed. The sky had turned slate gray, and the air felt moist. Lunch would clearly have to be indoors, in the Rathskeller. I hustled down Bascom Hill, spurred on by a boom of thunder over the lake. Rain pelted down just as I reached the side door of the Union. I quickly ducked in, brushed raindrops off my backpack, and headed for the Rathskeller.

"The Rath," as it's affectionately called, is a faithful replica of a German beer hall, replete with dark tables and chairs, rustic light fixtures, multiple arches, and whimsical murals featuring gnomes and German drinking adages in Gothic lettering. Beer steins of every size and description are on display. If you let your imagination wander, you can picture huddled plotters in lederhosen planning a putsch. On closer inspection, they're just students with their caps on backward playing poker and listening to rap, not marching songs.

The place was crowded but I spotted Toby waving from across the hall. He had snagged a table and was sitting with Helen and a man I assumed to be her companion. I made my way over.

I'd guessed right. "Professor Barnes, this is my friend Alan Knight," Helen said, looking proud of her man.

"Please call me Nora," I said to Helen. And to Alan I said, "I'm with him," pointing to Toby.

Alan stood and offered his hand. "Glad to meet you." He was a large, barrel-chested man with curly gray hair and a trim white beard. He must have been Helen's age, but like her he seemed gifted with the energy of someone younger. "We've been gossiping about our professors," he said, grinning, as I pulled up a chair.

"Does that mean I should leave?"

"Not about you," Alan reassured me. "We've been venting about our eccentric Professor Arp."

I plopped down into a chair and shook myself like a dog to rid myself of rain. Toby said, "Helen has only good things to say about your class."

"That's true," she confirmed.

Compliments tend to throw me off-kilter. I mumbled a simple thanks. Glancing over a menu encased in plastic, I asked, "Where's Maureen?"

Helen replied, "She had to stop at the bookstore, but she'll meet us here."

Judging from the empty wrappings on their trays, the three had already finished lunch. On the table was a pitcher of beer that had made the rounds and plastic cups for the contents. "What did you have to eat?" I asked Toby.

"The Bucky Burger. A hands-down favorite." Bucky Badger was the campus mascot, and his name was stamped on everything as a marketing device.

"What's on it?" I asked.

"What isn't?" replied Toby. "Cheese, of course. Two slices, as this is Wisconsin. Choose which kinds. Then lettuce, tomato, caramelized onions, condiments, and a secret sauce. No badger meat. Just beef."

"I'll have a salad and a Diet Coke," I said.

"Just as I thought," said Toby, rising. "I'll get it for you."

"Care for beer?" Alan said, lifting the quarter-full pitcher.

"Cold caffeine's my poison," I replied.

Toby went off to get my meal. "Helen told me you live in Madison," I said to Alan, as he poured more beer for Helen and himself.

"Yep. Never left. Did she mention I was a conscientious objector during the war? After college, I did my alternative service as an aide in the psychiatric unit at Madison General. Got interested in psychology while I was there and trained to become a psychotherapist. I had a practice here for forty years."

"And you knew Helen in college?"

"Yes, but we weren't a couple then. Just part of a group of friends."

Helen took over. "My mistake. I got married right after graduation to the wrong guy. It ended in divorce. Then three years ago I ran into Alan at a conference in Chicago, and here we are."

Alan rushed to answer a question no one had asked. "Me? I never married. I guess all those years I was waiting for the right girl."

Helen reached for his hand and gave it a squeeze.

A few minutes later, Toby returned with my salad, accompanied by a man about Alan's age. "Look who I found," said Toby.

"Jimmy Montana," Helen declared. "Maureen's husband."

Jimmy said hello. He was short and slight, with bronze skin, fine features, and slick black hair graying at the sides. His dress was distinctive: a sort of big-game hunter's outfit. He wore a short-sleeved khaki shirt with button-down pockets on the chest. The shirt hung loose over khaki pants. Around his neck he wore a multicolored bandana.

"What's up? You look pissed off," said Alan, as Jimmy found a seat.

"I *am* pissed off. I was walking down the hill just now and saw a new plaque they put up marking the protests of the sixties. It says student demonstrations mobilized 'thousands for and against the war,'

ending with the bombing of Sterling Hall. 'For and against the war'—
I don't remember a single demonstration *for* the war, do you? They were
all against it."

"So much for attempts at evenhandedness," said Alan.

"So much for the truth," said Helen. "The bombing didn't put an
end to the protests. Students kept on demonstrating until the war
ended."

"But it did knock the wind out of the movement. You've got to
admit that," said Alan, glancing to check Helen's reaction.

Toby leaned his forearm on the table. "I'm an outsider, remember.
What bombing are you talking about?"

"The bombing of Sterling Hall, the physics building that housed
the Army Math Research Center," said Jimmy. "It was bound to happen. It was the summer of 1970. Campuses across the country were in
turmoil since that spring. Nixon had expanded the war into Cambodia.
In May, four students were shot and killed by the National Guard at
a peaceful demonstration at Kent State. Then came the shootings at
Jackson State. Students were enraged, holding protests every day. The
lid was about to come off."

Helen picked up the tale. "The center produced math research for
the military that helped the war effort. It was a prime target, but nobody
was supposed to get hurt. The bomb went off in the middle of the
night, when the building was supposed to be empty. Unfortunately, a
graduate student was inside and he was killed."

"Such a mistake," muttered Alan. "Shouldn't have happened. The
bombers were so naive."

"We knew one of them," said Helen. "He was Maureen's boyfriend."

"Ex-boyfriend," Jimmy corrected. "They were high school sweet-
hearts. Maureen followed him out here when he got accepted by Wisconsin. But they broke up way before the bombing. Maureen doesn't
like to talk about it."

"You can understand why," said Helen.

"What happened to him, the ex-boyfriend?" asked Toby.

"Nothing. He got away," said Jimmy.

Alan cut across Jimmy's last words with a warning: "Maureen's coming. Let's change the subject."

Interventions like that, though they may be well intended, make me uncomfortable. I dislike being deceitful, even in tiny ways. Thankfully, Jimmy took charge by introducing Maureen to Toby, and then Maureen lightened the mood at the table by reaching into her University Bookstore bag and bringing out a party favor for each of us—a compact red umbrella emblazoned with a white decal of Bucky Badger. "They were practically giving them away at the cashier's desk," she said as she handed them out. "I just couldn't resist."

"Thanks, sweetie!" said Helen. She bent to tuck the gift into her handbag.

"We could have used these Friday evening at the regent's speech, when it started raining bones," said Toby. He aimed his new umbrella at the ceiling.

Helen sat up straight and said, "I've been thinking about that. Is it a coincidence that a right-wing speech was sabotaged while we were holding a conference down the street on political protest? Isn't it just the kind of thing we might have done back in the day?"

Toby said, "I appreciate the symbolism, but I doubt that students were behind it. The police say it was an accident."

"Political theater," said Jimmy. "That's what we would have called it."

"Of course. That was your specialty," said Helen. "Weren't you up on the roof of Bascom on the Day of Dow?"

Jimmy put up his hands, arrest style. "Yes, officer—me and ten other guys. We went out on the roof to get a view of the crowd and the police outside the Commerce building, which was next door. One guy had a camera, and he got a great shot of police beating students with clubs. That was in the paper the next day along with a shot of me, with my bandana as a mask against the tear gas, looking crazed."

Alan asked, "Is that when they started calling you Bandana Montana?" He gestured to the cloth around Jimmy's neck.

"It was. From then on, I wore a bandana as a symbol of protest. When there was a rally, I was there and the photographers found me. Soon it looked as if I had some special role in the movement, which I didn't. I was just a kid with a scarf and a catchy name." His words were self-deprecating, but there was pride in the way he lifted his chin to display his bandana, stylishly knotted at the side.

"Come on, now, you milked it for all it was worth," teased Helen. "Bandana Montana was a hot image for a student activist. Even hotter for a young artist. I remember your senior exhibit. Bandanas everywhere. In the art, on the art, on you. You made Bandana Montana a brand."

"In psychology we'd call that a fetish." Alan grunted.

"You had one too," said Jimmy. "You had a peace symbol on a gold chain you used to wear around your neck."

"I remember," said Helen. "I had a cheap button with the same symbol. I pinned it to my hat. What ever happened to yours?"

"I wish I knew. I haven't seen it in years," said Alan.

"That bandana launched my career," Jimmy continued, as if he hadn't been listening. And he hadn't. Rather, he'd been thinking of what he was going to say next. "I went to New York as a man with a moniker. I padded my portfolio with newspaper clippings about me at demonstrations. But that got me noticed."

"And that's what we call commodification." Helen sniffed.

Jimmy frowned, but Alan interceded. "Look, guys," he said. "We have work to do this afternoon at the library. We should get going." Alan explained that they had assigned reading for their class on reserve at the Kohler Art Library.

Helen and I decided to stay for a hot drink while Maureen ate lunch. I waited at the table with our belongings while Helen fetched tea and Maureen ordered at the grill. Helen, back quickly, rushed into an apology. "I'm sorry if I let my annoyance with Jimmy show there for a minute. He's a fine artist, but so is Maureen. He's always had a flair for getting attention. Maureen's quiet. She needed calm and time to develop. But it was a three-ring circus around Jimmy from the time they left school. They were married a year later. I just don't feel she was ever nurtured."

I stayed quiet. This was a sticky conversation from any perspective. They were both taking my class. I didn't want to discuss one student's marriage with the other, even if they were the best of friends.

Helen looked thoughtful. Then she leaned forward, her dark, intelligent eyes searching mine. "Not that I had it any easier. My parents discouraged me from everything I had a passion for." Her expression was sober.

"I'm sorry to hear that."

"You know, they were products of their time. A nice Jewish girl didn't play basketball or blow the trumpet or go to civil rights marches. She didn't run for class president on a platform of abolishing the prom, either." At that memory, a grin tugged at her lips.

"You didn't!"

"I certainly did. I didn't win, but I made some interesting friends."

"Where was this?"

"Glencoe, Illinois, just north of Chicago." She waved to Maureen, who was arriving with her lunch and a stack of cookies. Once Maureen had settled in and declared that the sweets were for sharing, Helen resumed her story. "In high school, there was only one person who understood me, Mr. Steele, the social studies teacher. He taught the state curriculum, but he also exposed us to Marx and Engels, labor history, and issues of social justice. He liked my combativeness. When he told me I'd be happy at the University of Wisconsin, I believed him. I trusted I would find like-minded students here. And I did. Maureen and Theo, Alan, later Jimmy. It felt like a club. We were all asking questions that people back home didn't want to face."

It was easy to picture Helen as a young iconoclast, but not Maureen. She might have the red hair associated with firebrands, but everything else about her seemed placid and unassuming. She didn't live on restless energy, as Helen did. She was physically as soft and rounded as Helen was taut and angular. She didn't lead in conversation, and her voice was low. I'd heard her offer only one political opinion, and that was against the wisdom of the Dow sit-in.

I asked Maureen, "How did you happen to end up coming to Madison? Was it the political reputation of the university that appealed to you?"

She laughed gently, pushing back her plate and shaking her head. "I was against the war and against violence. But as for coming to the UW, the plain truth is I came for a guy," she said. "Don't laugh. It was the 1960s. Nobody had heard of Gloria Steinem yet."

"Was he a student here?" I asked.

"No, he was my boyfriend at home in Havertown, Pennsylvania. We went to the same church, and we took the same bus to school. He was at Monsignor Bonner High School for Boys, and I was at the twinned Catholic school for girls. In senior year, we were both getting pressure to apply to Catholic colleges, but we'd had it, Theo with the monks and me with the nuns. We wanted to break free and get a broad education and meet a wide range of people."

"Then why the University of Wisconsin? Pretty far from home, wasn't it?"

"That was because of Theo. He was a fanatic about rowing. His dream was to compete on a highly ranked college rowing team, and Wisconsin had that. I applied because he applied. When we both got in, I was thrilled."

"As I remember it," said Helen, "you came because of Theo, but you hardly saw him. He came to our parties, and we had some meals together, but most of the time he wasn't around."

"Theo had room for only one passion at a time, and rowing was it. If he wasn't studying, he was lifting weights or working out on those stationary rowing machines. It was all to earn a place on the team, and he did. I gave him the support I could, but I didn't demand much of his time. He was doing what he came to do."

"But I seem to remember he made time for activist work," said Helen. "He worked on protests and wrote for the *Daily Cardinal*. He covered SDS for them, so he must have been spending time at their meetings too."

"That was afterward, not till junior year," said Maureen. "When he was cut from the traveling squad, he had a real crisis. Don't you remember? For months he was angry and impossible to be with. We fought and broke up, and then he quit the team and transferred all his energy to the antiwar movement. It was like throwing a switch. That's when he started hanging out with the radicals on campus."

Tears were coming to Maureen's eyes, and she looked askance so we might not notice. "I just get so sad when I think of how such a good kid let himself be drawn into it. I have to think he was brainwashed somehow. There was a time when I really cared for him, you know. Even after we broke up, I wanted him to make a good life for himself. Instead, he committed an act that took the life of another person, and he ruined his own life in the process. It's a horror that I can't let go of. All I can do is pray that he repented and spent the rest of his days trying to make up for it."

"You can't make up for taking a life," said Helen.

Maureen looked up. "You can try."

"Did you ever hear from him again?" I asked.

She shook her head no.

Helen said, "There was talk at the reunion that if ever there was a right time and place for Theo to come out of hiding and turn himself in, this was it. We kept an eye out for him but he never showed up."

Maureen looked as if she were about to speak, but instead dabbed her eyes with a napkin and bit her lip.

5

I WAS CURIOUS TO LEARN MORE ABOUT the violent event that had touched the lives of these four friends. But my research into the bombing of Sterling Hall would have to wait until the weekend. Toby's class featured field trips to several of Frank Lloyd Wright's important buildings, and I was eager to tag along. That day they were visiting the First Unitarian Meeting House in Madison. I wanted to see the famous Meeting House and hear the infamous Professor Arp. My plan was to arrive a half hour before the group, explore the place on my own, then drift over to mingle when the tour began.

Wright designed more buildings for Wisconsin sites than can be squeezed into a three-week course—thirty in Madison alone. Some were never built, others were built but later demolished, and some are still standing. The surviving homes are privately owned and usually can't be visited. However, two of his public buildings are available and decidedly worth seeing: the meeting house and the Monona Terrace Convention Center, overlooking Lake Monona. Toby's class also had a visit planned to Taliesin, Wright's home and studio in Spring Green.

The First Unitarian Meeting House proved easy to find. From the university, I drove out Campus Drive, heading west, and took a right turn on University Bay Drive, which brought me to its door. The striking modernist structure stands on a rise a block away from what is now the emergency entrance of the University Hospital. I'd read that the meeting house was built when Wright was eighty-four. His parents had been among the founding members of the congregation.

The entrance is at the south side of the building, which abuts the parking lot and gives little advance notice of the space within. A pitched copper roof hangs low over the entrance. (Wright was short and liked low ceilings.) I climbed five shallow steps, went through a pair of glass doors, and arrived at a small vestibule. From there I passed through a narrow corridor that suddenly opened onto the sweeping space of the chapel, with its stunning prow of glass and wood soaring toward the sky. Magnificent walls of windows filled the hall with light—plain, ordinary daylight made extraordinary by the perfect geometry of the room.

I sat in the center of the last pew and spent some time taking in the visual effect. Then I moseyed about, poking in corners and looking at things from different angles until a chatter of voices from the corridor announced the arrival of Toby's class. I caught Toby's eye as the group wandered in, and he beckoned me over. Jimmy Montana and Alan Knight were standing with him. "Hello again," said Alan.

"Hi, guys," I said, lowering my voice. "I'm going to try to make myself inconspicuous since I'm not part of the group. Maybe we can catch up later."

"Got it," Jimmy whispered.

They both nodded as I backed away.

Magnus Arp had come in behind his students, pausing in the vestibule to sign them in. Arp was short and wiry, and he bounced with nervous energy. He had curly red hair that bunched out over his ears and a Vandyke beard of the same color, which gave him the appearance of a portrait by some minor Dutch old master who was having an off day. He wore jeans and a summer-weight sports jacket.

"All right. Spread out, please. Take the seats up front." Though not a large man, he had a loud voice. He mounted the stone pulpit and took out a sheaf of notes from the inside pocket of his jacket.

I moved to the back and sat down as if I had just wandered in and been captivated by a docent's interesting remarks. And to be fair, Arp *was* interesting. He certainly knew all about the building. He talked about the construction history of the meeting house, the changes in plans and budget, the cost overruns, the quarrels, the later additions to the building, the salient points of its architecture, and its place in Wright's career.

I'll say this for him. Arp had a real feel for Wright, a true affection. When lecturing on the glass prow, he quoted Wright saying, "More and more, so it seems to me, light is the beautifier of the building." Then he asked the class to name specific ways that light coming from the prow achieved that effect. The students saw bursts of beauty that I hadn't noticed, all over the room, highlighted by the streams of eastern light coming from the prow. Arp was a capable teacher, I had to admit, in spite of what Toby had told me.

After summarizing the students' findings and tying them to the main points of his lecture, he encouraged the class to walk around the Meeting House on their own and stay as long as they liked. A couple of students gathered around him afterward to ask questions. And when they were breaking up, I walked over and waited for Toby to introduce me.

"Professor Arp, I'd like you to meet my wife."

"I enjoyed your lecture," I said, offering my hand.

Looking pleased, he shook heartily.

Toby continued his introduction. "She's visiting in your department. Nora Barnes."

"Barnes?" he repeated. He took a step back.

"Please call me Nora. I'm replacing Eve Olson for the summer."

Arp's face darkened. "Only the summer? That's not what I heard."

Toby bristled. "You heard what?"

"That this exchange is just a stepping stone to get you an appointment in the department." Glowering at me, he said intently, "Don't count on it."

I felt a tightening in my torso, and I hated that he had scared me. If Arp was a sample of collegiality in the department, I didn't want to be there. I struggled for a civil response.

"I'm not a candidate yet," I said, "but I take it that you'd be against the idea?"

"We have no shortage of women faculty," he said.

The man had the subtlety of a rock. Of the full-time faculty in the department, there were four women and six men. I held my tongue.

"The fact is we have a cabal of feminists who are trying to take over the department and a weak chair who doesn't know how to handle them."

I felt Toby stiffen beside me. I touched his hand, letting him know I'd deal with this myself. "A cabal? You mean with secret meetings and devious plots? That doesn't sound like the Eve Olson I know."

"Ask her yourself! She holds the meetings at her house. They're prejudiced against me because I do traditional scholarship and I'm writing a book on Frank Lloyd Wright, a dead White male. So, don't be surprised if the prospect of adding another member to their caucus doesn't exactly thrill me."

I couldn't restrain myself any longer. "You can't have a hiring policy based on sex. That's discrimination, and this is the twenty-first century."

"I know what century it is. And I'm still entitled to an opinion. I won't be bullied."

Toby fixed him with a steady gaze. "If there's a bully in this room, it's you," he said. I was afraid Toby might take a swing at him.

Arp prudently took another step back. "I'm not going to stand here and be threatened. I have a class to teach." He turned his back to me and walked rapidly toward a group of students who were standing around the pulpit and pointing up toward the glass peak.

"Well, of all the goddamn nerve," said Toby.

"Let it go." I hadn't anticipated that my presence would cause a scene. One thing was now clear. Arp had a history with Eve that she hadn't shared with me, and it wasn't pleasant.

"I told you he was going to be trouble," said Toby. "Let's find Jimmy and Alan. I saw them go into the office wing."

Toby led me to an inconspicuous doorway, and we went searching, poking our heads into occupied offices and empty meeting rooms. We read signs on closed office doors and stopped to examine a Japanese print hung beside one of them. At the end of the hall, we found the room where our new friends had settled. Alan was seated at a small table, his head in his hands. He looked up when we entered, seemingly ashamed to have been caught in an emotional gesture. Jimmy, standing by the window, offered an explanation.

"We were reliving some powerful moments. This is the room where Alan did his counseling work on conscientious objection."

Alan said, "My family were members here, and there was a group who counseled conscientious objectors, including me. After I declared as a CO, I took up the work, too. I listened to some heartrending decisions in this room."

"About refusing to go to war?" I asked.

"Yes." Alan looked spent but gathered himself to answer me. "Finding your conscience isn't easy. It's an ordeal. We felt sure the Vietnam War was wrong and we couldn't morally participate, but we couldn't shake the guilt that others were being drafted in our place. I was lucky that my parents agreed with me. I had emotional support, but many COs didn't. Their families threw them out, their girlfriends left them, their friends disappeared, leaving them alone with their convictions and their doubts."

His big body bulged out over the Wright-sized table. "And then there was pressure from the other side. The militants in the antiwar movement attacked us for refusing to get our hands dirty even if we were against the war. Nonviolence didn't cut it for them. They wanted us to take up the struggle against the state, as they were prepared to do." Alan seemed anguished.

47

Jimmy said, "After graduation I had a student deferment for art school, but Alan caught it from both sides. The government wanted him to fight the war, and the radicals wanted him to fight the government."

Alan shared a look of dismay with Jimmy and then turned to Toby and me. "I think I told you we knew one of the gang who bombed the physics building, Theo Kearn. He was assigned to be my roommate during freshman year. I used to argue with him all the time. At his Catholic high school, he had studied "just war" theory with some monk who was into social reform. Here he fell under the spell of a radical professor in the history department named Harvey Goldberg, who justified violent revolution. But violence only begets more violence, I told him. I still believe that. By the time he was a senior, Theo had his mind set on striking a blow that would get the attention of the country: he would put an end to the Army Math Research Center. And look at the result. The bombing took the fight out of the protest movement, and when the smoke cleared, guess what? The war continued."

"You say you were roommates?" asked Toby.

"Just one semester," Alan replied. "We didn't have much in common. I don't think anyone was close to Theo except Maureen. He was basically a loner."

"What about you, Jimmy?" Toby asked.

"I didn't care much for him, either. With me it was personal. We were—what's the word?" He thought a moment. "Rivals. Theo was Maureen's boyfriend before I met her. When we started to date, I felt she was carrying a torch for him even though they had broken up. I wanted him gone. And then he *was* gone, after the bombing, when he was on the run. But if anything, it got worse for a while. She pined for him, worried what would happen when he got caught."

"But he never did get caught," said Alan.

"No." Jimmy looked at me. "Made my marriage hell, though, for a couple of years. It was like there were two of us plus a ghost."

"I had my own kind of hell," Alan said. I wondered what he meant by that. He looked around the room, then he stood. "Let's get back to the class. They must be getting ready to leave."

On Saturday morning I checked in with my sister. With so much happening around me, I had almost forgotten I'd promised to call her. It would be afternoon in Ireland now. Sensing that small talk could be painful, I took a direct approach. "Hi, Angie. Is everything OK? Your texts sound unhappy. What's up?"

"I don't know. That's just it. It's been so good here. But all of a sudden I want to go home." With those last words, Angie sounded like a little girl kept too long at a party.

I asked, "You mean, go home for a visit, or go home permanently?"

"I don't even want to think about that. I just want to be in Rockport with Mom and Dad. I miss them."

"It's been almost a year," I said. "Maybe it's time for a visit. Could be that the calendar's calling. It's time to take stock."

"Yeah, that and the ring thing."

"The ring thing? You mean your claddagh ring?" That was the only ring I'd heard about. At the beginning of their courtship, Angie and Bobby had given each other a traditional Irish friendship ring.

"Bobby's been asking me to wear it on my left hand, which you do when you're engaged, but I've been putting him off. I don't really see the point. To switch it to my left hand, I'll have to get the ring made smaller. Later, if we get married, I want to have a gold wedding band on the left hand. Then I'd have to get the claddagh ring made larger again, to wear on the right hand. That's crazy. It makes more sense to leave the claddagh rings be, on our right hands."

I couldn't help hearing this the way Bobby might. What stood out for me was the "if" in "if we get married." Something needed clarifying. "What's the holdup, Angie?"

There was silence, and then she said, tentatively, "I think . . . it's making the commitment to Ireland. If I marry Bobby, I'm marrying Ireland. You know, at the end of this trial year, I feel I belong to Bobby and the farm and the sheep and the island. But I don't feel Irish, not even with my citizenship papers. I still feel American, and I still miss home."

"Well, for now it sounds like you're either going to miss the States or you're going to miss Bobby. Do you know which will hurt more?"

Again there was a silence. "It sounds awful, but I really don't."

"Then maybe you should come back to the States for a visit and see how it feels from here," I suggested.

"That's not a bad idea," she said. "I've been thinking about it, actually. If I did it soon, could I come to see you in Madison before I go home to Massachusetts?"

"Of course you could. I'd love to see you. I know Toby would too. We have plenty of room. When are you thinking of?"

"I'm not sure. Maybe in two weeks? I could look into flights."

"Great. Just let us know."

"I will." She sounded happy again.

It was still early enough on Saturday for me to walk to the farmers' market on the Capitol Square, which I'd been told not to miss. It's billed as the largest producer-only farmers' market in the United States. I had already been impressed by the State Capitol building, a stylistic twin to the US Capitol in Washington, DC, set on a square lawn, each side of which is two blocks long. The mass of shining white marble surrounded on four sides by red, white, and blue canopies casting shade on tables piled with fruits and vegetables was a stirring sight. Approaching, I felt elated by the colors and drawn into the crowd, where I became part of a counterclockwise procession around the four sides of the Square.

Midwestern geniality kept lines of customers from becoming obstructions to the general progress, and orders were filled with smiling efficiency. The biggest knots were at the bakery carts, so I skipped those and searched for products from the earth. By halfway around the Square, my burlap bag was heavy with asparagus, new potatoes, blackberries, rhubarb, and a pot of basil. I decided to make one last purchase, a carton of blazing red strawberries, which I would carefully cradle at the top of my bag. Waiting in a short line, I overheard a conflict at the next stall. A large man in a white apron and a black fedora was telling a customer to "mind your own business." It wasn't the kind of exchange you'd expect at a food stall, in this case, a cheese stand. Tacked to the stand was a hand-lettered sign that proclaimed: "Cheese made with milk from contented cows." It was my turn then, and my vendor tipped his head and said, "Don't mind my neighbor. He's always causing trouble. His cows may be contented, but he never is." I laughed, made my purchase, and cut out for home before the pleasant vibe of the market could be spoiled.

That evening we drove out to Spring Green to see a performance of *Waiting for Godot* at an impressive outdoor theater. We would be back again in just a week to visit Taliesin, but a separate trip to attend the American Players Theatre was well worth it. The site, built against a hill with the stage at the foot of it and rising tiers of seats for the audience, forms a natural amphitheater. The professional acting company was top-notch and the setting idyllic: the moon rose as if on cue as the play began.

In *Waiting for Godot*, two tramps are rooted to the spot where a mysterious figure has promised to meet them, though he never shows up. The tramps discuss leaving but can't bring themselves to go. The play is dark but has its comic moments, which the lead actors played to the hilt. The time comes when one character says to the other, "Let's go," and the other agrees but can't move because his pants have fallen down around his ankles. The audience loved it. On the drive home, Toby scratched his neck and remarked, "It's a brave actor who goes on stage every night and drops his pants for a laugh, with the mosquitoes out."

6

ON SUNDAY TOBY WENT OFF TO SCOUT ANTIQUES and I set out to learn what I could about the bombing of Sterling Hall. Eve's study provided the perfect ambiance for a day of research on the internet. The house was a two-story clapboard bungalow built in the 1920s on the near east side of town. Eve had remodeled the attic into a study. It had a wide-planked pine floor, built-in bookcases, and two skylights that brightened the room with natural light. The desk was centered in a curved nook in front of an eyebrow window, which looked out on Rutledge Street and offered a glimpse of Lake Monona through the treetops. I opened my laptop and settled down to work. Here's what I learned.

On August 24, 1970, at 3:54 a.m., a Ford Econoline van crammed with two tons of nitrate-rich fertilizer and fuel oil pulled into an alley next to Sterling Hall. The building housed the physics department of the university, as well as the Army Math Research Center, which was the target. The bombers chose the middle of the night on a Sunday, between the end of summer session and the beginning of student move-in week, assuming that the building and surrounding area would be deserted.

They were wrong. The blast killed a young physics researcher who was working through the night to finish an experiment, and it seriously injured three others, including a night watchman, who was permanently maimed. The explosion was heard ten miles away; it damaged twenty buildings and shattered windows throughout the city. It was the worst domestic terrorist bombing in the nation's history, prior to the Oklahoma City bombing in 1995.

Fleeing the scene with his coconspirators, Theo Kearn was said to have burst into tears when he heard on the car radio that a person had been killed in the explosion. A life had been taken; and if caught, the bombers could be charged with murder. There were four of them packed into a small Chevrolet Corvair. Two were brothers, local boys raised in a working-class family in Madison. The older brother had been to the university but dropped out. The younger one was drifting. He held odd jobs and sold street drugs. The third conspirator was just eighteen, a freshman from a middle-class family in Delaware, a top student. His job was to call the police with a warning to clear the building, but the warning did no good, since the bomb went off prematurely before anyone had a chance to respond. The fourth gang member, Theo Kearn, was twenty-two, from a respectable family on Philadelphia's Main Line. A former altar boy, he had started college in the Marine ROTC. Now they were all fugitives.

Theo had been a reporter for the *Daily Cardinal*, the student newspaper. He'd started out writing about sports, particularly rowing. He was proud of having a slot on the junior varsity crew. Just as Maureen told me, he had chosen Wisconsin on the strength of the reputation of its rowing program. The university was a contender for a national championship, and Kearn wanted to be on that team. He had spent his high school years building his skills on the Schuykill River, memorialized by Thomas Eakins as the birthplace of American rowing in a dozen exquisite oil paintings that glorify the physiques of young crewmen. But at just under six feet, Theo was considered small for collegiate rowing. Several of his Madison teammates were six feet six. He tried to compensate for his size by training harder than anybody else. Even so, he failed to make the travel squad in his junior year. He found a face-saving excuse to quit the team when the coach ordered everyone to get their hair cut short. He refused and left.

Kearn turned from writing about sports to reporting on the antiwar movement. He covered the violent suppression of student demonstrations and was radicalized by what he saw, once becoming part of the story when he was beaten by police. His teammates later spoke of Kearn as if he'd become a different person. If he hadn't quit the team, one said, he never would have joined the plot to destroy the Army Math Research Center.

Within an hour of the bombing, an all-points bulletin went out for the fleeing suspects. A patrol car stopped the dinky Corvair on Highway 12 leading out of town, and the four men inside said they were going camping, though they had no camping equipment. Almost incredibly, the patrolman let them go. Realizing that a description of their car was now in the police database, the fugitives slipped back into Madison, switched cars, laid low for a few hours, then set out for New York. They split up in Toledo. Kearn continued on to New York by Greyhound Bus. In New York, he prevailed on a friend to drive him to Boston, and from there, he made his way into Canada.

Theo was last spotted eleven days after the bombing by the Royal Canadian Mounted Police. He was holed up in a rooming house in Peterborough, Ontario, a small town north of Toronto. Based on a tip, the police had staked out the house and were waiting for final authorization to raid it. He barely escaped by leaping out of a rear window. And then he disappeared.

The Wisconsin bombers were the subjects of an intense FBI manhunt. The two brothers were captured separately, a few years apart. At a high-profile trial in Madison, the older one expressed regret for the loss of life but said he would do it again. His lawyers thought he could turn the tables by putting the Vietnam War in the dock. Despite the courtroom drama, he was convicted and sentenced to twenty-three years in prison. On his early release after serving only seven years, he returned to Madison and opened a juice wagon on Library Mall. His brother was sentenced to seven years but served only three. He was arrested a second time for selling drugs and went back to jail. The third conspirator was captured in San Rafael, California, a few years later. He too served three years of a seven-year sentence.

As for Kearn, he remains on the FBI's wanted list and could well be their longest-running fugitive. His wanted poster shows a young man with a strong jaw, dark mustache and thin beard, glasses, a low brow, and thick, dark hair. His height is given as five feet eleven to six feet and his weight as 185 pounds. There have been reported sightings of him over the years—in Canada, Hawaii, Costa Rica, Cuba, Algeria, California, Colorado, Ohio, and Pennsylvania—but none of them substantiated. As far as the FBI is concerned, Theo Kearn is still at large.

Or dead. If I hadn't spent all day Sunday immersed in the bombing, I never would have made the connection. But on Tuesday, when I heard the conclusion of the forensic anthropologist's second report, one detail leaped out at me.

"Diane," I said, "Read that last part again." We were waiting to tee off at the first hole at Glenway. Diane had her cell phone in hand and was quoting the highlights of the latest report sent by the forensic anthropologist.

"Which part?" she asked.

"That last part about occupational analysis." We already knew the skeleton was that of a man in his early twenties about six feet tall with a robust athletic build.

Diane flicked the text on her phone with her forefinger to go back a paragraph. "'No signs of trauma, e.g. knife nicks, bullet holes . . .' Wait. Here it is. 'Signs of occupation include strong rotator cuff, deltoid insertion, pectoralis crest and vertical border of scapula, suggesting active use of upper extremities. Marks of identity include hairline stress fractures on the anterolateral aspects of ribs 5 and 7. Callus formation indicates that these fractures were antemortem injuries that healed prior to the time of death. Rib stress fractures stem from repetitive motion and are common injuries in sports such as golf, baseball, squash, and especially crew.'"

Crew—competitive rowing—is what sparked the connection. Before he turned to radical politics, Theo Kearn was dedicated to the sport and worked out relentlessly on rowing machines. His bones would bear the marks. He'd been missing for almost half a century, but what if he'd been in Madison all that time?

"I have a hunch we've found the skeleton of Theo Kearn!"

"Say who?" said Diane.

"Theo Kearn. The bombing of Sterling Hall. 1970." Stress fractures. Rowing. Canada. Vanished without a trace. I recounted everything I knew.

Diane took an audible breath. "Well, it's an interesting guess, I'll give you that. If it's him, how did he end up here? Last seen in Canada, you said."

"Maybe he doubled back. You know, hiding in plain sight?"

"I wouldn't call the bottom of a cistern hiding in plain sight."

Ahead of us, the green was clear now. Diane gripped her driver, wagged her hips, and whacked a beauty straight down the fairway. She pulled out her broken tee and slid the club back into her bag.

"Whoever belongs to those bones didn't crawl in there to hide. Or commit suicide, either. There are easier ways to do it than that. No, there's a crime involved. I can smell it." She looked at me. "You going to play, or not?"

I was too excited for golf. "Aren't you going to make some calls or something?"

"Sure, I'm going to make some calls. But it's a gorgeous day for golf. If this case is as old as you think, a couple more hours won't make a big difference."

"Why do you say that?"

"If the perp is still with us, he's probably using a walker. Let's see what you can do with that driver."

I flubbed the shot. "Not necessarily."

"What?"

"A contemporary of Kearn would be in their early seventies. Lots of people that age are still pretty active." I hooked my second ball onto the wrong fairway.

"All right," said Diane, "I see this isn't working. Let's play three holes and go back to the clubhouse."

The first hole we played was a lost cause. I dug and replaced divots. I did better on the second hole, since it was much like the first, but Diane still outdid me. She took honors and got to go first on the third hole. The tee was high above a gully, which rose steeply to a big sand trap on the right and trees on the left. The green was just behind the sand trap, and there was another trap on the other side of the green. All this—tee to hole—was compressed into a space the size of a basketball court. Using a five iron, Diane sent the ball on a lovely arc onto the green.

"This is more like miniature golf," I complained. Trying to imitate Diane, I teed off with a five iron and sent the ball soaring high over the gully—good. But it dropped suddenly into the first sand trap. Diane winced in sympathy. "It's a deceptive hole," she said. "Things aren't what they seem from the tee." Everything certainly looked different from the sand trap. And from the second sand trap. And from the green. I walked away chastened.

At the clubhouse we sat at a table on the patio and drank Diet Cokes. (I'm not advertising for that brand. I'm just sadly addicted.) Diane punched numbers into her phone and stood up when she reached the FBI. Whether for privacy or a better signal, she walked out to the parking lot and paced its perimeter. When she returned, she looked businesslike. "The FBI is sending an agent from Milwaukee to check out your tip. He'll be here day after tomorrow. Will you be available to meet?"

"If it's after class I can."

"I'll set it up. That gives me a day to get all my stuff in order, files, records, so on. They're going to want to meet with the medical examiner, too. And since no good deed goes unpunished, I get to make the arrangements."

"I'm sorry if I'm making work for you. It's only a guess."

She waved me off. "It's what I do. You say it's only a guess. But if you're right, this becomes a case for the FBI's Joint Terrorism Task Force. Tell you one thing—it's about to get very busy around here." She got to her feet. "Drink up, I've got to get back to the office."

That evening I met Toby for dinner at a Middle Eastern restaurant on State Street, not far from the Capitol Square. I talked while Toby ate. He listened attentively as I laid out the reasons for my speculation about the bones. With the edge of his fork, he slid juicy cubes of lamb kebob from their skewer and mixed them with rice and hummus on his plate. He chewed a chunk thoughtfully and dabbed his lips with a napkin. "It's either a brilliant deduction or off the wall," he said. "I wonder what Jimmy and Alan will have to say about it."

"Or Helen and Maureen."

"They all knew him. It's an odd feeling to be connected to a bag of bones. If it's him, that is. Theo."

"And if it's not? What if I'm wrong?"

"Nobody can fault you for trying to help. Besides, do the cops have any better leads?"

"Not that I'm aware of."

"Well, then. And consider the irony if you're right."

"What irony?"

"Remember, some people thought Theo Kearn might put in an appearance at the sixties reunion?" Toby speared a kebob cube with his fork and pointed it at me. "Can you think of a more dramatic entrance?"

After dinner, we strolled up to the State Capitol and circled the Square, watching the building's pale stonework change in color as we lost the light. Then we headed back down State Street to browse in shop windows. Madison has its sprawling malls and big box stores on its periphery, but the heart of the city beats on State Street. For Madison, it's downtown. The street, which links the campus and the Capitol, is pedestrian-friendly, and it's an easy walk from one end to the other. Many of the shops occupy low, two-story buildings. Some are historic. On early mornings when the sun falls on the old buildings, the street can take on the air of a lonely Edward Hopper painting. Nightlife draws the students. On weekends they line up outside the bars, skimpily dressed, waiting their turn to get in.

We spent an hour happily hunting in the narrow aisles of a used bookstore near campus and hauled home two plastic shopping bags of purchases. Toby found an out-of-print book on restoring vintage furniture. I found a gorgeous coffee table book on American impressionism, lavishly illustrated. It would have been too expensive to buy when new. Unlike used cars, used furniture, used clothes, and other worn-out items, a used book never really gets old. Even when it falls apart, its words continue to exist in some form, somewhere, perhaps in someone, a reader. A comforting thought.

7

THE NEXT MORNING, AS THE CLASS FILED OUT, I flagged down Maureen and Helen and asked for a word. "I have something sensitive to discuss with you," I said. "Could you sit with me for a few minutes?" I lowered myself into one of the student desks, and they did the same.

Maureen blurted out, "Sorry. I said I wouldn't talk in class, but today I was a chatterbox." She was blushing again.

"No," I protested. "On the contrary, you made a great contribution." We'd been talking about the work of Berthe Morisot, whose sister Edma had been a promising painter too. But Edma gave up her career when she married, while Berthe went on to become a prominent figure in the impressionist movement. I remembered Helen telling me that in the early years of her marriage, Maureen had put her career on hold to support Jimmy's ambitions. She had blossomed as an artist in her own right only in the last few years. I had hoped Maureen would share her personal experience with the class, and I was pleased she did.

"This is about something outside class." Helen squirmed in her seat, like a kid in the principal's office. Maureen sat still and waited for me to continue.

"I've had a conversation with the campus police that I think I should tell you about." As I talked, I realized how alarming my words sounded. "Nothing about you directly, but about your friend Theo Kearn."

Both women looked surprised, but only Helen moved. Her hands went up, palms bent outward in a gesture of wonder. "You went to the police with what we said about Theo over lunch? What did we say that could—"

"Let me finish. This has to do with the bones that were found in the Bascom Hall flood. I'm friendly with a detective, Diane Young, who's trying to identify the victim. I was with her when she got the forensic report on the bones, and there were details about them that clicked with what I knew about Theo. There's a chance that the remains may be his."

Judging from their reactions, both women were hearing this news for the first time. Helen was still for a moment. "No," she said. "I have a hard time believing that. Theo left town right after the bombing. There was a huge manhunt for him."

"I know," I said, "but he could have returned."

"Those can't be his bones," said Maureen firmly.

"Returned for what?" asked Helen.

I pressed on. "Could he have come back to see somebody, to settle things before he went into hiding finally, or to get money?"

Helen's hands crossed over her heart. "He would have contacted one of us," she said. "We never heard from him."

"Did you expect to?"

"No, but for all these years we've thought of him as alive in Canada," said Helen. "Now you say he's been rotting in a tank of water all that time. It's a terrible image."

"I told you already, those can't be his bones," said Maureen, getting up. She signaled to Helen that they were leaving. As they walked to the door, she turned and said, "I've seen him. Theo is alive."

61

That knocked me back a step. I felt besieged by a flurry of questions. Had I drawn the wrong conclusion and raised a false alarm that would make Diane look foolish for calling in the FBI? No, if Theo Kearn were alive, they'd want to know about it. And if dead, they'd want to know that too. If alive, where had Maureen seen him? When? Did she know where he was hiding? Or had she been mistaken? Had she merely thought she'd seen him? It was clear by the way she'd turned on her heel that Maureen had no intention of continuing the conversation.

Toby had agreed to meet me at Library Mall for lunch, after which I had a courtesy call lined up with my department chair. We'd been introduced briefly, but this was to be our get-acquainted visit. A variety of outdoor food wagons made the mall a good option for a quick lunch, since it was on the way to the department. I got there first, chose the Thai cart, and carried a plastic box of pad thai to a small wrought-iron table. I remembered that one of the bombers had run a juice cart at this very location after he was released from prison. It was hard to picture an ex-bomber as a benevolent dispenser of smoothies.

Toby arrived expecting to prep me for my meeting with the chair, but I could barely restrain myself from sharing Maureen's bombshell. "So much for my grand deduction. Kearn's alive! She claims she saw him."

Toby gave voice to several of the questions and objections that had been running through my mind. Where? When? "She could have imagined it."

"That's what I've been telling myself. But now I'm fretting over talking to the FBI. I've got Diane worked up about the bones, and they may have nothing to do with Kearn. On the other hand, would I be betraying a confidence if I passed on what Maureen just said?"

Toby frowned. "Betraying a confidence? Hardly. This guy is wanted by the FBI. You don't want to withhold information. Just tell them what you know."

I thought things over while Toby went up to the Mexican food cart and returned with a drink and a plate of tacos. "Will you come with me tomorrow to Diane's meeting with the FBI agent? I'd like you to be there."

"Sure," he said, "if they let me in."

I said I'd ask Diane. We turned to our food and ate for a while. Toby went back to the Mexican cart for more napkins. When he returned, he said, "Can we talk about this meeting you're about to have with your department chair? What would you like to come out of it?"

I sighed. "That's hard for me to say with everything that's going on. I don't know."

Toby took a swig of soda. "Well, pretend for the moment that nothing else is going on. How interested are you in a teaching job here? You didn't give Eve any encouragement when she raised the possibility with you."

"I still feel that way. But I wouldn't clap my hands over my ears and refuse to listen if they wanted to recruit me. There would be a lot to think about. It would mean moving up to the big leagues and all that would entail."

"Such as?"

"Bigger classes, and teaching assistants to train and manage. Prestige, but also pressure to perform. More money, though not that much more. Opportunities to teach graduate students and direct dissertations, although I'm happy as I am, teaching undergraduates. Greater emphasis on research and publication, with a lighter teaching load as a trade-off. Conferences, committee work, and sharper departmental politics. In other words, there would be pros and cons."

"So, you *have* been thinking about it," said Toby.

"Hard not to. How would you feel about it, though?"

"It would be your call. I mean that. It's your career. I could open a gallery in Madison, no problem. There's always a market for art and antiques in a university town, and this is a good-sized one. There's not that much competition from what I've seen. Housing prices are way cheaper here than in California. If we sold our house in Bodega Bay, we could buy a mansion here with the proceeds. Then there are the lakes, parks, even a zoo; museums, a symphony orchestra, opera and ballet, lectures, bookstores, professional theater. Good kebobs. All and all, a nice place to live. Madison reminds me of Berkeley but with parking spaces."

"Don't forget the winter."

"There's that," he acknowledged ruefully. "Now I'm thinking of Napoleon's retreat from Moscow." He faked a shiver. "On the plus side, you already have a friend in the department."

"And an enemy," I parried. We finished lunch, Toby wished me luck, and I went off to my appointment.

The Department of Art History is housed within the campus art museum. As you enter the building, a utilitarian glass door opens onto a high atrium with a wide stairway leading to the art collection. To the right of the stairway are doors to the Kohler Art Library. My mind flitted to the attractive prospect of having a library like that just downstairs from my office as a year-round aid to research and teaching. I mounted the stairs to the main floor of the old art museum, now the smaller part of an expanded complex named the Chazen. Access to the department from here is down a hall to the right. I entered the long corridor, found Eve's office, and closed myself in for a quick primp in the mirror that she'd propped on the bookshelf next to her desk. Then I headed for the chair's office.

Doug Harrison was a dapper man with a practiced evasive manner, a skill highly prized in an administrator. He had chestnut-brown hair, which he wore long, and dark eyebrows fixed above a pair of close-set eyes. Altogether, he reminded me of the sleek, well-groomed ermine in Leonardo da Vinci's painting of a lady holding such a creature as a pet. He invited me with a gracious gesture to take a seat in front of his desk. I noticed on the wall a framed doctoral certificate from the University of St. Andrews in Scotland, a prestigious institution, to be sure. Even so, hanging your diploma in the office isn't the custom at the institutions I'm familiar with. Some would consider the gesture boastful. It's true, I suppose, that different professions have different norms. Physicians display their diplomas (and lawyers do too) in order to inspire confidence.

A patient waiting in a doctor's office can say to herself, "Well, at least he's passed his coursework." Professors, on the other hand, don't usually hang up their shingles. I'm not even sure where my PhD diploma is these days—probably moldering in a box somewhere.

Harrison noticed me noticing. "A conversation piece," he intimated, swiveling in his chair and pointing over his shoulder. "People aren't sure where St. Andrews is."

"Scotland," I said.

"Yes," he replied, slightly surprised. "One of the best places in Europe for art history. Let me see. You did your work at Berkeley, if I recall."

"That's right," I said.

"Another fine program," he allowed, thumbing through my file, which he had open in front of him. "Who was your dissertation director?"

"Esther Raleigh," I told him.

"Hmm," he mused, scrunching up his lip, "I don't seem to recognize the name."

"She's written extensively on Mary Cassatt."

"Raleigh." He rose, crossed the room, and withdrew a massive volume from an oak bookcase. "Just curious. Let's see if she's in *Who's Who in Academe*." He returned to his desk with the heavy tome and fanned through the pages. "How do you spell the last name?" He made a show of checking the same page twice. "No," he said at last, "apparently she's not listed."

It was a safe bet to assume that *he* was listed. But all that meant was he'd responded to a flattering invitation to list his accomplishments and pay several hundred dollars for a copy of the volume in which his name appeared. For a little extra, there would be a plaque. Yes, there it was, on the wall next to the bookcase. It wasn't exactly vanity publishing, but it came close.

"I'll send you a link to the department's faculty bibliography," I offered, "if you're still curious."

"Yes, please do," he said. There was an awkward pause. I filled it.

"I wanted to stop by to thank you for helping to arrange my teaching exchange with Eve this summer."

"Not at all. It's a good opportunity for our students. And for the department too. Broadens our curriculum." He leaned back and clasped his hands on my file. "We're a bit light in our offerings in the nineteenth century. In fact, we might have a vacancy in that area coming up. Eve may have mentioned it."

"She did say something to that effect," I confirmed, neutrally.

"Of course, it's too early to say anything definite," he went on. "The executive committee will meet in the fall to set hiring priorities. Then the dean has to agree to authorize a search. It's not a given that we'll be able to list the position. And if we do get approval, I don't know whether the listing will be for a senior appointment or at the entry level. But then again, it might be."

A simple declarative sentence was out of his reach.

"Hmm." I nodded again.

"I'd be happy to keep you posted if you think you might be interested."

"That would be good of you," I said.

There was another lull. I concluded that the job interview portion of the meeting, if that's what this was, was over.

"So, how do you like Madison so far?" The small talk continued for several minutes. He asked about my course. I mentioned there were two older women in my class and wondered if that was unusual in the summer session.

"It's happening more and more. We get retirees coming to Madison for the summer. They take advantage of cheap rents in town and prevail on faculty to let them sit in on classes for free. It gives them something to do. You don't have to admit them."

"Oh, but I'm happy to have them," I said. "They add an interesting mix of perspectives. The students don't seem to mind having a few members of their grandparents' generation in the classroom."

"It's up to you. Not all the faculty like it."

I was about to reply when, without a knock, the door flew open and Magnus Arp barged in, red-faced and belligerent.

"What do you want, Magnus?" snapped Harrison, annoyed. "This is a private meeting."

"So I was told by your secretary," said Arp. He had the effrontery to pull up a chair, unasked. "If you're discussing the job opening, maybe it shouldn't be private."

"Professor Barnes is here on a courtesy call. We were discussing the summer teaching exchange."

"We can start there," said Arp. "Who authorized it? The department never voted to approve it."

"The dean approved it," said Harrison, scowling.

"What concerns me is that this exchange could lead to a permanent position," said Arp, talking by me as if I weren't in the room. "And I have a right to know who'll be sitting on the council of full professors when my case for promotion comes up."

So that was it. Arp was worried about his promotion from associate to full professor, and he'd got it into his head that the women faculty in the department were against him. That explained why he thought Eve was pushing to get me hired and that, if she succeeded, I'd join their ranks in opposing him.

"I have to say, Magnus, you're way out of line. As I explained to Nora here, we don't even have authorization yet to conduct a search, let alone at what level, so your anxiety on that score is premature. Now please go. I'll be happy to meet with you separately to discuss your concerns. In fact, you can set up an appointment with my secretary on your way out." Harrison pointed toward the door. "Please go," he repeated.

I clasped my hands on my lap and studied them. For a minute the scene was frozen. Then abruptly, Arp got up and left.

Harrison slumped back in his chair. "I have to apologize for my colleague. He's overdue for promotion, but the committee is waiting for him to finish his book on Frank Lloyd Wright. He's been promising to include a new discovery, but he hasn't found what he's looking for."

"I see," I said.

"He's very high strung." Harrison cleared his throat. "But that doesn't excuse his rudeness."

I said, "No. What's more, he seems to have something against women faculty."

"Really? That would certainly be wrong."

From there the conversation petered out until I sensed a decent interval had passed. "Thanks for making time to see me," I said, rising. "I'll let you get back to what you were doing."

What he'd been doing when I came in was looking through the *Chronicle of Higher Education*, spread open to the job listings for administrators. I guessed that he'd been daydreaming about a deanship somewhere.

Sometime later, Toby asked, "So, how did your meeting go with the chair?"

"Oh boy," I said.

"That bad, eh?"

"Lee probably had a better time at Appomattox."

"Come over here, you need a hug." He gave me a long, comforting squeeze, my head nestled against his neck. "Don't want to talk about it?"

"Later, maybe," I said. "I'm starving. Let's eat."

For dinner we picked up takeout from a good little Indian restaurant on Williamson Street, near Eve's house. It included everybody's favorite, chicken tikka masala, spiced-up rice, a creamed spinach dish that Toby likes, and ginger naan, all tasty. It was almost dark by the time we finished, but I was too hyped up to bring the day to a close. Toby was up for a bit of adventure. "How about a bike ride?" I suggested. Eve had left two bicycles for our use, hers and her husband's, and we had talked before about an evening ramble as a way to get to know the neighborhood. The weather was ideal, warm and dry. The sky was streaked with orange, and the crickets were starting their musical number. We donned helmets and rolled the bicycles from the garage to the street. They were really old models with three-speed gearshifts, which was fine with me, since I'm an unsteady biker. We checked to make sure the headlights were working and the taillight reflectors were in place, and then we set off.

Eve's house was located a couple of blocks from Orton Park in an older east side neighborhood near the point where the Yahara River meets Lake Monona. The streets were narrow, lined with mature locust trees and rows of cars parked nose to tail against the curb. The leafy streets were pretty, but the lines of cars parked on both sides made for crowded biking conditions. We could be squeezed into tight spaces by oncoming traffic or cars coming up behind us wanting to pass. Yet traffic was light at that hour, and drivers would surely be considerate. Signs admonished cars to yield to bicycles and pedestrians, and Midwesterners obey the rules.

Toby led and I followed, single file. We pedaled up and over the little bridge that crosses the Yahara, turned onto Riverside Drive, and rode alongside the park that borders Lake Monona, deserted at this hour save for a lone old man walking his dog. At the end of the street, we bore right and kept going until we found ourselves in a tangle of unfamiliar streets that took us forward, around, back, and every which way until we were lost. We rode for what must have been an hour. It was dark by then and the street signs were difficult to read. At last, we turned onto a street that Toby recognized and which he was confident would lead us home.

Suddenly—out of nowhere—a vehicle came up behind us with its headlights blazing, radio blaring, and engine revving. It nudged my rear tire and almost toppled me. "Toby!" I called out.

"Turn right at the next corner," he shouted back. "Let's get out of this jerk's way." Toby took the turn and I followed, braking to keep the bike from slipping out from under me. The phantom vehicle made the turn too. By then it was clear that the driver was maliciously stalking us. I twisted my head to try to get a look at him, but the beams from high-intensity headlights were blinding. The lights were placed too high for a sedan—judging from their height above the ground, it probably was an SUV. Its color was dark. That's all I could tell.

Toby waved his arm, signaling the driver to pass. But instead of passing, the driver flicked his lights as a taunt. Then he began closing the distance between us as I pedaled behind Toby. We were pinned in. We couldn't hop the curb to the sidewalk because of the parked cars, and it wasn't safe to cross into the lane for oncoming traffic. Next, I felt a bump on my rear carrying rack. I struggled to keep the bike upright. Another bump. Then the driver gunned the engine and rammed me hard enough to run me into the back of Toby's bike. We both went sprawling in an entanglement of wheels and legs. The driver pulled around us and shot off with a screech of tires.

Toby was up quickly, checking himself and me for injuries. My knees were scraped and so were the palms of my hands. My right hip was starting to ache. Later I looked and saw it had turned black and blue. Toby had a banged-up elbow that was bleeding. I staunched the blood with tissues from my fanny pack. Fortunately, we got away with scrapes and bruises. When we got back to the house, Toby called the city police. The young cop who responded arrived in a squad car in ten minutes. After he took our information, he told us there had been a spate of incidents in town of vehicles intimidating cyclists. Probably teenagers out joyriding. Best not to be riding our bikes at night.

"Teenagers," Toby repeated skeptically after the young cop left.

"You don't think it could have been Arp, do you?" I asked.

"I wouldn't put it past him," said Toby. "I'm also thinking it's a strange coincidence that someone comes after you—us—the day after you come up with your theory about the bones. Could be that someone doesn't want you probing the past."

"So far I've only told Diane."

"What about Maureen and Helen?"

"Yes, them too."

"That means the campus police know about it, and the alumni know about it. Word travels pretty fast these days."

It took me a minute or two to process that. Why not go for the simplest explanation? "Couldn't the cop be right? Teenagers?"

"The radio in that SUV was on pretty loud. Did you hear what was playing? I'm giving you a clue."

Toby took my hand. I thought for a few seconds. The Beatles. The title of one of their earliest hits, "I Want to Hold Your Hand."

"Right. And that's not what teenagers are listening to today. It's music from their grandparents' generation."

"I listen to the Beatles."

"So do I, but it's music from the past."

"And you're suggesting that means an older driver?"

"It's just a thought," said Toby.

8

HELEN WASN'T IN CLASS THE NEXT MORNING, and I wondered if her absence had anything to do with the bike incident the night before. "She asked me to apologize to you for missing class," Maureen explained when class was over. "A family matter came up. She'll be back tomorrow."

"I'm glad to hear that. I'd hate to feel I spoiled the course for either of you by speculating about your friend." We started walking down the hill together.

"They're not Theo's bones," Maureen said again, stopping short and looking me in the eye. "It's not him."

"We won't know for sure until the test results come in. Perhaps the tests will prove you're right."

"They will," she said, resuming her walk. "I told you yesterday. I've seen Theo. I know he's alive."

I meant to avoid pushing her further, but I couldn't keep myself from asking, "When was this? Do you mind talking about it?"

She pursed her lips and said, "It was almost two weeks ago, the Friday of the sixties reunion, at a panel on the Dow demonstration. Somebody asked for a show of hands of people who were there in '67. I was in a seat toward the front, so I turned to look around the room. There was Theo, standing at the back, next to the exit."

"Did you get a good look at him?"

"He wasn't near me, if that's what you mean, and when so many people turned around to look for raised hands, he left. I didn't get a long look, either, but I'm sure it was him."

"What makes you so sure?"

"Maybe it was the way he was standing or the way he moved. He was lean, with big shoulders like Theo. He had a beard and his hair was gray, but I thought I could still make out his facial structure. I've sketched that head so many times—the long face, with a bold nose, and a squared-off, jutting chin."

"You could see all that from the front row to the back?"

"In my mind I have a clear picture of him," she maintained.

We continued to walk as the lake came gradually into view. "I respect that you're convinced," I said. "But sometimes the eye sees what the mind wants it to see rather than what's there. Think about it: the reunion brought back memories of the old days, when Theo was in your life. People were talking about him, even wondering if he'd make an appearance. Theo was on your mind. You could easily have mistaken someone else for him."

"That's what Jimmy says, it was just my imagination. But I know better."

"Was Jimmy with you?"

"It so happens he was, yes. He says I was wrong. He thinks Theo is probably dead."

"I hope you won't be too disappointed if it turns out he's right."

"If Theo's dead, I'll be more than disappointed. I'll be grieving."

I let that declaration draw a line under the conversation. We were headed for the Memorial Union food court, taking the back way behind the theater and then across the Terrace. When we were in sight of the big oak under which we had our first lunch together, I was surprised to spot Helen, sitting at a table with a burly man of her own age, not Alan. He looked familiar, but I couldn't place him. Helen was leaning in, pointing aggressively at his chest, and he was recoiling.

"Don't look," said Maureen, catching me by the elbow and leading me away, so Helen wouldn't see us. "That's her ex-husband, Walt. He's the family matter that kept her out of class today."

"It looks a bit fraught."

"It always is, with Walt. He was a sweet guy once, but he soured when Helen left him."

"That was a long time ago, no?"

"Oh yes. Their daughter, Beth, was just a toddler." Maureen halted, remembering. "Helen moved out and took Beth to Chicago, but Walt stayed on the farm in Spring Green. He still lives there."

As she resumed walking, my memory clicked in. I had seen Helen's ex at the farmers' market. He was the disputatious vendor who was arguing with a customer.

"I can't quite picture Helen on a farm," I said.

Maureen chuckled. "She couldn't quite picture herself on one, either. That was one of their problems, but not the only one." She paused, recollecting, then continued. "Beth used to visit her father in summer and on some weekends. That kept Helen involved with Walt, however tense it was. They have Beth in common."

At the food court we picked up lunches to take to our spouses. Toby and I were scheduled to meet with Diane and an FBI agent to discuss my hunch about the bones. At the same time, I felt duty bound to report Maureen's claim of seeing Kearn alive. Before we parted, I mentioned that I would relay her sighting.

"Don't fret about that on my account," she reassured me. "If I had a dollar for every time the FBI came knocking on my door asking questions about Theo, I'd be a rich woman. The thing is, I don't know any more now than I did then."

The UW–Madison Police Department occupies a two-story gray-bricked building on Monroe Street, across from the football stadium. In a meeting room on the second floor, we sat around an oval table and introduced ourselves. Special Agent Daryl Whelk of the FBI took up more than his share of the space. He was tall—basketball player tall—and given to looming. Even when he was seated, his long torso projected forward over the table. His dark hair was styled short on the sides, with a pompadour swirled with gel so that it stood up like a scoop of ice cream, adding a superfluous inch to his height. His hair gel filled the room with the surprising scent of peaches. He wore a blue suit over an open-collar shirt and cowboy boots.

Toby and I wore casual summer dress. Diane looked sober but shapely in her uniform. "Thank you for coming," she began. "We're always glad for a chance to cooperate with the FBI." She passed around a brief agenda while we exchanged business cards.

Agent Whelk took his time reading Diane's and mine, but when he came to Toby's card, he frowned. He put a palm on the armrest of his chair and swiveled toward him. "Art and antiques," he read. His tone conveyed a smidgeon of disdain. "May I ask what your role is at this meeting?"

Toby knew when he was being disrespected, and as a result gave a smart-ass reply, pointing to me. "I'm with her." He settled into his chair possessively.

Diane quickly intervened to smooth things over. "Mr. Sandler is here at my invitation," she explained. "Toby and Nora have worked with law enforcement before and have helped solve important cases. They're a team."

"All the same, they don't have clearance from the FBI. As far as the bureau is concerned, you and I are the team," said Whelk.

"They're here as consultants, at my invitation," repeated Diane.

He shrugged. "It's your turf. I won't make an issue out of it. I'm just saying that if the FBI joins this case, I'll be working directly with you." He pointed a finger first at his chest and then at Diane's, obviously checking her out.

Diane straightened in her chair. "Without Nora's contribution we wouldn't be having this meeting," she pointed out.

"I understand that. But over the years we've had a series of false leads concerning this fugitive. This one may not pan out either." He turned to address me. "Look, the FBI welcomes information from the public, but whenever tips come in from amateur detectives, we tend to be skeptical. Too many people watch crime shows on TV and think they're Miss Marple."

Another gratuitous insult. Toby must have been fuming, but he remained on his best behavior. "We'll take our directions from Diane, if that's all right with you," he said evenly. "We're here to help and have no intention of getting in the way. If we aren't useful to the investigation, we'll disappear."

"That's the right attitude," said Agent Whelk, adopting a more cordial tone now that he had peed on the bushes and defined his territory. "As long as we keep things that way, we'll get on." As if to demonstrate his primacy, he then pushed back his chair, raised his long legs, and crossed his ankles on top of the table. Turning on the charm, he said to Diane, "Before we get started, how do you like my boots? I'm still breaking them in."

In the middle of the table, they were hard to ignore. "I didn't know that agents were allowed to wear cowboy boots," she replied, evading the question of her opinion. "Isn't there a strict FBI dress code?"

"Suits are mandatory, but we have some latitude when it comes to footwear."

"They look expensive," she observed.

"They would be, if you bought them retail. These babies are hand-tooled by a Navajo craftsman. Happens to be a friend of mine. If you're into leather goods or silver—bracelets, earrings, and whatnot—I can get you a super discount. He's from New Mexico but he's working in Chicago now."

The room was quiet. He looked around. "Okay, where were we?" he asked, as if someone else had derailed the meeting.

"The agenda?" said Diane.

"Right," said Whelk, taking up his copy.

"I'd like to add an item to it," said Toby. "Nora and I were stalked by a car last night. We were riding our bikes and almost got run down."

Whelk looked dubious.

"It was intentional," added Toby. He gave a short account of the incident.

Diane, with an expression of concern, asked if we'd been seriously hurt. Whelk asked if we could identify the driver. The answer to both questions was no.

"Then I suggest we file it and move on," said Whelk. "The cop who came to your house was probably right. Teenagers out for a joyride. You're lucky it wasn't worse."

Toby was indignant. "I mentioned the assault because it's obviously related to this case. I think someone was trying to scare Nora off, someone familiar with her theory about the bones."

"So noted," said Whelk, in a tone of forbearance, "but in the absence of any evidence, a connection between your bicycle accident and your wife's theory about the bones is hypothetical. The important question is whether that theory is correct. That's the reason I'm here."

Toby was inclined to continue his protest, but Diane asserted her authority. "Then let's move to the main item on the agenda," she said. She had listed two questions for me to discuss: Why did I think the bones were the remains of Theo Kearn, and how did I reach that conclusion?

I feared that by making me the center of attention, Diane ran the risk of rubbing Agent Whelk the wrong way. To reduce the friction to his ego, I adopted a deferential tone. And given his hostility to amateur detectives, I made no special claim to Miss Marple–like powers of deduction. Instead, I stressed the role of happenstance in leading me to my conclusion.

Step by step, I outlined the sequence of events that led me to hazard what was still only a guess. First, I was present at the discovery of the bones and naturally took an interest in the case. Next, I had recently learned about Theo Kearn from people who had known him personally. Curiosity prompted me to find out more about him, and that research prepared me to connect the dots in the forensic anthropologist's report.

Diane had copies of the report, which she handed out. Together we looked at the passage describing types of injury common in competitive rowing. I said I would have missed the significance of stress fractures to the ribs if I hadn't just been reading about Kearn's dedication to the sport. The conjunction of these events over a short period of time, I explained, is what shaped my thinking.

This approach had a positive effect on Whelk. He hadn't been taking notes, but he had been listening closely, looking over at Diane from time to time with more than polite interest. Still, I had engaged his attention. The result was a perceptible change in his attitude toward the team around the table, off which he took his feet.

"Fair enough" he said. "It's a credible theory."

"Nora's being far too modest," said Diane. "It took ingenuity to make the connection."

"Agreed. That is, if she's right. Stress fractures of the ribs, huh? It's not enough for a positive ID, but it's worth following up." He slapped the table. "All right, I'm in." Whelk leaned over the table again, stopping two inches from my cheek, forcing me to edge my chair back. "Here's the plan. We need to light a fire under the State Crime Lab, insist on jumping the line for a DNA test. I'll make that request on behalf of the FBI." He looked to Diane. "DNA may be the gold standard for identification, but it's not the only tool in the box. Do we have a jawbone with teeth?"

"We have a partial," she answered.

"Then we can try to run a dental X-ray comparison."

"Does the FBI still have Kearn's dental records after all this time?" asked Toby.

"They should. The bureau would have asked for a copy from his dentist when they put him on the wanted list. They didn't have DNA analysis back then, not until the early eighties. With two types of evidence, we'll know for sure if the bones belong to Kearn or to some other poor bastard." There was something new in Whelk's voice, a hint of excitement. The use of "we" was a positive sign.

"Um, there's something else I ought to tell you," I said with trepidation. I didn't want to set things back.

"What's that?" asked Whelk.

"There's an older woman in the class I'm teaching who thinks that Kearn is still alive. She says she saw him here two weeks ago."

His eyes widened. "A sighting? That's even better than a bag of bones. It means a chance to catch him. You should have told me that in the first place. What's her name? I'll need to talk to her."

"Maureen Day. You probably have a file on her already. She was Kearn's girlfriend in high school and college before he became radicalized. She's here for the summer with her husband and several friends. They were students here in the sixties, and they all knew Kearn."

"I'll need to talk to all of them. Can you get me their names?"

"Yes. I brought a list with email addresses."

"Good thinking. If Kearn is alive and in Wisconsin, he's mine. Do you know that movie *Les Misérables*? Normally I don't like musicals, but that one I saw three times. I'm like the inspector who never gives up the chase."

"Javert?" I offered.

"That's him." He gave a toothy smile.

"He's your hero?" said Toby. "He hounded a man for twenty years for stealing a loaf of bread."

"He didn't make the law, he was just enforcing it," said Whelk. "Anyhow, we're talking about domestic terrorism here!" He sprang to his feet and began pacing with gangly exuberance. "If I could bring in Theo Kearn, it would be the making of my career, even better than cracking one of those big cases on the East or West Coast. They get all the attention. They don't know you in the Midwest."

"Have you ever put in for a transfer?" asked Diane.

"I can't wander too far afield with an elderly mother to look after in Milwaukee. I'm tied to the Midwest." He sat back down. "But who am I kidding? I don't think there's a chance of catching Kearn. It's much more likely he's dead by now."

"Why do you say that?" I asked.

"Because if he were alive, we would have caught him years ago." Whelk's pride in the agency in which he served was rather touching.

"Well," said Diane, "let's get to work." To Whelk she said: "I'll start by taking you up to Bascom Hall to see the crime scene. With that, twisting arms at the State Crime Lab, and interviewing Maureen Day and her friends, there's a lot to do." She stood and said, "Thanks, you two. We'll follow through on what we've got so far. I suggest we touch base again next week. Same day and time? Can you all make it?" Toby and I said we could.

"I can if you let me take you out to dinner tonight," said Whelk, in a surge of boldness. His try at a seductive wink was met by a glare of rebuke. "All right. Yes, I can make it," he said, backing off and blinking rapidly to cover his ocular gaffe. As we exited, Whelk lingered behind.

"Phew! I don't know what to make of him," I told Toby. Whelk's unpredictable behavior had thrown me off balance.

Not Toby. "I know what to make of him," he replied. "He's full of himself. But I made up my mind not to let him rattle me."

I put my arm around his waist. "Thank you for keeping your temper. I'm sure Diane appreciates it. I know I do."

"So noted," said Toby with a wink, puffing out his chest. His imitation was spot-on.

After a few hours of class preparation at home, I found my mind wandering back to the meeting. Impulsively, I dialed Diane's number. When she answered briskly, I fished for something to say. "Hi. Um. I just wanted to check if you thought today's meeting went all right."

"Sure," she said, "if you make allowances for quirks. We followed up on the names you gave us, and we have interviews set up with three of the four."

"Quick work," I said. "It's only been a few hours."

"Quick work is Agent Whelk's strong point. I could have him arrested him for exceeding the social speed limit."

"How so?"

"He insisted on showing me his new smartwatch, which gives you a complete physical besides telling the time. For one thing, it gives your heart rate. He pushes a button and up comes a zigzag pattern on the screen with a number, sixty-four. Then he comes over and takes it again, eighty-two. 'See,' he says, 'my heart beats faster when I'm near you.'"

"What a line!"

"Then he starts in with personal questions, such as am I straight, am I single, and do I live alone, followed by a high-pressure renewal of his dinner invitation."

"What counts as high pressure?"

"He implied that leaving your visiting agent alone for dinner constitutes failure to cooperate with the FBI. Or at least a lack of basic hospitality."

"Where is he visiting from?" I asked.

"Just Milwaukee. He'll be spending most weeknights in Madison, but he'll return to Milwaukee on the weekends unless he's needed here."

"Then your dereliction of dinner-dating will be confined to Monday through Thursday. How long do you think you'll hold out?"

"Forever. Well, at least until the case is closed. That's my policy, and I'm sticking to it."

"It won't be easy. He strikes me as the persistent type."

"Well, if he tries to follow me home, I'll introduce him to my father. That should cool him off."

"I thought you lived alone."

"I do, but Pop lives right next door. That way I can keep tabs on his health, and he can keep tabs on my love life. Puts a crimp in dating, but the arrangement comes in handy on occasion."

"Then you and Whelk have something in common. He has a parent to look after too."

"Don't think I didn't notice. He gets points for that. But for all the time he spends with his mother, he should have learned how to approach a woman by now."

I heard her shuffling papers. "How did he behave on your trip to the Bascom attic?" I asked.

"There he behaved like a pro. He was fearless about going out on the planks that forensics set out. He wanted to see for himself how a person could fall over the edge and into the cistern. It's risky up there right now—even though there's been work to stabilize the structure. But he got right up to the tank and acted out scenarios that brought the crime alive for me. And for him too. I'm optimistic—we're going to determine who those bones belong to, and we're going to find out who drowned him."

I said, "Let me see if I can sum this up. You're a team but not an item."

"That's a good way of putting it," she said. "Remind me of that, will you, if I drop my guard."

9

IT'S AN EASY DRIVE FROM MADISON TO SPRING GREEN, a straight shot west on Highway 14. We were in a retired school bus with Toby's class, and it was nearly full, since spouses and partners had been included to help split the cost of the rental. At Taliesin the tour would be conducted by an in-house guide. On the bus, Arp stood in the stairwell next to the driver and spoke into a handheld mic, preparing the group for our visit. As he gazed down the aisle, he pretended not to see me. I pretended not to see him back.

Toby and I were sitting behind Alan and Helen, with Jimmy and Maureen a few rows behind us. Alan twisted in his seat and said over his shoulder, "So, you really think they're Theo's bones?" The word was out that I had prompted a visit from the FBI.

I said, "It's a possibility."

"The FBI seems to think so," said Helen, twisting around in her seat too. "We're all being interviewed next week."

"I'm to blame for that. I mentioned you all knew him."

"It's not a problem for me," said Helen.

Toby leaned forward and in a low voice asked the pair, "How's Jimmy dealing with it? I mean, with Maureen claiming Kearn's alive and she's seen him?"

Alan took a glance beyond us, to check that Jimmy wasn't listening. Then he said, quietly, "He's agitated. He gets strung out whenever Maureen starts thinking about Theo again. It puts stress on their relationship. He thinks she's imagining things, but that doesn't make it easier."

Helen interrupted in a hoarse whisper. "Maureen's just fine," she said, more to Alan than to us. "Jimmy exaggerates when he gets upset." With that, she turned to face front. Alan gave a mocking thrust of his chin before he turned too. He didn't like being contradicted.

We listened to Arp for a while, but the cranky sound system garbled his words. He was telling us about Wright's early years. I leaned back in my seat and watched the scenery go by—well-tended fields, red barns, a few tidy small towns, soft, rolling hills—a "green and pleasant land," to borrow Blake's description of the English countryside.

According to Arp, Wright roamed the hills and valleys of this corner of rural Wisconsin in his youth, observing and bonding with nature. Years later, at a critical moment in his life, he returned to build his home and studio in Spring Green. He had abandoned his young family in Oak Park, Illinois, and run off to Europe with the wife of a client, Mamah Cheney. He hoped the new home would be their refuge from the ensuing scandal. He called it Taliesin, which in Welsh means "shining brow."

Our bus delivered us to the visitor center, where we milled around in the gift shop, waiting for our tour to begin. All sorts of Wright merchandise were on display: mugs, puzzles, coasters, scarves, blankets, cushions, throw rugs, and whatnots bearing images of Wright's designs. I wasn't drawn to the souvenirs. The book section, however, lured me with its full stock of titles on architecture and Wright's life and work. I was thumbing through an attractive, well-illustrated volume, considering whether to buy it, when Jimmy approached me.

"Can I talk to you a minute?" he asked. He looked nervous.

"Sure. Is everything okay with you and Maureen?"

"It's this business with the FBI."

"I take it you got a call setting up an interview."

"That's right. The FBI agent mentioned your name."

"It's nothing to worry about," I said, carefully sliding the book I was holding back into its place on the shelf, but sticking out a bit, so that I could easily get back to it. I explained, "It's about Maureen saying she saw Theo Kearn at the reunion. They need to follow up on that, ask for your opinion, if you were there. Basic information like that. You're not in any kind of trouble."

He seemed to relax. "I *was* there. And the man we saw was *not* Theo. He was younger than Theo would be now, for one thing. There was a resemblance maybe. But we were too far away to identify him, and it was just a glimpse. For my money, it wasn't him."

"So that's all you have to tell the agent."

"Unfortunately, Maureen doesn't agree with me. She thinks it was Theo, and she's afraid."

"Afraid of what?"

"It's irrational," said Jimmy. "Like he's back from the past to haunt her."

"I'm sorry she's going through this," I said, "but maybe the interview will help. It may do her good to talk about it."

"Do you think so?" he asked, brightening a bit.

A bell chimed, and our tour was called. Jimmy went to detach Maureen from a display of silk scarves, and I joined Toby, who was at the counter buying a book on Frank Lloyd Wright's furniture. I glanced back at the books section, wondering if I had time to go back for the book I was interested in, and I noticed Alan standing there. Our eyes met for a moment and he turned away. I wondered whether he had been listening to my conversation with Jimmy. Just then the tour desk announced the last call for our group, and I decided to go back for the book later.

We were quickly herded into a shuttle bus for a five-minute trip to the main house. The Taliesin estate covers hundreds of acres and includes a number of buildings besides the main house and studio. We were taking the short tour, however.

As the house came into view, our new guide, a bright young woman, discussed Wright's use of local limestone and other natural building materials to blend his house with the environment. She explained how its flat, horizontal planes typified Wright's "Prairie style" of architecture; while a narrow, cantilevered balcony, called "the bird walk," thrust outward toward the valley in modernistic counterpoint. The bus crawled, so that we could appreciate the changing proportions of the house as we moved toward it. By the time we reached the courtyard, we were in a reverent mood, ready to explore the interior.

We entered the house through a small, dark hallway that opened into an enormous living room. The dramatic space was filled with light from a continuous series of casement windows that seemed to take the place of traditional walls, with a view looking out over the Wisconsin River. Wright gave the room a very high, peaked ceiling (cream colored with wood trim), a great limestone fireplace and hearth, wood floors, and a further row of windows at ceiling level. He wanted every element in the room to be part of an aesthetic whole. To that end, he designed the rugs, lamps, furniture, leaded-glass windows, even the table settings. In the brochure we were given, one critic called the result "the most beautiful living room in America."

However, tragedy struck the home in 1914. An axe-wielding handyman went berserk and slaughtered six people, including Mamah Cheney and two of her children. Then he set fire to the house and burned it to the ground. Wright, who had been in Chicago that day, was devastated. Yet he found the will to rebuild the house and expand it. Almost incredibly, Taliesin was nearly destroyed by fire two more times over the years. Each time Wright rebuilt and expanded the estate, so the Taliesin of today, with the main house and outbuildings, is the largest version.

Toby and I lingered in the living room after the rest of the tour moved on. The furniture drew Toby's attention. We had to hurry through the bedrooms to catch up with the group as the guide talked about a collection of Japanese prints that inspired Wright's designs. Before anyone was ready, our hour was up and we were back at the low door where we had entered.

Toby and I were the last to leave and the last to notice a stranger in the courtyard. He had been sitting on a low stone wall waiting for our tour to finish. I recognized him as the ex-husband Helen had been arguing with on the Union Terrace. Now he rose—rather, sprang—from his perch and grabbed Helen's upper arm, badgering her in a tone too low for me to hear. She shook him off and motioned to the garden toward the back of the house. She hustled down the garden path, apparently to avoid the embarrassment of a public argument.

The ex-husband lumbered after her, and I could make out some of what he was saying. "It's not your decision to make . . ." When he caught up with her, he grabbed her again, and I feared for Helen. He was a large man and looked strong. However, he dropped her arm once she stopped walking, and they fell into the back and forth of a marital spat, with voices rising and falling.

Meanwhile, Maureen, Jimmy, and Alan gathered at the entrance to the garden, and I guessed they were discussing whether to intervene. Finally, Alan, acting in his role as Helen's current protector, strode toward Helen and her ex. I knew enough to worry that the two stags were about to lock horns. But Alan surprised me. Instead of charging in with an aggressive shout, he said something inaudible and extended his hand, and after a brief hesitation, the other man shook it. With quick glances from one face to another, I tracked a fairly civil interchange between Helen and her two men. Alan was masterful. I couldn't imagine how he managed to bring down the temperature so quickly. I assumed that his experience as a peacemaker and a psychologist had been put to good use.

The trio continued talking until the shuttle bus pulled up into the courtyard. Then Helen whipped away from the two men and strode quickly toward us. She brushed past Maureen, saying, "I'm okay," and kept walking till she reached me. "Help me out, would you?" she said. "I don't want to be with Alan right now. Let's get in the bus and sit together." Toby heard, and he waved me on my way.

At the shuttle-bus door, the line parted like the Red Sea, and Ms. Moses marched through. People were giving way to the little lady who had held her own in a dustup with two men. Moving in her wake, I took the aisle seat next to her and waited for an explanation.

"I'm sorry to drag you into this," she said, "but you do make a great human shield. I can't face another word from Alan."

I didn't expect that. "Why? Do you think he was being overly protective?"

"Controlling is a better word."

"Are you saying that his rescue efforts were unwelcome?"

"I've dealt with Walt for fifty years without needing help. I'm used to him showing up full of bluster where he's not wanted, and I know he calms down quickly. He can go from rage to remorse in a minute."

"That's the classic pattern of an abuser," I said, lowering my voice. Out of concern for her, I pressed on into intimate territory. "Was Walt ever abusive in your marriage?"

Helen shrugged a shoulder in a gesture that said neither yes nor no. Then she said, "There was a lot of this kind of behavior—fuming and storming. That kept me compliant for the first few years. I stayed because of Beth, our daughter. I wanted her to have two parents while she was growing up. One night when he'd been drinking, it got physical. He shoved me against a wall and held me in a lock while he yelled at me. The next day, I packed up Beth and drove to my parents, and that was the end of the marriage." Her chin set in defiance.

"Maureen told me you left because you couldn't get used to life on a farm."

"Hell, yes. That was true too. I came out here with hippy notions. Everything I knew about farming I got from the teach-ins Walt led on Earth Day. I thought that Spring Green was going to be the site of an eco-revolution, and our farm would be the epicenter. What I remember is a lot of manure."

"Where's the farm located?"

"Just a few miles west of here. That's why it was easy for Walt to get on the grounds today. He knows people at Taliesin."

"How did he know you'd be here, though?"

Irritation caused Helen's voice to rise. "Beth must have told him. I think I mentioned the trip to her." Her words were muffled by the start of the shuttle bus taking us back to the visitor center.

"By the way, Beth wants me to invite you and Toby to her Fourth of July cookout. There'll be lots of people there, including us. The trouble is, she also wants to invite Walt. That's what we've been arguing about. I say it's not a good idea. Yes, he's her father. But any time he's with me and there's drinking, there's trouble."

I said we'd be delighted to come to the cookout. By way of reassurance, I added, "If there's any trouble with Walt, I'll bet Alan will defuse it and make peace, just as he did today."

Helen scoffed. "He didn't make peace between Walt and me. He took Walt's side, so of course Walt calmed down. Then they just wore me out. Two against one."

"Huh" was all I could say to that.

We were turning into the driveway to the visitor center, and I was ready to resign my role as human shield and confidante. "You'll patch it up with Alan," I told Helen, "and the sooner the better. I'm going to nap on Toby's shoulder on the bus home."

At the visitor center, I went back to buy the book I'd been looking through when Jimmy had cornered me. It was a large, hardcover volume and rather expensive, but it covered Wright's whole career, and the photographs were stunning. On impulse, I also bought a set of coasters illustrated with geometric designs inspired by Wright's stained-glass windows.

Paired up again with Toby on the bus back to Madison, I shared the gist of my conversation with Helen. "That's interesting," said Toby. "I sat with Alan and, according to him, it's Helen who's controlling. She's terrified to let Walt be himself, so she sets rules for him, shuts him out, doesn't even answer his phone calls. I wouldn't count on Alan to control Walt at the cookout, or Helen, for that matter."

"Why do you say that?"

"Because Helen usually gets her way. And for all his ballyhoo as a peacemaker, Alan doesn't seem to be at peace with himself. Something's nagging at him."

It had been a long day, and when we got home, I was looking forward to a hot bath, a light dinner, and an early bedtime. First, though,

I wanted to show Toby my last-minute purchases at the visitor center. I set out the coasters on the dining room table, and they looked great against the dark oak surface. I hauled out my new Frank Lloyd Wright tome and started thumbing through the illustrated pages. A postcard fell out and tumbled to the floor. I bent to retrieve it. The card had a photo of Taliesin on the picture side and a chilling one-word message on the other. Printed in capital letters, it said, "STOP."

10

"STOP." IT MIGHT HAVE BEEN A WARNING. It might have been a plea. Anyone on the tour could have slipped it between the pages of the book while it was lying on the counter next to the cash register. I had left it there when I went back to get the coasters.

"That clinches it," said Toby. "It wasn't teenagers out for fun who rammed our bikes. Someone was delivering a message. And now here's a second one."

"The message being?" I asked.

"Stop digging into the past."

"Or stop thinking about a job here, if the messenger is Arp."

"That could be," said Toby. He was thoughtful. "We probably should notify Diane."

I tried her phone, but it went to voice mail. I asked her to return my call when she was free.

"Meanwhile," Toby said, "the best thing we can do is put those messages in the mental trash can, get a good night's sleep, and try to enjoy the weekend."

To my surprise, I did sleep soundly. In the morning I awoke remembering that I'd promised to call my sister on the weekend to discuss her upcoming trip to Madison. It was Saturday already. I had pushed it to the back of my mind. My days had been crowded with thoughts about a skeleton, teaching, an investigation, a threatening bicycle incident, a possible job offer, a sinister postcard, new acquaintances. With so much happening, I hadn't been able to give Angie the attention she deserved.

It was early in the morning in Madison, which made it about lunchtime in Ireland. I took out my phone, put in my earbuds, took a sip of tea, and called Angie. She was bubbling with excitement, having finalized her travel arrangements. I took down her flight information and said of course we'd pick her up. She'd arrive on Thursday evening on a flight from Dublin to Madison, with a connection in Chicago.

I cut to the chase. "So, what's going on? Has Bobby proposed to you?"

The pause was slight but significant. "No, not really. No. Not an out-and-out 'Will you marry me?'" She sounded surprised at her own answer. "But recently he's been talking like he assumes we're getting married. He'll say things like he knows the kitchen needs remodeling but we should wait till after the wedding. He said that in front of his mother last weekend, and this morning she introduced me to one of her friends as her son's fiancée."

"How did you feel about that?"

"Mortified! I just stood there like a statue in the middle of the grocery aisle."

"You didn't correct her?"

"Yes, I did, when the friend asked about the wedding date. I told her we weren't that far yet and we haven't gotten formally engaged. We hope to be doing that in good time. I tried to smile and make like everything was rosy."

"So maybe that was a fortunate run-in," I suggested. "It gave you a chance to clarify that you're not yet engaged. The trouble is, Bobby's mom and her friend and you know it, but Bobby might not. There's your next step. You need to talk to Bobby—fast, before his mother does."

Angie moaned. Then she said, "Okay. Thank you." She was gone.

I sat for a while, sipping my tea and trying to interpret the quick hang-up. Was my advice too intrusive? Had I failed to show support? Or was it something else, like Bobby walking into the room? Maybe it was best to believe that. I waited an hour and called again. I caught her just coming in for lunch.

"Bobby's warming up soup," she said. "I can't talk long."

"Okay," I said. "I just want to know you're not angry. You got off the phone so fast just now."

"You scared me skinless when you said I'd better get to Bobby before his mother did. I dropped the call with you so I could find him and talk."

"Oh." My stomach clenched. "How did it go?"

"Not great," she said. "At first he didn't see what all the bother was about. He said that for his mother we're as good as married and she thinks of me as her daughter already. But that's a problem for me. I haven't agreed to tie the knot. I haven't even been asked. I had to say that straight out to him."

"Oh, gosh."

"Yeah, it wasn't good. He felt attacked, like I was saying he wasn't sure enough to make a proper proposal. Really, I meant the opposite— neither of us is sure yet. We love each other. We love working together. We love living together, even with his mother in the house. We are almost there, but not quite. I guess that's how I would describe the situation."

"I think I get the picture, Angie. Let's talk this out when we see each other instead of trying to do it over the phone."

"Okay. Can't wait to see you!"

"Me too. Meanwhile, stay safe. Have a good flight."

We ended the call affectionately, wishing each other a great day. After breakfast, I would be planning a class on Monet's women. After lunch, she would be weaning lambs.

That evening we drove out to Spring Green again to see *The Importance of Being Earnest*, by Oscar Wilde. Toby thinks it's the funniest play in the English language, and I had never seen it, so I said let's go. It opens with two upper-class layabouts named Jack and Algy, who spend their days eating muffins, chasing young ladies, and thinking up clever things to say. The ingenues they are in love with, Gwendolen and Cecily, both intend to marry a man named Ernest, a name that inspires confidence.

The wit is dazzling, and the plot is delightfully contrived. The hero, Jack, is a foundling who was left in a handbag in the cloakroom of Victoria Station by an absent-minded governess. She mixed up the baby with a novel she was writing, and the manuscript wound up in the pram. Gwendolyn's mother is not about to let her daughter form an alliance, as she puts it, with a parcel! But it turns out that Jack, the parcel, is Algy's long-lost brother. And what's more, at birth he was christened Ernest, so all ends well! I laughed so hard, my sides ached, and I wondered—could uproarious laughter cause stress fractures of the ribs?

On Sunday, Toby invited me to tag along on his hunt for antiques at bargain prices to resell in his gallery back home. On an auction website, a profusion of Sunday estate sales and auctions dotted the map of southern Wisconsin. Toby had his pick. He printed out the map and circled an auction near the town of Mount Horeb that looked rich in possibility. It featured various collectibles, plus smaller pieces of country pine and oak furniture, known as "primitives" in the trade—cabinets, chests, benches, trunks, small tables, and the like—which, when refinished or restored, would fetch a tidy profit.

Toby rented a small van for the day in anticipation of a good haul. We headed south out of Madison on Highway 151 on a sunny afternoon. The road was banked by lush fields and farms, and the only sound was the thrum of the tires on the pavement. We drove for about fifteen miles before turning off onto County Road PD, where we began a search for the address. The auction was held in an old red barn that had been repurposed as a sales venue. Signage above the entrance confirmed that we had reached "Nielsen & Son's Estate Liquidations: Farm Machinery, Household Goods, Antiques, Old Tools, Toys, Gold & Jewelry, Firearms, Real Estate." Presumably, no single auction spanned the entire menu. A field adjacent to the barn served as a parking lot. Cars and pickup trucks were parked at all angles. The Nielsens had attracted a sizeable crowd.

Inside, the goods to be auctioned lined one wall, each piece identified by a tag with its lot number. Clients were cautioned to inspect each item carefully before bidding. Everything was to be sold "as is." That happens to be the mantra of every auction house in the land from the humblest to the most exalted. If Sotheby's sells you a painting that perchance is misattributed, or one that has a patched-up hole in the center of the canvas, they will remind you that you bought the work "as is," meaning as it was on the day of the auction, not as you wished it were.

The bidders at this rural auction were a mixed group of city folk, tourists, and farmers, seated on metal folding chairs arranged in rows. The barn still had its earthen floor, and wisps of errant hay covered the ground as reminders of the structure's original use. Up front on a raised wooden platform sat the auctioneer. Nielsen the elder looked to be in his eighties and was coping with the onset of infirmities familiar to his age cohort. He welcomed bidders, complained about his aches and pains, and passed the mic over to "& son." The younger Nielsen was hefty and had a rumbling smoker's voice, punctuated by an occasional cough. He wore a straw hat and sported a yellow-stained walrus mustache.

I took a seat near the front and saved one for Toby, who went to examine the goods to see which pieces interested him. Even though the auction had started, people wandered in and out of the barn. Some came and left early, some arrived later; it depended on the order of the lots they would bid on. They had timed their arrival and based their estimates of price on the catalog of works to be sold. At the fancy auction houses, these catalogs are expensive productions with glossy pages of color photographs. Here, the catalog was simply a typed list of several pages, duplicated and stapled.

Holding a folded catalog containing his penciled annotations, Toby squeezed into the row to claim the seat next to me, stepping over the feet of several competitors.

"Did you find anything interesting?" I whispered. Prospective bidders shouldn't broadcast their intentions to the bidders seated around them.

"I did," he said, so softly that I had to lip-read. "Several pieces I could easily resell if I get them at a good price, and one very special piece that I want no matter what."

"Which one?"

Shielding the catalog list with one hand, he pointed to Lot 142.

I took the list and read silently: "A Primitive Nineteenth-Century Pine-and-Poplar Schoolmaster's Desk. Estimate: $300–$600."

I leaned in close to him to ask, "What makes it so special?"

"I'll show you if we get it," Toby said, a look of mischief on his face. "It's a surprise." Meanwhile, he set his phone low on my thigh and pointed to a photo he'd just taken. The piece reminded me of those all-in-one seat and desk combinations that used to be common in children's classrooms. This one, however, was made for an adult. It was a stand-alone desk with no seat attached and had a hinged, slanted top that flipped open to reveal a storage space. The tilted top was the desk's most notable feature. The wood was acorn brown and had the appealing patina that comes only through age.

I agreed that it was a very attractive piece. "How high are you willing to go on it?"

"I don't know. I'm still thinking about it." That wasn't typical Toby behavior. He's usually decisive in these situations. Rarely has he returned from an auction gnashing his teeth because he paid too much for an item or kicking himself for losing a prize to another bidder. He usually sticks to his price limit with the assurance that he knows what he's doing and that he'll win some and lose some but come out ahead in the end. This time he seemed anxious.

By the end of a couple of hours, he had done very well. He'd lost three of the lots on his acquisitions list but had picked up four—an early American cherrywood candlestand, a turn-of-the-century leaded-glass table lamp, a nineteenth-century pine four-drawer chest, and an appealing steamship painting from the China Trade era. Now, as the auctioneer approached Lot 142, Toby tensed up. He clenched his pencil in his fist and tapped it nervously on the catalog on his knee.

"Next lot. Number 142. A primitive nineteenth-century pine-and-poplar schoolmaster's desk," read the auctioneer. "I'd like to open the bidding at two hundred dollars. Do I have two hundred?"

There wasn't any movement in the room. The auctioneer swept his gaze from one side to the other. Each bidder had a paddle with a number on it. To bid, you raised it in the air. Toby's number was thirty-six. He was waiting for someone else to start the bidding so he could top them.

"All right," the auctioneer relented. "I'll open at one fifty. Do I have—yes, one hundred fifty dollars, bidder thirty-six. Thank you." That was Toby making sure the lot wasn't withdrawn because the bidding hadn't met the reserve (the minimum price the owner was willing to sell for). "I have one fifty, now what about two?" the auctioneer called out, and we were off to the races. From there, the bidding rapidly escalated at fifty-dollar increments, with five or six bidders in contention. Despite a faltering beginning, in no time at all the bid to beat stood at eight hundred dollars.

"Toby," I reminded him, "the high estimate on this lot is six hundred."

Up went his paddle. "Number thirty-six, eight hundred and fifty dollars," the auctioneer acknowledged.

"Check around the room," urged Toby. "How many others are still bidding?"

"Four, I think, although there's someone sitting behind a post, and I'm not sure if he's still in or not."

"Okay. Keep your eye on him."

The auctioneer announced a bid of nine hundred dollars.

The bidding was nearing a line in the sand. A thousand. That's the point when you expect the faint of heart (or sound of mind) to throw in the towel. To add to the pressure, the bid increments jump from fifty to one hundred dollars once you cross that line.

The next bid, of nine hundred fifty dollars, came from the back of the room. Toby weighed his options. With a bid of one thousand, he would either prevail or enter a bloody bidding war with no early victory in sight. He raised his paddle in one quick move, as a warning to any would-be opponent that his determination was unshakable and that they'd better think twice about continuing.

It didn't work. "I have eleven hundred dollars. Back to you, sir," said the auctioneer.

"Twelve hundred," said Toby loudly as he raised his paddle again. The audible part was equivalent to a gorilla pounding his chest.

"Thirteen," came the voice from the back.

"Can you see who that is?" asked Toby.

"I can't see him clearly because of the post," I said.

"Fourteen."

"Fifteen."

"Wait, he's moving. Now I see him." I got a glimpse of curly red hair and a Vandyke beard. "Oh no. I don't believe it."

"Who is it?" asked Toby.

"It's that weasel, Magnus Arp."

And just like that, we were at two thousand dollars.

"The shackles are off," muttered Toby. The gleam of battle was in his eyes.

The bid increment jumped to two hundred dollars, and with just the two of them remaining, the action went awfully fast. Two, four, six, eight, three thousand, back to you, sir. Two, four, six, eight, four thousand. "This is crazy," I whispered to Toby, to no avail. They went at it with the determination of trench warfare, trading one charge after the other across no-man's-land.

Toby finally broke him (and us) at five thousand dollars. Arp angrily tossed his paddle aside and loped out of the barn, snarling. He paused to kick over an antique milk can that was standing by the doorway. The clatter was such that even people in the front of the room turned their heads. I hurried to the back and followed him with my eyes. It was easy to track him as he strode across the field, looking for his car. In a minute, he found it: a dark SUV, just like the one that rammed my bike. Why was I not surprised?

I wondered if he had followed us to the auction. More likely, someone had tipped him off, had told him that an item of interest to him would be on the block. But why was he obsessed with the schoolmaster's desk and willing to venture thousands of dollars to get it, when the auction house had valued it in the hundreds? And speaking of obsession, what impulse drove its spurs into my husband's flanks and urged him to match Arp dollar for dollar until he had driven him from the field? Male pride? Ego?

"Both," Toby conceded when I put the question to him. "But something else, too. I know why Arp wanted the desk so badly—for the same reason I wanted it. Let me show you what I found when I was looking the piece over before the auction." The sale was winding down. We were collecting our purchases, having paid for them. "Two things, really," Toby continued. "First, take a good look at the outside. Walk around it. Do you notice anything out of the ordinary?"

I followed Toby's instructions and looked the desk over—the top, the sides, the back, the legs—and then I saw it. One of the legs was charred black from the bottom to about seven inches up. "That leg looks like it's been burned," I said.

"My guess is that the desk was salvaged from a fire," said Toby. "And not just any fire. Look inside."

I lifted the tilted top. Again, it took me a minute to see it. Carved into the board forming the inside of the back of the desk, in the space below the hinges for the lid, were the initials FLW. The "F" was larger than the other two letters and more distinctive. Two horizontal bars of the letter crossed the vertical bar and extended on both sides, the top bar much farther out to the right. Later, when it came to his full signature, the top bar of the *F* would extend far enough to cover the *k* of "Frank," sheltering the letters of his name like the roof of one of his Prairie style homes, or the cantilevered balconies of Taliesin and Fallingwater.

"I think this came from Taliesin," said Toby, "from one of the fires. And I think it may be one of Wright's earliest drafting desks."

97

11

"YOU DID KNOW WHAT YOU WERE DOING. How much do you think it's worth?"

"That I don't know," said Toby. "To a Wright afficionado, probably double or triple what I paid for it, but I didn't buy it to resell. I bought it for myself. The more I learn about him, the more convinced I become that Wright really was a genius, certainly the greatest American architect we've ever had. To own something of his, a desk he actually may have worked on, would be amazing. I guess I've become a total fan."

"You used to be a cynic when it came to fans."

"Sports fans, yes. They get all worked up over issues of little consequence. 'A' wins today. 'B' loses tomorrow—what real difference does it make? But genius is a special case. A genius changes the way we see the world. They make it new. That's true in art as well as science. Tell me, who's your favorite artist?"

I shook my head. "There are too many of them. I can't pick just one."

"Then give me a list of five without thinking much about it, off the top of your head."

I tried. "Okay." I started counting on my fingers. "Vermeer, Brueghel, Van Gogh, Monet, Berthe Morisot. Now, she might not be on other people's lists, but she's on mine."

"Good," said Toby. "And say you had a chance to own an easel that she used when she was painting. Think about it. What would you do with it?"

"I'd buy it if I could," I said. "I'd keep it in my study and look at it every day for inspiration."

"Exactly." Toby ran his hand across the top of the little desk. "And that's why this piece will have pride of place in my gallery when I get it home, but it won't ever be for sale."

We collected Toby's purchases. The first order of business was to wrap them for protection in the sheets and blankets we'd borrowed from Eve's closets. (The auction house provided no packing material.) Then the challenge was to arrange the items securely in the back of the van. After a prudent drive home, avoiding swerves that could shift the contents, we unloaded the van carefully and stored our finds in the house.

We were able to return the van before the rental office closed, thus avoiding an overcharge. Toby suggested we spend the hypothetical savings on a quick meal out. We were huddled over tacos and our phones when Maureen called. Toby saw her name on my screen, and he signaled me to take the call.

"Hi, Maureen," I said. "What's up?"

"I'm sorry to bother you on the weekend," she replied, "and I apologize for a last-minute request. But I'm wondering if we could have lunch tomorrow. I'd like to talk with you before my interview with the FBI."

"Ah. Well, sure. I've got things to do at the office, though. Let's make it simple and close to the museum." We settled on that.

Toby watched me put the phone down and turn off the ringer. He said, "Sounds like you're meeting Maureen. Is that such a good idea? You're already more enmeshed with her than you want to be."

That thought had flashed through my mind, but my habit of kindly cooperation had me agreeing before I could stop myself. Now I felt embarrassed. Toby was sure to see this as another instance of my not being able to say no. And in this case, hasty agreement could have serious consequences. What if Maureen was the one who left me the order to "STOP"?

Defensively, I said, "It's just a quick lunch tomorrow. She wants to talk with me before her FBI interview."

"Maybe she wants to tell you something."

"Or try out a line she's planning to take with Whelk." We both knew I shouldn't be coaching her.

Toby looked at me sympathetically and said, "Tread carefully. You're about to step in hot tar."

The next day, after managing a lively class discussion, I turned to my lunch companion with apprehension. Maureen looked her usual self—calm, sad, and softly beautiful. However, she wanted something from me, and I didn't like not knowing what it was.

We walked down Bascom Hill and through Library Mall to State Street, chatting about our visit to Taliesin. While Toby and I had focused on the living room, Maureen had been drawn to Wright's drafting studio. On the subject of drafts, she also told me she was working on a pencil portrait of Theo Kearn from memory. It wouldn't serve any purpose in the investigation, but she felt compelled to do it and to get it right. I would have liked to hear more. However, we reached our destination, a salad bar, and went inside. Once our meals were in front of us, she got to the point. "I'm sorry to pull you into my dilemma about the interview tomorrow, but since you got me into it, it seems only fair."

"Don't put that all on me, Maureen. The FBI was bound to include you in their interviews."

She cut me off. "You were the one who told them I was in town and that I had seen Theo. And you put the finger on Jimmy and Helen and Al. Yes, we all knew Theo, but we never knew anything about the bombing or how he escaped. He didn't want us to. That's what I told

100

the FBI the first time they came knocking on my door, which started soon after the bombing. They searched my room and took my scrapbook from high school. I had pasted a Valentine's Day card inside it that Theo once sent me with some strands of his hair, like the Romantic poets. They said they needed the hair and an example of his handwriting for identification purposes."

And so, I thought, when DNA testing came into use, the FBI had a hair sample for analysis.

"They've been poking into my private life ever since." She stabbed her salad.

She had a point. I didn't say anything. But I noted that this was a turnabout from the other day when she said she was used to FBI scrutiny.

"If I seem annoyed, try to imagine living your whole life with the knowledge that the FBI has you in its sights. Out of the blue, they would show up, asking about a piece of mail I got from Canada or a phone call I'd received from Helen. That's how I knew they were monitoring my mail and phone and email traffic. I suppose it's never going to be over." She sighed. "At least give me a heads-up. This Agent Whelk—what's he like, and what does he want from me this time?"

What was he like? A fast operator and a bit of a doofus, but that was an opinion best kept to myself. This much I told her: "Don't be fooled by his outward manner. He's shrewder than he appears to be. Just answer his questions truthfully, and you'll be fine."

"What do you suppose he's going to ask?"

"That should be obvious—why do you insist that Theo is alive? You're the only person who claims to have seen him, and here in town, no less. That would be my first line of questioning if I were interrogating you. You said before that when you saw Theo, he was some distance away. And it's been decades since you saw him last. What makes you so sure you recognized him?"

"We were a couple for five years. That makes a difference. I know his walk and everything else about how he looks."

"That's a good answer. But even so, what if it turns out you were mistaken—you know it's possible—and the skeleton is his? That raises the question of who hid his body in the cistern. Think back to when you were all in college together. Did Theo have any enemies then? Anyone you were aware of who wished him harm or who might have wanted him out of the way?"

"You mean, aside from Jimmy?" Maureen looked distraught.

"Yes. But since you mentioned Jimmy, did he and Theo ever come to blows?"

"They both knew I would never stand for that."

"So, who else might have wished Theo harm?"

I waited a moment for her to compose herself, then said, "That's bound to be Whelk's second line of questioning. If those are Theo's bones, he didn't die of natural causes. You'll have to face that, Maureen. Who could have wanted him dead? Someone with a political motive? Is there anybody you've ever wondered about?"

Her expression was guarded when she said, "Not on that account."

I could just imagine Agent Whelk reacting to that. "You *have* wondered about somebody. Who?"

She put her fork down and swabbed her lips with her napkin. "It's not right for me to say. It's somebody else's story to tell, a very private story, and I only know it secondhand."

"You can bet that won't be a problem for Agent Whelk. If you dangle your story in front of him the way you just dangled it in front of me, he'll pounce and devour you before you've blinked."

"Enough, Nora. Please. I've had all I can take of this for now." She made two fists and placed them on the table. "Theo isn't dead. That's what I'm going to say tomorrow." She pushed up and started to walk away, mumbling, "He's not," more to herself than to me.

After a few steps, she turned around and sat back down. "I'm sorry. I'm a bit upset. You just can't know how it was back then and how it's been for me for so many years." She sat up straight, as if to summon her pride and conviction.

"No apologies necessary. I'd be upset too, if I were in your shoes."

She took another leafy bite of her salad and looked around the room. Then she teared up again and choked out, "This is where I used to work, back in the day." I must have frowned, not understanding.

"Not in this chain salad bar. This space used to be Gino's, where we all came for pizza, when we had the money. It was an authentic Italian restaurant. There was a real Gino, and the food was great. I waitressed here my senior year. I was back home already at the time of the bombing. A waitress I'd worked with phoned me, long distance—that was a big deal then. She was working lunch the day after, and she heard over the kitchen radio that Theo was one of the accused bombers. I felt sick when I got that news, and I still feel sick whenever I think about it."

That ended our lunch, but we saw each other later in the afternoon at a Wright exhibition in the art library. It was a small show that Arp had arranged for his class, consisting of Wright memorabilia borrowed from a private collector. There were three horizontal display cases at the back of the reading room. Toby, Helen, and Alan were leaning over one, and Maureen and Jimmy were inspecting another, holding hands, looking lovey. I had the impression they had just quarreled and were making up. Arp buzzed around like an annoying red insect, pointing things out.

Toby came over and asked how my lunch with Maureen had gone. I gave him a quick report, and together we browsed the displays. In the first case were some dramatic black-and-white photographs of Wright taken by Pedro Guerrero, Wright's favorite photographer. In the second case were a few miniature models, made by a student, of projects designed by Wright that had never been built. One was a boathouse for the Wisconsin rowing team. In an accompanying letter, Wright vowed that when his alma mater called, he would always be ready to "design anything from a chicken house to a cathedral."

The third case had a selection of Wright's architectural drawings. There were fine sketches, some in colored pencil, of buildings both constructed and imaginary. As an artist—and he surely was one—Wright drew with a line that was delicate and precise. His shading could be as soft as Constable's, his grasp of perspective as strong as Piranesi's. One of the drawings included a landscape developed in exquisite detail. Others were flat, neat, and bold, like the Japanese prints he so admired.

After the group had browsed the exhibit on their own, Arp led them to the stacks where the books on Wright were shelved. There he talked about issues of scholarship and bibliography. I had work of my own to do, which took me to the opposite side of the reading room. I was planning to assign a paper requiring research in the library, and I wanted to know exactly what my students could expect to find. The catalog system in the art library was the same as the one for the main library and would be easy for them to use. I had catalog numbers for books included in the assignment, and a chart told me they were all in the north stacks.

I remembered from my last visit that these bookcases were motorized. From a distance, they looked like floor-to-ceiling metal lockers, with just a few of them open to show loaded bookshelves. Up close, each unit had its label for call numbers and a touch pad for ordering the stack to move right or left. Unlike fixed bookcases with permanent aisles between them, these massive stacks moved sideways on their tracks to open or close an aisle as needed. Push a button, and they moved apart to open up the aisle. Push another button, and they squeezed together like the pleats of an accordion. When the stacks were closed, the aisle between them disappeared. The design was a great space-saver.

After familiarizing myself with the operation of the system, I went to work.

Gauguin was the last master on my list, and I found his section near the end of an aisle flanked by movable units on both the right and left. I stepped into the aisle. I was pleased to see that there were quite a few books on Gauguin at the deep end. Several were piled on the top shelf reserved for very tall books. I popped out of the aisle and found a shin-high metal stool, which I dragged back with me. Tall art books tend to be generous with full-color illustrations, and I was eager to see the Gauguin volumes. I stepped up on the stool and started flipping pages.

I was leafing through the last of the tall books when I felt a rumbling and heard the sound of moving stacks. That must be the unit next to this one, I thought, in the first instant. But the book in my hands fell toward my chest, pushed by the shelf in front of me. The heavy, book-laden stack was closing in on its neighboring stack—and on me! I cried out, lunged off the stool, and leaped toward the opening, which was narrowing fast. In horror, I sensed that I wasn't going to make it. Then suddenly the lumbering bookcase balked and shook to the sound of scraping metal. I just managed to squeeze out, tearing my blouse. Turning around, I saw the stack pulsing against the stool, which was sandwiched between two walls of bookshelves, with gears grinding loudly. Without the blockage caused by the little stool, the monster of a moving bookcase would have closed on my body and crushed me like a character in some horror tale by Edgar Allan Poe.

With adrenaline driving me, I ran toward the center of the reading room, heedlessly bumping into someone emerging from another one of the bookshelf units. We grabbed at each other for balance. It was Magnus Arp, with one hand on my shoulder and the other flailing for support.

"You again!" I choked out, pushing him away.

Ahead I saw the student worker from the information desk coming to the rescue. From behind, he took Arp by the elbow and ordered, "Let her go!" But then he saw Arp's face and recognized him. "Professor! I'm sorry! I thought—" He looked at me, taking in my torn blouse and panicked face. "What is this?" he asked. "Are you hurt?"

"Somebody tried to crush me between the bookshelves," I blurted. I pointed back to the unit I had escaped. It was still rumbling, trying to close on the metal stool.

The student left us and went to the offending unit. He looked in, shook his head, and reached out to press the operating button. A soft whir replaced the rumbling, and the bookshelf drew back. "That is *so* not supposed to happen," he said, walking back to us. "I better report this."

By then, other people were upon us. Helen was first, then Alan and Jimmy. Toby was struggling to get past others who had heard my cries. Everyone was asking what had happened, and I started to say, but my student rescuer took over. "Please don't use the stacks! There's something wrong with the rolling bookshelves. Step aside. I have to get help." He wriggled away, leaving me to the care of the crowd. Toby was quickly at my side, his eyes interrogating the circle of onlookers.

In that crowd was someone who had pushed the button to close the heavy shelves on me. It couldn't have happened spontaneously. Was it Arp? He wanted me gone before his promotion case came up. Toby's winning bid for the Frank Lloyd Wright desk might have been the last straw for him. But my conversation with Maureen had raised another possibility. There was someone she knew who harbored a secret that might shed light on the mystery of Theo Kearn's disappearance. Did that person fear my prying enough to stage this accident?

The candidates stood before me, almost as in a police lineup. Helen looked concerned but prepared to act; she was capable and strong-willed enough to do a thing like this—but why would she? Alan stood behind her. He struck me as too passive to launch an attack against me, but maybe I was wrong about him. Jimmy had his arm around Maureen, shielding her from trouble; I knew little enough about him, other than that he loved Maureen loyally. Would he hurt me if he thought it would protect Maureen from harm? Finally, Maureen herself. Her face was a study in sadness, as if she knew the reason for all this distress but lacked the power to prevent it.

We were told a detective from the campus police was on her way to take our statements. It was a comfort to see Diane. When she arrived, she and one of her officers questioned the bystanders and then let most of them go, after taking their names. Arp and I and the student worker stayed, retelling the events. Toby stood by me for support, while Arp cast himself in the role of hero. According to his statement, he heard me scream and was coming to my rescue when we collided. Either that, I thought, or he was fleeing from the scene of the crime. I held back from accusing him or anyone else, but I thought of them all, one by one, and realized that my circle of suspicion had widened.

12

TOBY COOKED ME A DINNER OF NEW ENGLAND comfort food: codfish cakes, Boston baked beans, and warm chocolate pudding for dessert. The tastes of home soothed me, and that night I slept nine hours.

I made it through teaching on Tuesday, but I was still shaken. Maureen and Helen stayed after class to express their concern, and when I got home Toby catered to me. Diane called to ask how I was and to let me know the results of her questioning. Unfortunately, no one had seen the person who pushed the button that sent the stacks closing in on me. I asked if it could have been an accident, the result of someone passing by and brushing against the button unintentionally. Not very likely, she thought. The system was designed to prevent that kind of mishap. She cautioned me to stay on the alert.

Wednesday was the Fourth of July. That meant no class, and a good thing too, since I was still feeling rattled from my misadventure. I wasn't really in the mood for a party either, certainly not one where I would see four of the people who might have trapped me in the stacks. But I had accepted Helen's invitation, and to bow out now would be awkward. At breakfast, Toby agreed that we should go, and he blithely went out to mow the lawn.

I was left at the table, in need of a diversion. I had been curious about the Wisconsin State Historical Society, which occupied a building of classical proportions on Library Mall. I passed it every day on my way to the office but had yet to go inside. The historical society was closed for the holiday, but it occurred to me that I could visit its website and conduct a virtual tour online. I wasn't looking for anything in particular, just skimming the collections to get a sense of what a researcher might find.

I was impressed. Through the society's website, Wisconsinites can trace their family trees, delve into the state archives, or browse a wide range of special collections, including, to name but a few, a guide to Wisconsin newspapers from 1833 to 2004, a trove of memorabilia from Wisconsin's very active role in the Civil War, and a database of Wisconsin shipwrecks. I had to think twice about that last category, but then I remembered that the state borders two of the Great Lakes.

What drew my interest was the huge database of historical images, including thousands of old photos that had been digitized. Guessing, I launched a search for images of student demonstrations in the 1960s, and soon I was following a thread that led me to the Dow Chemical protests of 1967. The newspapers called them "riots." A sequence of black-and-white photos brought the past to life. First there was a bird's-eye view of marchers packing State Street all the way from the Capitol to the foot of Bascom Hill. Then there were shots of marchers on the hill clashing with a phalanx of police amid swirls of tear gas. There were disturbing photos of students being swatted to the ground by helmeted cops wielding batons. And there were several close-ups of protestors assembling in groups before the march began.

One of these caught my eye. The figures in the foreground looked familiar even before I clicked on the icon to enlarge the image. And there they were—Jimmy, Alan, Maureen, and Helen, inhabiting their younger selves. Alan and Maureen were holding cardboard signs, which for now rested on the ground. Alan's, which said "Up Against the Wall! Mother Dow," was crudely lettered (and the punctuation was off). Maureen's sign showed real skill. "No to Napalm" was its message, accompanied by a drawing of a peasant hut in flames. The young Maureen looked radiant, a midwestern Joan of Arc, inspired with hopeful passion. Young Helen, standing next to her, had a fist raised. Jimmy, a bandana on his head, was looking at the camera, and Alan was looking at Maureen. He had turned toward her and was staring with unabashed yearning.

I printed the picture from my screen and waited for Toby to come in. He was hot and sweaty from his yard work. I gave him a chance to grab a cold drink from the fridge, then showed him the photo. "What do you think?" I asked. "I'd say Alan had a crush on Maureen at the time."

"I'd say you're right," Toby agreed. "The poor guy looks poleaxed." He took a gulp from his glass of cold water. "Maybe we all look ridiculous at that stage."

"You didn't."

"What, look ridiculous or ever look at you like that?"

"That's privileged information," I said. "Go take your shower."

Beth Foreman, Helen's daughter, and Beth's partner, Anne Howard, lived in a narrow, two-story house on the south side of Lake Monona. From the street, the place looked small, but if you followed the walkway to the back, it held a surprise: a generous screened-in porch and a lawn that ran down to the lake, with a splendid view of the State Capitol on the opposite shore. The yard had been lovingly landscaped, with three sitting areas, each with a magnificent view.

For the party, red, white, and blue crepe-paper bunting had been tacked to the porch, in counterpoint to old-fashioned red rosebushes and white benches facing the lake. Near the screened porch, a circle of whitewashed Adirondack chairs was shaded by a venerable old spruce. All seats were taken. Midway down the lawn, a group gathered at a stone campfire circle. The host, Anne, had a grill going there, and the smell of fat dripping from sizzling meat permeated the air. At the end of the lawn, wooden chairs down at the dock had attracted the water lovers.

I was standing by the porch with my hands occupied by a tray of store-bought cupcakes, which was my small contribution to the cookout. The smiling woman who came toward me was obviously Helen's daughter. She was tall, like her mother, and had Helen's thick, wild curls—only they were black.

"Welcome to the party! You must be Mom's professor," she said, "and you've brought sweets! Thanks! I'm Beth. Come up with me to the porch. We've set the buffet there." She led me up the stairs and showed me where the desserts were tucked away. Other women were putting finishing touches on the main buffet table, tossing salads and checking that every platter had its serving utensils.

"Mom is in the kitchen," said Beth, just as Helen came through the doorway with a bucket of ice. She squealed at the sight of me, set the bucket on the floor, and corralled her daughter and me in a group hug.

"I was afraid you wouldn't come," she said.

Beth laughed, used to her mother's enthusiasms, and gave in to being introduced while secured in an embrace. When Beth stepped back, her smile matched Helen's, right down to the blood red of her lipstick. I had no reason to question her sincerity, but I was no longer completely sure about Helen's.

"I owe you thanks," said Beth. "Your course has kept Mom in Madison this summer, and we've had more time together than in years. How about making this an annual thing?"

"That's nice to hear, but it's her old friendships that sparked the summer plan. Right, Helen?"

"True," she said. "The reunion brought us here, but your course was an incentive to stay."

"Speaking of getting people to stay," said Beth, "we'd better get the meal going or we'll lose our party. Can you help me carry the rest of the meats down to the grill? It's time for Anne to play Top Chef." We went back to the kitchen for brats, hamburger patties, and serving plates and then moved down the lawn, like a caravan bearing its trade on the route to Samarkand.

At the fire circle we delivered the goods, and Beth introduced me to her father, Walt, and to her partner, Anne. Anne, lean and long-legged, was dressed for the part. White-aproned from shoulder to knee, she looked very like a TV chef. Anne taught physics at the university and had just conducted a little experiment, she said. She explained to Beth that her test run had shown that the burgers did best on the gas grill, which had temperature control. She would be the designated grill master. Walt, his bulk protected by denim overalls and his head sporting a black fedora, would stoke the coal fire and sear the brats. The two looked an unlikely pair, but they shared a mission, and they got right to it.

While they did their work, Helen and I visited the various clusters of guests, letting them know it was time to mount the porch steps and fill their plates with everything but the main course. For that they would line up at the grills. It was a nice way to be introduced to strangers, who would associate me with the aroma of brats and burgers. And it was a good way for Helen to gather her friends together. She had reserved a picnic table expressly for us.

When we were finally seated with food and drink, Helen asked the question she'd been holding back. "I suppose you all saw this morning's paper?"

Jimmy put down his brat. "We don't get one at the apartment."

"We do," said Toby, "but who reads the paper on the Fourth of July? It's nothing but ads. What was in it?"

Frowning, Alan reached into a plastic bag at his feet, pulled out the front section of the *Wisconsin State Journal*, and handed it to Helen. She opened it to page 3, folded it once, and pointed to a drawing.

"It's Theo," she said.

"Helen!" Alan spoke sharply. "That's not what it says." He looked directly at Maureen. "It's an artist's version of what the man in the cistern might have looked like based on a reconstruction of the skull they recovered. The FBI has just released the sketch. They're asking the public to help identify the victim."

"Let me see that," Jimmy demanded. He took the paper and held it between Maureen and himself, and they took a long time studying the sketch. All of us had stopped eating.

Jimmy looked at Maureen with worry. "What do you think?" he asked her.

She raised her eyes from the page and said, "There's a resemblance, but it's not him."

"Are you serious?" Helen sounded irritated. "It's Theo all over. The long face. The Marlboro Man chin. Look at the photo of Theo from the web. You'll see."

Jimmy spoke up. "That's the photo the FBI used for the wanted poster back in 1970, and it's misleading. Theo's almost smiling in it, looking like your friendly camp counselor. He hardly ever smiled."

Maureen stood up. "I've got something to show all of you. I've been working on a drawing of Theo as he was when we were seniors in high school. I did a dozen of them back then. I thought his face would come back to me from muscle memory, and it did. I'll get it. It's in the car." Jimmy rose to go with her.

Leaving, he turned the newspaper back to Helen, who handed it to me. My opinion didn't matter much, but I did see parallels between the artist's reconstruction and the FBI wanted poster. Yet what if the artist had let the poster photo influence her work? While Toby and I read the article, Helen and Alan spoke quietly. He seemed to be urging her to go easy on Maureen.

When the couple returned, Jimmy was carrying a medium-size artist's pad.

"Clear a space," he said. "We don't want to get mustard stains on this."

Toby and I removed our dishes and used napkins to wipe off the end of the table. Jimmy then propped the pad on the edge and let it fall back on his chest, while Maureen raised the cardboard cover to reveal her portrait of Theo in his teens—rawboned, gawky, yet stolidly stern. He was wearing the same round glasses as in the FBI wanted photo, but instead of smiling at the camera, he was gazing off to the side with a fierce intensity. Maureen had caught her subject in a moment that revealed the man he would become, a man capable of a terrible act.

"That's the real Theo," said Jimmy. Maureen hung back.

"Wow," said Helen. "I remember that look. Used to creep me out."

Toby put the newspaper article flat on the table next to Maureen's drawing. The comparison was hardly fair. Maureen's drawing had the conviction of life; the other was dead in every sense.

Jimmy asked Helen, "Well? Are they similar or different?"

"I see the similarities," said Helen, tracing with her finger on the police sketch. "The face is long, almost horsey, you know, except that the jaw is so squared off. The cheekbones are prominent in both drawings."

"But the middle of the face is different," said Jimmy. "The face in the reconstruction has a long, thin nose. That's part of what gives it the horsey look. That's not Theo's nose at all. You can see that in Maureen's drawing."

"A nose is mostly cartilage, not bone," Maureen interrupted. "The forensic artist would have to guess at the shape, based on the small bits of bone that are at the top of the nose—if they even survived. The nose is the least reliable part of any facial reconstruction."

"Well, then, that backs me up," said Helen. "The face could be Theo's. The artist just guessed wrong about his nose."

"The hair is different. The lips are different. The eyes are different," said Jimmy.

"There are more similarities than differences," said Helen. "I see the similarities."

Alan sounded annoyed. "Why be so insistent about it?" he asked Helen. "Is there a reason you prefer to think of him as dead?"

Before Helen could gather herself to answer, a male voice boomed from behind me. "I'll tell you who prefers to think of him dead. Me. I'm sick of hearing Theo Kearn idolized by a bunch of washed-up radicals."

I turned to see an unsteady Walt, carrying a platter of cooked brats akimbo. Right behind him was Beth, evidently there to prevent damage. She took the platter from his hands and offered it to Toby, who was the only one at the table who had finished his meal. "We have seconds," she said, acting as if she hadn't heard Walt's slurred remarks. "But it looks as if some of you haven't done justice to your firsts."

"I'll tell you why. They're too busy raking over the coals of the past," said Walt, leaning over the table and getting a look at the portrait that Jimmy was still propping up. "What the hell? Are you setting up a shrine? To him? Listen to me. Nothing remotely good ever came out of that man. Nothing!"

Helen's eyes darted to her daughter. For a second or two she seemed about to say something, but whatever it was, she held it back. An awkward moment passed. Then she said to Beth gently, "Maybe your father would like a nap before the fireworks. Why don't you help him inside?" I expected some protest from Walt, but Helen's suggestion worked like a secret code the three had used to see them through the years. Walt shuffled off with Beth and disappeared with her into the house.

No one seemed inclined to resume the conversation. During the pause I tried to read each face around the table, wondering again who could have been so cold-blooded as to close the moving stacks against me at the art library. It might have been one of them, but no one was acting uneasy with me.

Unsmilingly, Helen offered the platter of brats and, getting no takers, took it off to another group. Maureen folded up her sketch pad and gave it to Jimmy, who returned it to the car. "I shouldn't have brought it," she said. "I should have let a party be a party."

"It's not your fault," I replied. "With the FBI interviews taking place this week, the subject was unavoidable. Maybe that's what stirred up all that feeling in Walt. I assume he was called in, just as you were. How did it go, your interview with Agent Whelk?"

The setting sun was in Maureen's eyes. She turned to face east, and the strain lessened in her face. "All right," she said.

"Well, that's a surprise. You were nervous enough about it on Monday."

"He didn't ask me anything I wasn't expecting, thanks to our little practice session."

"That must have been a relief," I said, regretting now that I'd taken that lunch with her.

"I won't be relieved until all this is over."

"You may not have to wait much longer," I told her. "The university police expect DNA results to be available soon from the State Crime Lab."

"It can't be soon enough for me," she said.

"The results might not be what you want to hear."

Maureen rose. "How about helping me get the dessert course ready? Something sweet. That's what I could use right now."

By the time the desserts had been set out, the sun had dropped to the horizon, casting orange rays across the lake. I spotted Toby down on the dock with Jimmy, talking and enjoying the sunset. I ambled down to let them know the desserts were ready. As I neared them, I overheard Jimmy answering a question that Toby had asked him. I stopped and listened.

"The last time I saw Theo? Yes, I do remember. It was another Fourth of July party, our last summer here. Maureen was with me, Helen was with Walt, and Alan was with a date, no one special. I remember it because Helen and Walt had a fight—about what, I don't know—and Walt stormed out the door. About an hour later, Theo showed up. He was pretty wasted from smoking pot. First, he tried to get Maureen to leave with him. She told him they were over. She was with me now. I stepped in and said the same thing, and he backed off."

I moved forward and joined them on the dock. Jimmy nodded to acknowledge my arrival, then continued. "It must have been around 2:00 when the party broke up. I was surprised to see Helen leave with Theo. She was still steaming about Walt, did it to get back at him, I figured. And Theo was trying to make Maureen jealous. Helen and Theo? I don't know what went on between them after they left the party. Later, Helen told Maureen that nothing happened, that Theo just walked her home. Maybe that's the way it was. Maybe there was more to it. When Walt heard about it, he swore he'd beat Theo to a pulp if he ever got his hands on him. Of course, he never got the chance. That was the last time any of us saw Theo—the Fourth of July after our graduation. In August, we went our separate ways. Helen married Walt, Alan stayed in Madison, I went to New York to start art school, and Maureen went home. And then Theo and those other goddamned idiots blew up the physics building, and he disappeared."

No one said anything as we walked back to the house. My mind was racing. I thought, that must be the story Maureen didn't want to tell me: Helen and Theo. She was protecting Helen's privacy, but at the same time covering up a motive that Walt may have had to hurt Theo. According to Jimmy, Helen told Maureen that her walk home with Theo was innocent. But Jimmy heard that story secondhand. What if something *had* happened between Theo and Helen, call it a one-night stand—would Helen have told Maureen the truth? Would Maureen have shared the full story with Jimmy? Apart from gossip, what did Jimmy actually know? And why was he telling this story to us now?

13

AFTER DESSERT, TOBY VANISHED FOR A WHILE. I finally found him in the kitchen, seated at a small table with Anne Howard, the physics professor. They were drinking beer from the bottle and seemed to be enjoying each other's company.

"Pull up a chair," said Toby. "We're talking about quantum mechanics."

"A conversation stopper if I ever heard one," I said, joining them. Toby, who was an English major, never took a physics course in college, but lately he's developed an interest in physics and cosmology. He subscribes to several popular science magazines. Me? I know zilch about those subjects.

"It's my fault, I guess," said Anne. "With all the talk about whether Theo Kearn is dead or alive, I couldn't resist bringing up Schrödinger's cat. It's a famous thought experiment in physics involving a cat who's said to be both dead and alive at the same time."

I must have looked blank. Toby took over. "It's based on a theory of quantum mechanics. The cat may exist in more than one state until a scientist opens the cat's box, which either kills him or saves him."

"That makes no sense to me," I said, drawing up to the table.

Anne laughed and said, "Let's retrace our steps for Nora's sake, so she doesn't think we've gone off the deep end." She pointed toward Toby with an open hand. "Why don't you recap the experiment? I think you've got it. If I keep lecturing, we could be here all night."

Toby, encouraged to explain a new idea, was in his element. "All right. But remember," he said to Anne, "this is an English major's take on a problem in physics. It's bound to be watered down." He hesitated. "I'm not sure where to start."

"Try the beginning," I suggested. Now Toby laughed. I could tell they'd been having a good time.

"Okay," said Toby, gearing up. "The beginning was in the early twentieth century when quantum mechanics overthrew the classical model of the atom. The old model pictured an orderly system with electrons orbiting a nucleus like planets orbiting the sun. But in the new model, electrons jumped from one orbit to another, unpredictably and on a random basis. Each jump involved a new energy state. A quantum refers to a packet of energy."

"Is that where the phrase 'quantum leap' comes from? From electrons jumping out of their orbits?" I asked.

"I'd say yes." Toby looked to Anne for approval. He got a nod and continued. "Einstein wasn't happy with this new model, which described a universe dependent on chance. Neither was his friend Erwin Schrödinger, who said he didn't believe an electron could hop around like a flea. They both found one proposition of quantum mechanics particularly troubling, the so-called Copenhagen interpretation, which claims that particles exist neither here nor there in reality until they are observed."

Toby saw me frowning.

"I know. As far as I can make out, what that means is that a particle can occupy multiple states of being and positions until a scientist pins it down by observing it, at which point the multiple states 'collapse' into a single state, a thing."

"Holy cow," I said.

"It's hard to wrap your head around," Toby acknowledged.

"You're doing great," said Anne.

"To me it sounds pretty mystical," said Toby, "like emanations from the One to the Many in Hinduism, only in reverse. At the subatomic level things seem to go in the opposite direction, from the many to the one when they collapse into a point—whatever that really means."

"Remember, you're trying to translate mathematical equations into metaphors, using words without the math," cautioned Anne. "If I were to describe what happens when a particle is observed as 'the statistical collapse of a wave function,' would that be helpful to you?"

"Not in the least," said Toby.

"Me neither," I said.

"Sorry," said Anne. "In that case, let's move on. Go ahead, Toby."

Toby raised his bottle to his lips and took a sip. He was about to press on, but I stopped him. "Wait. I have two questions already. One. Why is it called the Copenhagen interpretation? And two. Where's the cat?"

Toby laughed again. "I'm coming to the cat. As for the Copenhagen interpretation, the leading proponents of the theory were the Danish physicist Niels Bohr and his circle in Copenhagen. Bohr and Einstein went head-to-head on these issues. Their debates are famous."

"Got it. Sorry for the interruption. Please go on."

"Now for the cat. Schrödinger decided to satirize the theory by means of a clever thought experiment. The thing is, a lot of smart people missed the satire and took the experiment seriously. You can make up your own mind about it." Toby finished his beer and rolled the empty bottle in his hands.

"In the experiment, a cat is sealed in a box along with a small lump of radioactive material. Also in the box is a Geiger counter, a glass vial containing poison, and a Rube Goldberg–type contraption that connects a hammer to the Geiger counter. If an atom decays while the cat is in the box, the Geiger counter will detect it, the hammer will break the vial of poison, and the cat will die. If no atom decays while the cat is in the box, the cat will live. Since radioactive decay occurs on a random basis, the fate of the cat is up to chance."

"That's cruelty to animals," I said. "How long does the poor cat have to stay in the box?"

Anne elaborated. "It depends. The time is set in relation to the rate of decay of the radioactive material, so that there's a fifty-fifty chance of radiation being detected during the experiment."

"Is there food and water in the box?" I asked.

"And kitty litter?" Toby chimed in.

"It's a thought experiment," said Anne, a little sharply. "As far as I know, nobody ever tried this with a real cat."

"I should hope not," I said.

Toby continued. "There's more. So, the life of the cat depends on a random event—the decay of a particle. According to the Copenhagen interpretation, a particle exists in multiple potential states until it is observed. Those states include decayed and not decayed. The cat, whose fate depends on the atom, exists in multiple potential states, as well. Those states include dead and not dead, which is why the cat is said to be both dead and alive. The situation changes when an observer opens the box. The act of observation pins down the cat to a single state." Toby paused and lifted his forefinger to pontificate. "The multiple of the possible becomes the actual of the factual."

"Just a minute, Toby," I said. "That sounds like another line you've made up."

"It's new to me," said Anne.

"Sorry," he apologized. "It popped into my head. The point I was about to make is that the outcome isn't decided *before* the observer opens the box. Rather, opening the box plays a role in the outcome; the cat's life depends on the observer too. At least that's my understanding," Toby concluded. He turned to Anne. "How did I do?"

"Very well!" she said, clapping with one hand against the beer bottle in the other.

I said to Toby, "You get high marks for the recital—maybe an A minus with the wordplay—but if you ask me, there's something basically wrong with the experiment. First of all, isn't the atom going to do its thing whether or not someone looks in the box?"

"Good point," said Anne. "That objection has been raised by others."

"And secondly, the whole premise is absurd," I said. "Maybe a particle can exist in multiple states at once, but in my experience, a cat can't. Isn't Schrödinger mixing apples and oranges, or something like that?"

"Yes, he was having fun with words, like Toby," said Anne. "My own take is that he mixed apples and oranges, as you put it, to make a point. He wanted to satirize the theory and remind us that the micro and macro worlds don't follow the same rules. Animals don't behave like subatomic particles. Neither do we."

She continued. "Take your elusive fugitive, Theo Kearn. He belongs to the macro world, our everyday world. You can ask if he's dead or alive, but you can't say he's dead and alive at the same time. In our everyday world, he's one or the other. That you're looking for him, I guess, puts you in the role of the observer, but I doubt it will determine the outcome."

"Maybe not," said Toby, "but how do we know if Kearn is dead or alive unless he's observed? He hasn't been seen in all these years. As far as we know, maybe he exists and maybe he doesn't, like Schrödinger's cat, and that will remain the case until we can make an observation."

Anne scratched her mop of short blond curls.

"If physics can't settle the matter," I said, "I hope biology can. We're awaiting the results of a DNA test on the bones."

"I guess that will be the equivalent of looking in the box," said Toby.

I continued listening to Toby and Anne talk about physics and criminology until the subject shifted to the uncertainty principle. I'd had my physics lesson for the day.

I was retracing my steps to rejoin the company on the porch when familiar music coming through the house speaker system stopped me in my tracks. It was the overture to the Beatles' album *Sgt. Pepper's Lonely*

Hearts Club Band. Although the music was upbeat, it brought back the frightening memory of the car that rammed my bicycle and drove off into the night. The driver of that vehicle had his music turned up full blast and was playing the Beatles. Was it purely a coincidence that I was hearing the same music now? Of course, that's just what it could be, a coincidence, I reminded myself. *Sgt. Pepper* is one of the most popular rock 'n' roll albums in history. Still, it felt strange to hear the Beatles again so soon after that incident, their youthful voices tinged with insouciance despite a bleak vision. "I read the news today, oh boy."

In the living room, I found Walt stretched out on a lounge chair, yawning as if the music had awakened him. "Hello," he said when he saw me. "Did you put on that CD?"

"It wasn't me," I said.

"Oh, then it was Beth. She likes to play it for Helen when she comes over. Helen's such a fan. The two of them can sit there listening to the Beatles for hours." He straightened up. "Mind you, I think the Beatles are pretty great too." As if he felt the need to explain his liking to me, he added, "They're the voices of my generation, along with Dylan." He got up and walked around the room, scratching the back of his neck. "Funny, I was looking for that CD earlier today, but I couldn't find it."

I took a shot in the dark. "Maybe it was in Beth's car. I think I saw her carrying some CDs in from her car just as we arrived."

"Could be," said Walt.

He found my made-up explanation plausible. That meant that Beth routinely transferred CDs from the house to her car and back. Did it mean that she or someone else with access to her car had been behind the wheel the night we were run off the road? I didn't want to think so.

"Were you looking for it for a particular reason?" I asked.

"There's a song on it I've always liked," he said. He sang a bar in a reedy, plaintive voice: "Will you still need me, will you still feed me / When I'm sixty-four?" He smiled ruefully. "As a couple, Helen and I didn't make it to sixty-four. When we were young, we thought we would. At least I did. The first year we were married, that was our song." He hummed a few more lines. "Let me see if I can find the right track."

Walt disappeared around a corner into the den where the sound system was located, and soon the wistful tune, with its follow-the-bouncing-ball rhythm, was coming through the living room speakers. He returned in a different mood, visibly pained by the music he craved. His eyes had teared up, and his fists were clenched. He didn't want me there. I left the room quietly.

On the porch I found Helen and Beth deep in conversation. "Sorry to interrupt," I said, "but I thought I'd tell you that Walt is up and about."

"And up to no good, no doubt," said Helen.

"Mom, cut it out. Dad will be all right."

"If you can keep him away from the beer," Helen countered.

"If you can keep him away from your guests," Beth retorted. She quickly whipped into the house.

I felt responsible for the scene. I hadn't needed to report on Walt's awakening. Doing so implied that he might cause trouble, and that attitude put me on Helen's side, against Beth. I should have kept my mouth shut, per usual. My apology collided with Helen's. "I've broken every rule in the Amicable Divorce Handbook," she confessed. "Don't speak ill of your ex-spouse to your child. Don't disparage him in front of his friends. Don't try to control his behavior. You'd think I was new to this."

"You didn't need me waltzing in with Walt's name on my lips."

"It was just the match that lit the fire. We were already talking about touchy stuff. Beth was blaming me for Walt's outburst at the picnic table."

That didn't seem fair. "How could that be your fault? He blew up when he heard Alan mention Theo's name."

"Beth said that's because I bring up Theo whenever I get the chance, which is the opposite of true. Walt always hated Theo. I learned a long time ago not to mention him."

"What was behind his animosity?"

Helen looked to the door, as if she feared that Beth or Walt would overhear. Lowering her voice, she said, "Everyone blamed the bombers for giving the antiwar movement a bad name. For Walt, it went deeper. He was active in a movement to benefit small farmers like his father. He opposed government policies that favored megafarms and uniform products. The antiwar movement for him was only one part of a larger revolution. When the bombers took a life in Sterling Hall, they undermined the whole revolution. That's what Walt thought, and he was furious."

Or was his fury the result of a personal animus? I remembered Helen looking at her daughter when Walt said that no good ever came from Theo Kearn. Helen had been about to say something but stopped. I wondered what she left unsaid.

At a quarter to ten, it was finally dark enough for the fireworks to begin. Everyone sat on the lawn looking out over the lake, where the sky show would display. Some guests had brought blankets to recline on. Others, like us, took bath towels provided by our hosts and made like we were on the beach. Toby and I laid our towels on the grass next to Helen and Alan. He had his arm around her shoulders. Jimmy and Maureen were sitting in front of them, a little to one side. Walt was sitting with Beth and Anne farther down the sloping lawn. Maureen laughed as she sprayed Jimmy with mosquito repellent. Then she turned to me and offered her plastic bottle of OFF!, which we used and passed on to Helen. The aromas of DEET and marijuana hung in the night air.

The first rocket tore through the darkness and exploded into a fountain of diamonds pouring into the lake. The second rose higher and flared into a crimson shower. The third whistled as it rose and then unfolded into a shimmering golden ball that lingered in the heights. Each effect outdid the other. Then the bursts came faster, flashing like strobe lights, alternating between darkness and light. During one spectacular burst, I noticed Alan gazing intently at Maureen. In those few seconds of illumination, I studied his face. It bore the same slack, bovine expression as in the photograph taken so many years ago at the Dow demonstration.

It's true that observation is a potent force. In physics, they say, it can kill a cat. With people, it may lay bare a hidden truth. My observation of Alan Knight came with a frisson of guilt for having spied upon his inner life and glimpsed a secret that he'd kept from the world since his college days.

14

WHEN WE ARRIVED AT THE CONFERENCE ROOM the next afternoon, Agent Whelk was already there. He and Diane were sitting at opposite ends of the table, separated by a wall of silence. She looked indignant. He was sulking. His pompadour looked askew, listing to one side like a fallen battle flag. I guessed he had tried an assault on the citadel and had been repelled. "There you are," said Diane, expressing relief. "Right on time."

"Is everything all right?" I asked.

"Yes. More or less," she added, a little flustered.

Whelk did what he could to look professional. He buttoned his jacket and straightened his cuffs. Diane got right down to work. She handed out a short agenda with an attachment. She'd been counting on the State Crime Lab to tell us whether the bones were Theo Kearn's, but the news from that quarter, she announced, was disappointing.

"They did move us up to the front of the line, but we don't have decisive results. Let's start with the dental records. They outsourced the report to a forensic odontologist in Green Bay. I've attached it. You can skip to his conclusion."

The document was three pages long. I skimmed the last two paragraphs:

"According to procedure, I have transmitted a digitized file of the postmortem DPR to the National Crime Information Center, to be matched against the digital records in their database. Meanwhile, as you requested, I have conducted a visual comparison of the postmortem and antemortem DPRs."

"What's a DPR?" asked Toby.

"A dental panoramic radiograph," Diane explained. "In other words, an X-ray of the mouth. He's compared an X-ray of the remains with an old X-ray of Theo Kearn's teeth."

The odontologist concluded: "In my opinion, the two radiographs are consistent, taking into account the teeth that are missing in the post-mortem sample due to decomposition of the periodontal ligaments that attached them to the jaw. In principle, the greater the number of altera-tions we find, or problems with the teeth, the greater the potential for a positive identification. In this case, however, both radiographs show sub-jects in their early twenties with generally healthy teeth and the absence of significant dental work, making a positive identification difficult. Still, a dental finding of 'consistent' may be an important contribution to the process. It may be used in combination with other forms of identifica-tion, such as DNA analysis, and serve as corroborating evidence."

Diane read the last sentence aloud and added, "Could be, possibly, may be, but can't say for sure. He's stopped short of an identification and is kicking the can down the road to the National Crime Informa-tion Center."

"He does say that his finding could be used as supporting evidence, along with a DNA result," I pointed out.

"That's the trouble," said Diane. "We don't have a DNA result. The State Crime Lab reports that water degrades DNA, and these bones were submerged in a water tank for decades. The lab couldn't recover enough usable DNA to sequence a genome, which they need to do in order to create a profile."

"That's devastating news," said Toby. "Where do you go from here?"

"I wish I knew," said Diane. "I'm stymied."

At this, Agent Whelk stirred from his sulk as if prompted by a cue. He sat up in his chair, reminding me of his height. "There's no need to give up yet," he announced. "The facilities at FBI headquarters are state-of-the-art. They have a new system for extracting damaged DNA using silica-coated magnetic particles. Don't ask me to explain how it works. The process can retrieve DNA fragments under the most difficult conditions, and it's been used successfully with old bones."

"That's more like it," said Diane. "So, what's the next step?"

"I've already taken it," said Whelk, wrapping himself in the cloak of authority. "We follow the DNA trail. I've been in touch with headquarters and tasked with collecting new bone samples from the State Crime Lab. I'm flying them to Quantico this evening as a special courier. I've got fresh sections from a femur, the pelvis, a rib, and a molar to deliver. They're sitting right over there." He pointed to a nondescript black roller-type suitcase standing in the corner.

"You mean you're getting on a plane with human bones in your bag?" asked Toby.

"I didn't stuff my socks with them, if that's what you mean. They're packed in special containers to protect and keep them dry. I'd show them to you, except it's illegal to break the sealing tape until they're delivered."

"What happens when you go through security?" I asked.

"No problem. I take the containers out and put them through the X-ray machine just as you do with a laptop. I have documentation with me, of course."

"What time is your flight? My sister is coming in this evening from Dublin by way of Chicago. I could give you a lift to the airport."

"I've got a seat on the 7:05 to O'Hare. Thanks anyway, but I'm going to the airport right after this meeting to see if I can get on an earlier flight."

That simplified things. Angie wasn't due in until later.

"But say, if you're interested in the subject, I've got something to show you."

"What subject?" I asked, like a stooge in the audience at a magician's show.

"Transporting bones." He reached into his jacket pocket and brought out a hard plastic glasses case. He handed it to me. "Take a look." Whelk had recovered by now from his earlier contretemps with Diane. His personality had reverted to its default setting as life of the party.

I pried open the glasses case. Inside, on a background of black velvet, were the bones of a complete human finger. I yelped and dropped the case, which shut with a snap that almost took *my* finger with it.

"Very funny, Whelk," said Toby.

Diane, appalled, said, "Did you take that bone from the crime lab? You could get in trouble for that."

"Relax. It's a fake, made out of plastic. I got it a couple of years ago at one of those pop-up Halloween stores that sell masks and costumes and practical jokes. It looks real, doesn't it?" He bent down and picked it up from the floor. "Scared you, I bet," he said to me.

"I'll say. You scared the hell out of me," I admitted.

"What are you, twelve years old?" said Toby. "Grow up."

"I was just having some fun," Whelk said.

Diane took charge. "I'm going to pretend I didn't see that happen." She was shaking her head. "I assume you'll let me know immediately if the bureau can extract usable DNA. Good luck with your trip. Now, let's move on to other matters. The police artist's sketch was published in the newspaper over the holiday, with a request to the public for help in identifying the victim. We've already had a few calls. Nora, I'm wondering if your alumni friends have seen it?"

"Yes, and they had quite a debate over it. They're divided as to whether it looks like Theo. Helen is a definite yes. Maureen is a definite no. Jimmy won't go against Maureen, so that's another no. And Alan kept his opinion to himself. Not what I'd call a slam dunk."

"No," said Diane. "What can you tell us about your interviews, Agent Whelk?"

"No breakthroughs there. Maureen Day is the most interesting subject. By the way, a very attractive older woman. How old would you say she was?"

"Too old for you," said Diane. "Get on with it."

Whelk said, somewhat chastened, "She's adamant in her statement that she saw Kearn alive during the sixties conference here. She seems sincere in her belief."

"But no one can corroborate her statement. Am I right?" said Toby.

"That's true so far in my investigation," said Whelk.

"Jimmy, her husband, was with her at the time," Toby added. "He says she was mistaken. So, the evidence for a sighting is limited to one person who was hoping and half expecting to see her ex-boyfriend again, and who conjured him up in her imagination." Toby tossed his pencil on the table and sat back in his chair.

"What else do you have?" Diane asked Whelk.

"Jimmy Montana seemed nervous all the time we were talking. I don't know if that means anything. And Magnus Arp is your typical academic eccentric. His explanation checks out, though, for his trips to the Bascom attic. They were research related. That's about all I've got. We're short on other clues or leads."

Diane looked around the table and came back to Whelk. "That leaves a lot riding on the FBI's ability to salvage DNA. That's the only way we'll ever be able to identify the bones with certainty."

"You'll never have certainty," said Toby, "even if the bureau succeeds. The best you can hope for is high probability. That's how genetic profiles are assessed."

"What's that supposed to mean?" asked Whelk testily.

Toby didn't answer him directly but continued to address Diane. "Anyhow, the standard of truth in a court of law isn't certainty, but likelihood—proof 'beyond a reasonable doubt.'"

"I know that," Whelk grumbled. Toby was getting under his skin.

"The point is," Toby went on, "DNA matchups are expressed in terms of probability." There was no stopping him now. He continued. "The person conducting the test compares an unknown sample of DNA to a known source. If the sample and source overlap, the next step is to rule out coincidence. You do that by calculating the probability of a random sample giving the same result as the test sample. Say the odds of that work out to be a million to one. That means a one in a million chance that the DNA match is coincidental. And if the probability of coincidence is that low, then the probability of a genuine match is extremely high. But that's as much as science can say."

Throughout Toby's explanation, Whelk had been squirming in his chair. "Thanks for the genetics lesson, Mr. Furniture Salesman," he said.

"Antiques," Toby muttered under his breath. He was stung.

"Whatever. That still makes you an amateur."

"Stop it," Diane chided.

Toby's ears colored red, but he held his tongue. I recognized that "he'll-get-*his*" expression and worried what might come of it if the meeting went on much longer. It's a good thing it didn't.

Toby was in a lousy mood when we got home. He had goaded Whelk and in return had been insulted. The experience left a bitter taste. I sent him to the den to watch some escapist TV, while I turned to the task of preparing class for the next day and as much as possible for Monday. Everything had to be ready, because Angie would soon be with us, and Angie can be a full-time occupation. Understanding that, Toby prepared his own dinner and delivered a tuna sandwich to my desk. He left me alone and brooded until it was time to pick up Angie.

We arrived at the Madison airport early and settled into the waiting lounge, where deep-pillowed leather chairs were arranged as in a cozy living room, except that they all were pointed toward the escalator that would deliver arriving passengers to the lobby. The style of the lounge paid homage to Frank Lloyd Wright, with low proportions, warm wood, and a wall of sand-colored brick. We weren't the only ones content to relax there while we waited for a family member to appear.

At Angie's scheduled arrival time, I got up to check the monitor. Her flight's status was just being changed from "On Time" to "Arrived." Leaving Toby to his reading, I found a place to stand watch. A young mom and her redheaded toddler were doing the same, positioning themselves just out of the way of escalator traffic, at a convenient spot for a family hug. I scanned for Angie, who is always easy to find because of her height, but my only significant sighting was a redheaded man, already waving. For a wild second, I thought it was Arp. As the man descended and then threw his arms around his wife and son, I continued searching the top of the stairs. The number of passengers thinned, and I began to worry. I pulled out my phone and looked for a text from Angie. Nothing. I texted her: *Arrived? Where are you?* Straightaway she replied, *Wait I'm here.* Meaning where?

Toby appeared at my side as I was texting back, and he was the one to spot Angie at the top of the escalator. "There she is!" he said, lifting his arm to wave.

Angie didn't return the gesture. She stood ramrod straight, with both hands gripping the handle of her carry-on. Instantly I sensed that something was wrong. When Angie is very upset, she goes dead still. She had that look, right then: shoulders locked, face pale, eyes fixed ahead, mouth grim.

"Let me handle this," I said to Toby. He looked puzzled, having noticed nothing amiss. What he saw was a tall young blond woman with the poise of a fashion model, coming down the escalator in camera-ready posture.

As we hugged, I felt her stiffness. I asked, "Angie, what's wrong?"

"It's this suitcase," she said. "It's not mine." It was a plain black roller bag, carry-on size.

"What? You took the wrong suitcase off the plane? We can go back there and get the right one." I started grabbing for the bag, but she held it back.

"No, it's the bag I put on the plane. But something happened in Chicago." She choked, and tears came to her eyes. "I was accosted at O'Hare."

I put my arms around her. "Oh, honey, we'll take care of you." I held her while sobs began, and then I got her to sit down, along with me. Toby took the bag and stood beside us. "Tell us what happened," I urged.

She used the tissues I handed her and managed to get control of her voice. "A guy started hitting on me, and when I tried to get away from him, he chased me. I was scared to death!" Her face crumpled up, and she paused while tears fell. Then she sniffed and continued.

"I ran through the whole terminal and turned into the next one. Before he could make the turn, I ducked into a women's room, and I hid in a stall until I thought he was gone. And he was."

"But didn't you have to go back to the gate, to catch the plane?" I asked.

"Not that one, the gate had changed." She closed her eyes and pressed her hands to her cheeks and blew out. Then she opened her eyes and said, "Let me start over. I was sitting at the gate, waiting for my flight to Madison, when a plane landed and the passengers started filing out. This one guy was in everybody's way. He was arguing with the attendant at the gangway door, and she was trying to get him to stand aside so people could pass. Then he went to the counter and got in the face of the other attendant. Everyone could hear him saying, 'You can *too* do something!' and 'That's not good enough.'"

"Is this the guy who hassled you?"

"Yes. So finally, he tones down, then he turns around to his little audience in the area and makes a V for victory sign. People pretended not to notice him, but he was tall and hard to miss. I was up front and couldn't help but notice, and he noticed me. Maybe I half smiled or something, just to be polite, but he took it for an invitation and walked right to me. There were lots of empty seats, but he took the one right next to mine, and he leaned in and started talking, while the counter attendant was working on getting him on a flight on another airline. He talked nonstop, like a salesman. He said I had a sympathetic face and that I could be a model. Was I interested in fashion? How did I like his boots? Hand-tooled by a Navajo friend of his. Did I like Navajo jewelry? He could get me a discount."

Toby clapped a hand to his forehead in astonishment.

"All the while," Angie continued, "I kept thinking there was something off about the guy. I finally got my courage up and asked him to leave me alone."

"But he didn't?" I asked. Of course, by then I had worked it out, too.

"No, he got worse. He said, 'Don't worry, you're safe with me. You're talking to an FBI agent! Couldn't get safer than that.' And he shows me an FBI badge, fake of course—holds it right in front of my face, trapping me in the chair. He boasts that he's working on one of the biggest cases in FBI history, and he has the bones of a terrorist in his suitcase. I should have run right then, but I was frozen."

Angie was so distressed by her own story that she didn't notice the glances that Toby and I exchanged. I was dumbfounded. But a small tug of a smile appeared on Toby's lower lip.

Angie plowed on: "'I'll show you,' he says, and he unzips his carry-on. He points to a white package. 'I can't open that,' he says, 'until I get to FBI headquarters,' and he zips the carry-on back up. 'But this will show you what's in it.' And he hands me a glasses case. You'll never guess what was in there."

I didn't have to guess. But I waited for her to say it.

"A finger bone!"

I didn't fake surprise, but an expression of dismay was an appropriate reaction, and she continued. "I mean, he could be a monster, a serial killer, I thought. Jeffrey Dahmer—wasn't he from Wisconsin?"

"How did you get away?" I asked.

"I was so lucky. My phone beeped, with a text from the airline that my gate had changed. I sprang up, grabbed the handle of my suitcase—only it was the wrong one—and ran like a rabbit, pulling it behind me. He was on my tail, but I was faster. I don't think he saw me slip into the women's room. I waited in there as long as I could, and then I raced to my new gate. Thankfully, he wasn't there."

"When did you find out you had the wrong bag?"

"In the women's room. See, the suitcase I left behind wasn't my own to begin with. I borrowed Bobby's, because his is better for international carry-on than mine. Bobby's is black and the same size as the bone guy's, pretty much identical. But when I looked over the bag, I saw that the name tag was wrong. It had a cover on it. When I flipped the cover up, it didn't say Bobby Colman."

I asked to look at the bag, and I checked the tag. Sure enough, the name was D. T. Whelk. Then I unzipped it and spotted the white packages inside, secured by yellow tape that said "FBI Evidence." I closed the bag quickly.

"Bones present and accounted for," I said to Toby.

"But what about their courier?" he replied. "I wonder if Whelk went on to Quantico without them, and if so, what story he told when he got there. Or maybe he's hiding his head somewhere in shame."

Angie's voice cut through. "What are you talking about? You know the bone guy?"

"Enough to wish we didn't," Toby said.

"He's investigating a case we're looking into," I clarified. "We'll have to see that the bones in this suitcase get to the FBI lab he was headed for."

"Wait. He's actually an FBI agent?" Angie looked aghast.

"Yes," Toby said dryly, "though perhaps not an example of the bureau's finest."

Angie looked down at the suitcase. "That makes this FBI property. I swiped FBI property and fled the scene!"

"Don't say that," I cautioned. "It was a mix-up, and Agent Whelk caused it."

"God help me. I hope the government sees it that way." She put her hand on the suitcase handle, and it was shaking. "So, what do we do with this?" she asked. "Turn it in to baggage claim? Leave it in the women's bathroom? Call the police?"

"Those aren't good options under the circumstances," said Toby. He rubbed his lower lip, considering. "Remember the mix-up of the baby and the handbag in *The Importance of Being Earnest*?" he said to me. "I guess Oscar was right. Life does imitate art sometimes!" Then he patted the roller bag and said to Angie, "As for the suitcase, we can handle it ourselves. We'll take it home, keep it safe, and I'll find a way to return it, once I establish you won't get in trouble."

"And what about *my* suitcase?" Angie said. "How am I going to get that?"

"I have a feeling Agent Whelk will hold on to it," Toby said. "We'll try to work out a trade. Meanwhile, if he tries to trace the owner, he won't get very far. The bag belongs to a Mr. Bobby Colman from Achill

Island, Ireland, but no passenger of that name was registered for a flight. Mr. Colman didn't arrive in, or depart from, Chicago. The FBI agent doesn't know who you are."

Angie turned to me for confirmation. What could I do? I nodded. Inside me, a voice was whispering, "Federal crime! Halt!"

"Let's get out of here, gang," Toby said.

At home, in between finding Angie a clean toothbrush and lending her a nightgown, I told her the story behind the bones in the black bag. Toby interrupted when he appeared in the hallway outside Angie's bedroom. "I've stashed the suitcase in the attic. Tomorrow I'll stay here with Angie and guard the treasure until you get back from teaching. Then we can strategize about the give-back."

"But isn't tomorrow your class trip to Monona Terrace? You don't want to miss that," I said.

"We can go another day. I've had enough of Arp, anyhow."

I turned to the last task of the day—picking out clothes for my bagless sister. A sundress that hit me mid-calf would skim her knees. I gave her that, a pair of stretchy yoga pants, and some tops. Then, in the bathroom we three would share, I gave her access to all my toiletries. There's nothing like sharing a hairbrush to bring two sisters together. We said good night giggling.

I opened our bedroom door, expecting to see Toby reading, waiting to review the day with me. Instead, I found him lying on his back, with eyes shut, his Kindle in his hands but fallen to his chest. His lips were moving slightly, in dream talk. I watched for a while, wondering if he was half-awake. But no. His lips parted, even showing a bit of tooth. No doubt about it. Toby was grinning in his sleep.

15

Friday went much as Toby had planned, except that Angie didn't stay at home with him. When I came into the kitchen to make my morning tea, she was at the little table wearing my night-gown, knotted at the waist, over yoga pants. She'd scrounged around and found the coffee stash. Her cup was half-empty, and she was reading the morning paper.

"I hope you don't mind that I made myself at home," she said, with confidence in the answer. "I was pouring my coffee when I heard the paper arrive on the front porch. That kid comes early! Let me tell you, no one on Achill Island is working at six in the morning. We stay up late and we start work after the morning drizzle—nine or ten-ish."

"You're up early, then." My watch said six twenty.

"On Achill, it's lunchtime."

"You'll adjust fast," I said. "You're young." I liked to tease Angie about being my kid sister; there's a twelve-year difference between us.

"If I feel tired later, I'll take a nap. But if I'm sleeping when you get home, wake me up. I don't want to miss any sister time. We've got so much to talk about."

While I was teaching, Angie walked all around the neighborhood and discovered the used-clothing shops on Williamson Street. At St. Vinny's she found her fashion hub and a means to replenish her wardrobe. But by the time I got home, jet lag had bested her, and she slept straight through until the next day.

On Saturday morning, Toby made a weekend breakfast that was fit for two Wisconsin milkmaids: buttermilk pancakes, maple syrup from upstate, Dane County raspberries, whipped cream, and crisp bacon from Oscar Meyer (till recently, Madison's anchor industry).

"What are you trying to do, seduce me away from the Full Irish Breakfast?" Angie asked.

"He didn't even pull out the stops," I answered. "Absent are the eggs. He must be saving them for tomorrow."

"Egg-zactly," said the chef. "The Full Irish is just too full."

"And too Irish," added Angie, with a pout, as she drizzled deep golden syrup over her puffy pancakes. "Irish bacon is too big and hammy, Irish sausage is too greasy, and who wants baked beans at breakfast?"

Tightening the screw, I added, "Then there's black pudding. When I heard that the key ingredient is pigs' blood, I couldn't even try it."

Angie dolloped whipped cream onto her pancakes and laughed. She savored her bite, licked whipped cream off her lips, and said, "Yes, but it's not just a difference in food. For months I worked at trying to learn the local ways, the local words, even the Achill Island accent. I thought it was going pretty well, but one night, after a family party, Mary took me aside and said, 'Angie, love, it's no use trying to blather like us. You sound like you're slagging us, half the time.' Nora, I was so hurt that I burst into tears."

"At least Mary is a straight shooter," I said.

"That she is, and thank God for it. The next thing she said has become my mantra. 'My son fell in love with an American girl, Angie. Don't forget that.'"

Toby raised his coffee cup. "American girls are the best. I married one myself." He looked pleased to see Angie's smile. But then her face clouded over. "What are we going to do about the FBI bag with the bones in it?" she asked Toby.

"Leave it to me. Don't give it another thought today. Instead, why don't you and Nora plan an activity that you'll enjoy?"

"Now that sounds like a great idea," I said. Angie agreed.

Toby doesn't dawdle over breakfast, since it's already late by the time he begins it. At times, he has startled houseguests with his quick clearing of the plates, but Angie was used to him and kept up with his pace. She helped him clear and shooed him off so that she and I could do the dishes together. Over suds, we planned an outing to Yahara Place Park and then east along the lakeshore for a mile to Olbrich Gardens, the City of Madison's horticultural showpiece.

"That sounds perfect," Angie said.

I surprised myself by playing the enthusiastic walking guide. I had been in Madison only a month, but I'd grown fond of the place, and I found myself selling it to Angie. I'd initially turned up my nose at the mishmash of styles in Eve's neighborhood, but I'd come to delight in the variety of houses, most of them built between 1890 and 1930. You'd find an imposing brick Georgian Revival and a small Queen Anne bungalow on the same block. On other streets, bungalows in the Arts and Crafts style dominated, some boasting a second story and attic, like Eve's house. I pointed these out to Angie, but she was more interested in the gardening. Few of the houses had much of a front yard, but many of the small plots were planted like bouquets, with an eclectic mixture of daisies and lilies, zinnias and marigolds, tall cosmos and dwarf delphiniums.

Stopping at a shady walkway lined with impatiens, Angie said, "I've missed gardening."

"You're on a farm," I said. "There must be a garden."

"Sure, for vegetables. I want flowers. Mary says that a farmer doesn't have time for flowers. When she got married, she planted white lilies next to the house, and they're still there, thick and hardy without work. That's her idea of the perfect flower garden. I prefer this." She pointed to the lush violets and pinks of the impatiens border.

"I see the problem. You're dying to put in color, but it's Mary's house, not yours. You're not even a daughter-in-law yet. You don't have planting rights."

"And that's one of the things I'm worried about. I'm living in his mother's house, and that won't change if Bobby and I get married. I'll never get a chance to create a home. It's already created."

"Hmm. Let's keep moving and try to think." I gestured toward the park, where a vista of Lake Monona came into view and opened a sense of freedom and possibility. We picked up our pace and took the footpath at waterside. Families of mallards glided close by on the placid water.

I said, "Do you really have to live with your mother-in-law?"

"I do. It's expected. And before you start, I know that I don't have to conform to everyone else's expectations. But in this case it's expected for good reasons. When Bobby's father died, he took over his father's work, raising the sheep for wool and for sale to butchers. He saved the family ranch and made it possible for his mother to keep her home. Bobby says it's essential for him to live on-site, next to the animals, if he's to manage them, and I've seen how that's so, especially this spring with the lambing. And he's good company for Mary."

"So, everybody's happy again, and along comes Angie."

"Yeah, and Bobby assumes he'll reach the next level of happiness simply by adding me to the equation and helping me adjust. That's what he's been working on for a year. Now I know how to contribute and get along, but there are times when I feel like a hired hand, that's all."

We were beyond Yahara Park and had walked to a grassy hill looking out over the water. A small iron sign proclaimed an effigy mound constructed by first peoples. I thought of the waterside graveyard we'd visited with Angie on Achill Island, where bereaved families had erected monuments to the victims of mass drownings. Both cultures honored the dead by placing them in an open spot, near water but protected from its erosive force by height and earthwork.

Thinking of Achill brought me back to Angie's dilemma. I asked, "Why don't you ask Bobby for more of a role?"

"The setup goes against it. I was supposed to be spending a year finding out if I liked the life enough to marry a sheep rancher. If I asked for a definite stake in the work of the ranch, it would be pushy. That should come once we know we're getting married."

"Who says? You won't feel confident about getting married until you and Bobby talk about this. I'll bet Bobby would back you up and get Mary to join you in some planning sessions—but you won't know until you ask."

Angie nodded and we continued for a while without speaking. Soon our destination was in sight. At the east end of the lake, we spotted the glass conservatory of Olbrich Gardens shining in the sun. An attendant at the door asked us where we were from. I was glad to hear Angie's firm answer: Ireland. Once admitted, Angie headed straight for the roses, acres of them. Red, white, pink, and coral. Long-stemmed, short-stemmed, and shrubby. Angie declared that it was roses she dreamed of adding to Mary's front yard, and she was looking for a type hardy enough to withstand island conditions. But after much roaming and considering, she reluctantly concluded that it would be better to search on Achill Island for a native rose that thrived there and a homeowner who knew what nurture it required.

With Angie's mission aborted, we randomly took paths through patches of Wisconsin wildflowers and by clusters of perennials from all over the world until we came upon the Thai Pavilion. Eve had told me it was her favorite place in Madison, a gift to the city from the Thailand chapter of the university alumni association. The delicate pavilion, carved of wood and painted red and gold, was first built in Thailand and then disassembled. A team of craftsmen was sent from Bangkok to Madison to reconstruct it, and it is now one of the city's most popular attractions, a gathering place and site for meditation.

Heading south, we followed signs to the pavilion grounds. High bushes and trees screened the building from full sight until the moment when we reached a wooden bridge, where the view opened to a sunburst of gold, surrounded by an acre of green park. The many-paneled roof of the pavilion gave it the illusion of flight, each orange-gold tile catching the light and the eaves curving up to a peak. The open-air structure, with its intricate carvings on gilded columns and pediments, seemed like a mirage rising by some act of legerdemain out of the midwestern soil.

"It's dazzling," Angie said. "I feel dizzy." She walked slowly to the middle of the pavilion floor and lowered herself into a yogi's meditating position. When she didn't move after a few minutes, I decided to walk around the grounds and contemplate the building. My admiration for it grew with each new perspective.

Angie continued to meditate for a good while. When she met me by the reflecting pool, she looked resolved. "I've learned something from this place," she said.

"What's that?"

"If this pavilion could be moved thousands of miles to a radically different culture and still keep its power, I guess I can move to Ireland and continue to be me."

"Meditating in the pavilion told you that?"

"Yes, that and our conversation on the way here and then reading the panels on the other side of the building. They stressed that it was crucial to prepare a foundation that would withstand Madison's freezing weather. That's what I've got to do with Bobby and Mary—lay down the conditions that will let me thrive."

There was so much good sense in what she said that I was struck by its applicability to me. Could I move to a large university in the middle of the country, to a major research institution with a different teaching environment and its own culture and expectations, and still remain myself? I didn't know.

Sunday we had an adventure of a different kind, a retreat to our girlhood Catholicism, but thoroughly updated. Angie asked me to take her to Sunday assembly at Holy Wisdom Monastery, an ecumenical community of Benedictine Sisters, located on the north side of Lake Mendota. She had booked a mini-retreat to help clarify her decision-making. The package included an overnight stay on Sunday and two sessions of "spiritual guidance" involving prayer and meditation, one after the service on Sunday and another on Monday morning.

With visits to the Thai Pavilion and the Holy Wisdom Monastery under her belt, Angie felt that she had covered her spiritual bases. For good measure, we added a stop at James Madison Park to visit the Gates of Heaven, Madison's first synagogue. Now if only Toby could finesse the return of Whelk's bag without landing Angie in a federal lockup, I'd say her visit to Madison was a success.

The meeting with Whelk on Monday had been scheduled before his departure. Its purpose was to hear about his trip to Quantico. I wondered how he would explain the loss of his bag, or whether he'd even show up. Toby assured me he was prepared for any eventuality. We arrived at university police headquarters ahead of time, with Toby pulling the roller bag bouncing behind him. He left it in the care of the receptionist at the welcome window, after exchanging a few words with her about an imaginary trip. He thanked her for keeping an eye on it, and we marched upstairs.

Agent Whelk was seated with his elbow on the table and his head leaning on his fist, looking thoroughly downcast. He reminded me of Van Gogh's portrait of the melancholy Doctor Gachet sitting in his garden, bearing (in Vincent's words) "the heartbroken expression of our time." Whelk barely acknowledged our entrance. He was so dejected that his once prominent pompadour had dwindled to a cowlick, which he brushed away from his forehead with a dispirited gesture.

Diane, seated facing him, was at a loss. She greeted us with a sigh. "We've run into some trouble," she said. "Unfortunately, the bones never made it to Quantico. Agent Whelk, could you start over again, please, for the benefit of Toby and Nora? He was just beginning to tell me what happened."

Whelk looked up and floated a pained glance in our direction. At first his voice was almost inaudible, but gradually it gathered volume as he went along. "As I was telling Diane," he began, "there was an awful mistake with the baggage. My plane to Washington was full—we were packed in like sardines. Because I just managed to get on at the last minute, I got stuck way in the back, in a window seat. I couldn't budge." He searched our faces to see if we got the point. "The overhead bin was full, so a stewardess, over my objection, took my bag and put it in one of the bins up front. She promised she'd get it down for me before we landed. Well, she didn't." He threw up his hands. "As soon as we got to the gate, some wise guy sitting in the row beneath the bin jumped up, grabbed my bag, and hurried off the plane with it. I assume it was by mistake, but he disappeared into the crowd before I could reach him."

So that was Agent Whelk's story. It was a clever mixture of truth and fabrication to make it appear that someone else was at fault for losing the bones. It was true that a stranger had grabbed his bag by mistake, but it wouldn't have happened if he hadn't been flirting with an attractive young woman and showing off. In this edited version of events, the loss of his bag would still be an embarrassment, but it would go even harder with him if the facts were known. I wasn't about to correct the record. His story put the blame on a fictitious flight attendant—and let Angie off the hook. Any way you looked at it, though, Whelk was in hot water. A courier isn't allowed to lose his cargo.

Diane had been thinking the same thing. "What did they say at Quantico? Are you in trouble?"

"Am I in trouble?" He rolled his eyes and raised a forefinger and thumb to his temple in a pantomime of a handgun. "Just shoot me. I've been reprimanded and suspended, pending a hearing. So, this isn't an official meeting. It can't be. I'm just here to tell you face-to-face what happened."

"I'm sorry," said Diane. "What's the chance of finding this person who took your bag? By now he must have realized his mistake."

"I've been in touch with the airline. Nothing yet. I'm working with a copy of the passenger list to track him down."

That didn't ring true. There was no such "him" to track down on Whelk's fictitious flight.

"He's probably afraid to turn it in because of what might happen to him," said Diane.

"He should be," said Whelk, adopting an aggrieved tone. "I'll find him, and when I do, I'll charge him with stealing government property, tampering with evidence, impeding a federal investigation, fleeing from a federal officer, and I don't know what else." He paused, remembering his current status. "At least that's what I'll do if I'm reinstated."

Oh boy. As long as Angie was at risk of being charged with any of those crimes, we had a problem. I whispered to Toby that this wasn't the time to bring up the return of her suitcase. Whelk had erased Angie from the story, and I hoped we could let that stand.

Toby patted my hand in agreement.

Diane persisted. "What happens now with DNA testing of the bones?"

"They'll have to start over. The bureau will send another agent to collect new samples to bring to Quantico."

"How long will all that take?"

"It depends on how long it takes them to replace me." His expression was glum.

"I'm sorry," Diane said again.

Toby chose this moment to make his move. "Whelk, what would you say if I told you I could restore your bag to you today with the contents undisturbed?"

"What are you talking about?" he said gruffly. "What do you know about it?"

"Before I go any further, you'll have to agree to a single, nonnegotiable condition, and that is: no questions asked. No questions about who took it or found it or how I came to know about it. No recriminations, and above all, no criminal charges. The only acceptable response would be your gratitude. What do you say?"

Diane dropped her pencil.

Whelk blustered. "What? How? If you have it—"

Toby stopped him with a finger to his lips. "I'll repeat my offer one more time. I can return your missing bag with its contents undisturbed on one condition: no questions asked. Do we have a deal?"

"If I were you, Agent Whelk, I'd say yes," Diane prompted.

Any inclination he might have had to resist leaked out of him like air from a punctured balloon. "All right, yes," said Whelk, "no questions asked." He looked weary.

"Good," said Toby, "I'll be back in a wink." He left the room and returned in a few minutes, tugging the roller bag behind him. "Is this it?" he asked, turning the bag over to Whelk. "Go ahead, open it to make sure."

Whelk zipped it open to reveal the sample containers unopened, their sealing tape intact. He slumped back in his chair. "What the—! Yes, everything's here."

Diane said to Whelk, "You should let them know at Quantico that you've recovered the bag and the bone samples. They might still accept them."

Toby suggested, "You might even get yourself reinstated. The recovery of the contents should count for something. You can say you tracked the bag down on your own initiative."

Whelk slowly rallied. His eyes focused and color crept back into his cheeks. "Do you think so? Maybe if I appealed in person." He looked at his watch. "I can still make a flight to Washington today. You don't think I'd look foolish?"

"Take a chance," I said.

"Good luck, Daryl," said Diane. "I'll be pulling for you."

"Then I'll go." He paused, then said to Diane, "You know, that's the first time you've called me by my first name." He looked bemused.

"Humph. If you're going, you better go," she said.

"I will. There's just one thing." He turned to Toby. "I know I agreed to your terms, but I'm dying to know. How in the hell did you do it?"

Toby let the question hang in the air and savored it for a moment before he answered. "We amateurs have our methods."

Whelk had the good grace to incline his head in a gesture that said well played. He gathered his things and hustled out the door, his bag bumping along behind him. As soon as he was gone, Diane asked, "All right, are you going to keep me in the dark too?"

I recounted the highlights of Angie's story for her—how Whelk had flirted with her at O'Hare while both were between flights; how he had scared the daylights out of her with his fake finger bone; how she had run away, grabbing his bag instead of hers; how there had been a chase through the airport; and how the bag ended up in our house. When I finished, all she said was, "The big dope."

"Why, Diane, I believe you're beginning to develop a soft spot for him."

"Don't be ridiculous," she said, ignoring my inquiring look.

"Just how will this affect the investigation?" asked Toby.

"There will probably be another delay. The FBI may want new samples for DNA testing, whatever they decide about Daryl."

"Even though the seals on the containers were intact?" asked Toby.

"Probably. The bag was missing over the weekend. That means the chain of custody was broken, compromising the samples as evidence. I didn't mention the issue to Daryl because I didn't want to discourage him or mix it up with his attempt to get reinstated."

Toby said, "Maybe he'll get by with a slap on the wrist. If the FBI can manage to get usable DNA from the bones, they'll be able to build a genetic profile and compare it to any samples they may have of Kearn's DNA."

I mentioned the hair sample that Maureen had disclosed.

Diane nodded. "And if the bones aren't his, the FBI can upload the data to the National DNA Index System and look for a match there. Meanwhile, I've got my hands full here, running down tips in response to the sketch that was in the newspaper."

"Do any seem promising?" I asked.

"None so far. I don't mind telling you, Nora, that I'm drawn to the idea that we've found Theo Kearn. We just don't have proof. And until the remains are formally identified, the investigation can't move ahead."

Toby was feeling awfully pleased with himself by the time we got home. I warned him against gloating. "You brought that bag to the department knowing full well you were going to give it back. You could have just returned it without dragging things out. Why did you?"

"For one thing, I needed Whelk to agree not to press charges against Angie, so I stipulated that as a condition. It worked. For another, I needed to protect myself. That worked too. And for another, he deserved it."

"You enjoyed toying with him, didn't you?"

Toby folded his hands and looked skyward, like a kid playing an angel in the school play. I wasn't going to let him off that easily. "You know what, Toby? I'm beginning to wonder if the man I married is a bit of a sadist."

Toby looked struck for just an instant. Then I saw a naughty twinkle in his eye. "A sadist, am I? Say that again and I'll spank you."

I said it again. Two can play this game.

He twirled an imaginary mustache like a stage villain and intoned: "'Do you go to women? Do not forget the whip.' The quote is from Nietzsche."

"Nietzsche never got anywhere near a woman. The quote is from Nora."

"Tosh, woman. Upstairs with you!" he ordered in his stage villain voice, pointing to the bedroom.

"Angie might be up there, back from Holy Wisdom," I objected.

"All right, then downstairs with you!" he ordered, pointing to the basement.

"Are you kidding? There are spiders down there."

He was running out of directions. He asked in his normal voice, "Should we skip the whole idea?"

"Give me a minute. Let me check upstairs," I said. I did a quick reconnaissance and returned. "The coast is clear."

"Then let's go."

I started up but languished on the landing.

"Yes? Am I supposed to carry you up like Scarlett O'Hara, or perchance, do you want me to make love to you right here on the stairs?"

I considered the offer. I pictured the posture.

And while I was doing that, the front door flew open, and Angie called out in her loudest voice, "Hi, everyone, I'm home!"

16

IT WAS THE MIDDLE OF THE NIGHT. Angie was at my bedside, shaking me by the shoulder and urgently whispering, "Nora, wake up!"

"What is it?" I whispered back, groggy, propping myself up on one elbow. Toby was still asleep at my side.

"Someone's in the house. He's downstairs. A burglar, or that crazy FBI agent who chased me in the airport. Maybe he's tracked me down. Listen, you can hear him!" In the silence that followed, I heard a soft *thud* of someone bumping into a piece of furniture. No light had been turned on, but there definitely was someone there. "We've got to wake Toby up." Angie kept her voice low.

Toby was already stirring. He rolled over on his side and rubbed his eyes. "What's going on?" he asked, crabby at having his sleep disturbed.

"Shh," Angie warned.

"There's someone in the house. You can hear him moving around downstairs," I said.

He sat up in bed. The three of us held our breath and listened. Then I heard a click, like a door shutting. "Look around up here for something I can use as a weapon," Toby whispered, "while I get some clothes on." On warm nights he sleeps in his shorts. He pulled on a pair of pants and a T-shirt and slipped on a pair of rubber-soled moccasins while Angie and I scurried about as quietly as we could, looking for some object he could use for defense. There was nothing immediately at hand. A lamp? Too clumsy. A shoe? Too flimsy. A vase? Too delicate. Finally, Angie stood in the doorway to our bedroom clutching a wooden cylinder with a rubber cup attached to one end.

"A toilet plunger? Is that the best you can do?" sputtered Toby.

"Yes, as a matter of fact, it is," said Angie. "It won't help you on offense, but it might help on defense. Like, if he has a knife, you could fend him off or keep him at a distance with the rubber end."

"What if he has a gun?" whispered Toby.

"Then we're in trouble," she said.

"Better take it," I advised. "There's nothing else." And that is how Toby ended up creeping silently down our staircase with a plunger raised above his head. In the outline of his shadow, he looked like an ax murderer. Angie and I huddled at the top of the stairs. I could see the beams of a flashlight bouncing around below. I followed Toby's progress halfway down and watched him crouch and move in the direction of the light source. He made a determined lunge, there was a grunt, and the flashlight beam hit a spot on the ceiling and then went out.

"Get the lights!" Toby shouted.

In the excitement of the moment, I forgot where the switch was, not being in my own house, but Angie was standing next to it at the top of the stairs. She flicked it on to reveal Toby grappling with a figure dressed in black from head to toe. He wore a balaclava pulled down over his face. They struggled indecisively until Toby stepped back, gained a purchase with his toes, and shoved the plunger squarely into the prowler's chest. As an instrument of propulsion, it worked according to design. Toby put his weight behind his thrust and drove the intruder back against the wall, then wrestled him to the floor. There followed a flurry of arms and legs. At one point, Toby had his man in a hammerlock, but his opponent squirmed out of it. They rolled over several times until, finally, Toby emerged on top. From then on, he had the upper hand. The brief struggle ended with Toby sitting on the prowler's chest, pinning him to the floor by pressing his wrists down on either side of his head. "Pull this damned head thing off," said Toby, trying to catch his breath, "so we can see his face."

I tugged the cords of my bathrobe tighter, knelt, and pulled the balaclava off in one swift motion, as you might a sock. A mop of red hair was the giveaway. Magnus Arp was twisting to no avail in Toby's grip.

"Damn it, Arp, it's always you!" I shouted.

"You know this person?" Angie asked.

"He's a colleague in my department," I said.

"I'm taking a course from him," said Toby.

We spoke over each other at the same time.

Angie shook her head in disbelief. "What's up with these oddballs from Wisconsin? There must be something in the cheese."

Toby ignored the comment. "How did you get in here?" he demanded, glaring down at his pinned adversary.

"Through that window in the dining room." Arp pointed with his chin. "The screen is loose, and the window wasn't locked. You might want to beef up your security."

Toby's face flushed with anger. "This is the last straw, Arp, breaking into our house in the dead of night. You've been hostile to us since the day we arrived, and dangerous, too, trying to drive Nora out of the department. You're the one who ran her off the road when we were biking, aren't you? And when that didn't work, you tried to flatten her between the moving stacks in the art library!"

"And I thought *I* had problems trying to fit in!" said Angie, to the room at large.

"Those are reckless charges," Arp retorted. He was defiant. "You don't have any evidence to back them up. I could sue for defamation."

"You do that. This time we're calling the police," said Toby. "But there's one thing I want to do before they get here." He raised his fist.

Arp flinched. "You wouldn't hit a man when he's down, would you?" he squeaked.

"Ordinarily, no," said Toby, and punched him in the nose.

The blood began to flow immediately. Toby reached into his pants pocket and produced a handkerchief. "Here. Take this. It's clean. That was just a half punch, by the way. It could have been much harder." Toby stood up. "Better lie there a few minutes until the bleeding stops."

As he lay there on the floor, Arp resembled a dazed turkey on the chopping block, the red handkerchief dangling from his nose like a wattle. The discarded plunger was lying at his feet. "Is that a toilet plunger you shoved me with?" he asked in an offended tone.

"We couldn't find anything else," said Angie apologetically.

"If it's beneath your dignity," said Toby, "try breaking into a better quality home next time. You might get shot."

Arp shuddered and spread the handkerchief over his eyes. Angie concluded that the fight had gone out of him and announced, "I'm going back to bed," which she did.

I was seething but also puzzled. "What was the point of breaking in here tonight, Magnus? Just to rattle me some more?"

"I know what he's after," said Toby, "but before I change my mind, let's make that call."

From his prone position, Arp waved an arm, signaling stop. "Don't call the police. That would ruin me. I'll make you a deal."

"What kind of deal?" asked Toby.

"I'll tell you what you want to know about those incidents you mentioned, if you agree not to press charges."

"The bike ramming and the art library?" said Toby.

"Yes, and I swear I won't bother you again."

"This will be the end of your harassing us?" I asked.

"You have my word."

"So," said Toby, "we let you go and you confess, that's the deal."

"You could put it that way. Help me up."

Toby clasped his hand, pulling Arp to his feet and sealing their verbal agreement at the same time. We moved to the dining room table. Arp still pressed a corner of Toby's handkerchief to one nostril, though the worst of the bleeding was over. "I suppose I could make a pot of tea," I said. Both men nodded. I put the kettle on.

"You have to understand I never meant to hurt you," Arp began, addressing me, "only to discourage you from coming here. The fact is I'm in trouble. My career is on the line. I'm coming up again this year for promotion to full professor. I failed to get it last year for the second time. The vote was close. One more hostile woman on the council of full professors would kill my chances."

"How do you know how I would vote if I were in the department? I don't know myself. I haven't studied your case."

"You're a friend of Eve. She could easily prejudice you against me."

"I like to think I'd form my own opinion. I consider myself a fair person."

"I don't know you, maybe you are. I couldn't take a chance." He folded up the bloody handkerchief and returned it to Toby.

Impatient, Toby said, "So you mounted a campaign of intimidation to scare Nora away. You've already admitted that."

"I went too far. I'm sorry for that, but I still say I never meant to hurt you. That night when I nudged your bike with my car, it was just a tap. It's an exaggeration to say you were rammed."

"We crashed just the same," Toby fumed. "It's pure luck that we weren't badly hurt."

Arp whined, "I said I was sorry."

"When you just 'tapped' my bike, as you put it, I remember hearing music by the Beatles playing, with the car radio turned up loud," I said. "What was the point of that?"

"No point at all. I don't remember what was on the radio. I sometimes listen to a station that plays 'golden oldies.' Whatever they were playing that night was up to them. I admit I did turn the volume up loud."

"And the art library—" Toby began, but Arp interrupted.

"I know those moving stacks look dangerous, but there's an automatic safety device that cuts the power if they run into an obstacle. I knew they would stop before you got hurt."

I didn't remember it that way. I recalled the sound of the motorized stack grinding and whirring against the stool that I managed to wedge between the bookshelves.

"It was a reckless thing to do," admitted Arp. "I'm sorry."

I said, "And it was you, I suppose, who slipped the warning note that said 'stop' into the book I bought at Taliesin."

Now Arp looked perplexed. "What note? I don't know anything about that."

I believed him. He had already confessed to greater offenses; why deny the lesser? Someone else had delivered that message, and it could have been anyone in our tour group.

The kettle was whistling. I turned it off and poured hot water into a pot with several tea bags and let them steep. We stopped talking. When the tea was ready, I set out mugs and poured. There was a tinkling of spoons and some fussing with a plastic squeeze bottle of honey. We sipped, then resumed. Toby and I had additional questions, and Arp had something on his mind he hadn't disclosed. Toby pressed the questioning. "What about tonight? You were after the Frank Lloyd Wright desk we fought over at the auction. Am I right?"

"Not the desk itself but something hidden inside it—Wright's concept drawings to replace the dome on Bascom Hall that burned down a hundred years ago."

"Ah. Now it's beginning to make sense. What's the connection to my desk?"

"A hunch I have, and I admit it's a long shot. I've turned up several pieces of evidence in my research. One is a photograph of an apprentice at Taliesin who is shown working at that very desk—or one just like it. His name was Herbert Powers. I have a copy of a letter he wrote to his mother dated June 1, 1936. In it he said that Mr. Wright had drawn some sketches for a dome to be built at the university and Wright assigned him to work on the project."

He took a sip of tea and continued. "I also know that Wright mentioned the idea to Alexander Meiklejohn, the director of the Experimental College. Meiklejohn was a frequent guest at Taliesin. On Wright's behalf, he persuaded Glenn Frank, the president of the university, to back the idea. But Frank ran afoul of the regents and was fired in 1937. The project lost its patron. Then came World War II. Powers joined the navy. Unfortunately, his ship went down somewhere in the Pacific. By then the drawings Wright had made for the dome had disappeared. But there's a connection between the last person who had them—Herbert Powers— and that desk. It may be a long shot, as I've said, but it's worth a look."

"That's quite a story," said Toby. "And with all that knowledge, you had the gall to sneak in here like a thief in the night to steal whatever you could find."

Arp cringed at the word "steal."

"Indulge me," Toby went on. "I'd like to know why you've spent so much effort on a relatively minor project in Wright's career. Replacing a structure on an existing building doesn't compare with designing the Jacobs House or, say, the Johnson Wax building. Yet you were prepared to commit an act of desperation, breaking in here tonight to rummage for the plans. I don't get it. There must be more to it than meets the eye."

"That's just it," said Arp. "There's much more to it. Have you noticed that from Bascom Hall, you can see all the way to the end of State Street and the dome of the State Capitol? It isn't accidental that the buildings are aligned. Originally their two domes were in synchrony. Wright developed his idea for a new dome on Bascom while he was working on his civic center for the city, Monona Terrace. He designed a beautiful dome for that building, as well. For Wright, the three domes of the city—the Capitol and two of his own design—would symbolize the interrelated ideals of democracy, culture, and education. He believed that architecture could express the connections."

"Impressive," said Toby. "What happened to the dome on Monona Terrace? There isn't one there now."

"No. It wasn't included in the final version of the building, which was constructed by Wright's associates after his death. Had it been built according to Wright's original plan, Monona Terrace would have rivaled his greatest buildings," Arp declared. "On the roof there would have been a plaza with fountains and a glass dome in the center, close to the dome of the State Capitol a few blocks away."

"Your point being that restoration of the Bascom dome was part of this grand design," said Toby. "A trilogy."

"Precisely. With the Capitol dome and Monona Terrace, democracy was linked with art and culture, but education was the missing element in the scheme. Without it, Wright believed, democracy and culture decay."

"Is that the theme of the book you're working on?" I asked.

"Yes. And you can see the importance to my work of discovering Wright's original intentions for the project."

"Well, Professor. You've convinced me of the significance of those drawings, if they still exist," said Toby.

"Then let's take that desk apart and look for them!"

"Not so fast." Toby shook his head. "That doesn't mean we're partners all of a sudden or that you're forgiven for breaking in tonight and for all your other crap. You're not." Arp looked at the floor.

"It's very late and I'm tired," Toby continued. "I'll conduct a professional search in the morning but without your help. I shudder at the thought of letting you tear apart a valuable and historic piece of furniture. I'll search *my* property in *my* house by myself, if it's all the same to you—which it isn't. I know that. But I'll tell you what. If I do find any plans or drawings, I'll share credit for their discovery with you, and I'll see that you're the first person to get copies to work with."

At first Arp didn't say a word. Then he said, "That would be incredibly generous of you." Suspiciously, he added, "Why would you do that?"

Toby looked him in the eye. "Because despite what I think of you personally, I'm impressed by your scholarship. I'm impressed even more by your passion for Wright. Because the search for knowledge is a noble pursuit, and even though you're a conniving pest and a pain in the ass, I can see that you're dedicated to it. And finally, because you have a contribution to make to your field, and I don't want to stand in the way of it."

I never felt prouder of my husband than at that moment. "Toby, I apologize for calling you a sadist yesterday. That's a wonderful thing to say—not the pain in the ass part, I mean the rest of it."

Toby, while pleased, has an aversion to sentimentality, and before things could go too far in that direction, he scooped Arp up by the collar, hauled him to his feet, and started frog-marching him toward the front door. "Lest we forget, you're still a prowler, and I reserve the right to kick your sorry ass out of my house."

In the doorway, Toby fumbled with the lock. He was using one hand and holding Arp by his collar with the other, with Arp squirming to break free, when a gold chain that Arp was wearing around his neck came loose and slipped to the floor.

"What's this?" I said, picking it up.

"It's mine," said Arp. "The clasp is loose. I need to get it fixed." At the end of the chain was a gold pendant in the shape of a circle. Inside the circle was an upside-down *Y*. It looked familiar.

"May I see it?" asked Toby.

Holding the pendant by its chain, I dropped it in his cupped hand. Toby checked the clasp, then ran his finger around the surface of the circle. "It's the old peace symbol, remember?"

I did remember, and I remembered Helen and Jimmy in the Rathskeller talking about Alan sporting such a pendant back in the days of the campus demonstrations. "May I see it again, please?" I asked Toby. I held it up close. On the back of the stem of the *Y*, faint but still visible, were the engraved initials "A. K."

"Where did you get this?" I asked Arp.

"It was a gift," he said.

"Where did you get this?" Toby repeated in a no-nonsense tone. He had seen the initials too.

"All right. I found it. There was no place to return it, and I liked the look of it, so I kept it."

"Found it where?" said Toby.

"Up in the Bascom attic where I was taking measurements for the dome, if you must know. I moved a couple of boards and found it underneath. It was covered by a thick layer of dust, so it must have lain there for years. How was I going to find the owner?"

"When was this?" Toby continued the grilling.

"About six months ago. Look. You don't have to make a federal case out of it," he whined.

"I've got news for you. It's already a federal case," said Toby. "Don't be surprised if the FBI comes knocking on your door."

"What for? It can't be that valuable."

"It might be evidence, though, related to the bones that were discovered in the cistern. I'm going to keep it to turn over to the university police."

"The university police!" Arp swallowed hard. "Can I just go home now, please?" He looked exhausted.

"Go," said Toby. If he had planned on physically kicking Arp out, his heart wasn't in it now.

"Don't forget your balaclava," I said, pointing to it on the floor.

Arp sighed, retrieved it, and left, without being further molested.

"He won't be back." Toby turned to me. "Are you thinking what I'm thinking?" he asked, holding up the pendant.

"It's the first piece of physical evidence we've had in the case. And it places Alan Knight at the scene of the crime."

17

IT WAS ONE OF THOSE HOT WISCONSIN SUMMER mornings so quiet outside it seemed the birds slept in. Yet we were up with the sun (a notable feat for Toby), prompted by the enticement of a treasure hunt. Toby prepared the coffee the way he liked it while I made us a quick breakfast of scrambled eggs and toast. I felt sticky already because of the humidity. Angie snoozed on, oblivious to the activity downstairs. I had my class to teach at eleven, but neither of us wanted to wait until I got back to search for the missing Frank Lloyd Wright drawings. The desk was in the closed-in porch at the front of the house. Toby carried it into the middle of the living room, where there was more space to examine it. "These schoolmaster's desks sometimes had false bottoms," he said, running his hand under the old desk. It didn't have a drawer. "I'm looking for a catch or release." He pursed his lips in concentration and ran his hand back and forth slowly, exploring every gnarl and burr. "Nope." He repeated the survey using his fingertips. Still no result. I felt his disappointment. But he said, "Let's not give up yet."

He turned his attention from the bottom of the desk to its top. He lifted the lid, which stood open vertically on its hinges without requiring support. The underside was streaked with cracks and scratches and areas of discoloration. Toby checked it visually, moving his eyes slowly back and forth across the surface. Then he ran his fingers across the edge of the lid, eyes closed. He repeated the examination, attending to the sides of the lid, then back to the top. Something—he stopped. He wasn't sure. Lightly again using his fingertips. "Yes." He beamed. Between forefinger and thumb he had found the tiniest of latches on the lid. It had a miniscule wooden release. When he applied the nail of his forefinger, it dropped open, revealing a narrow space like a separator in a briefcase. "I've never seen anything like it," said Toby.

"Well, fine," I said, "but is there anything inside?"

He reached in and withdrew four sheets of tissue-thin tracing paper, allowing them to flutter to the bottom of the desk. I separated them gingerly and held each one by two corners up to the light. The graceful drawings had a lifelike immediacy and freshness. They were delicately done, outlined in India ink and softly shaded using colored pencils. I'm not an expert on Wright, but to me the drawings, rendered in the sure hand of a master, had the strength of authenticity. Certainly, they were consistent with the drawings I had seen at the Wright exhibition at the art library. One sketch showed the facade of Bascom Hall with the proposed new dome in place, restoring the building's original proportions. Another showed the dome in larger scale. A third imagined a bird's-eye view of the dome looking down through it to the rotunda below, and a fourth sketched the view from inside looking up.

It took me a while to realize that Wright's design envisaged a dome with a top that was made of glass. The footprint of the old dome was still visible in the building in the form of a rotunda on each floor below. Wright's design called for opening each rotunda to the floor above it, with the top floor letting the daylight in. The concept was daring. He used this idea again on a much grander scale when he designed the

Guggenheim, with its spiral galleries leading the eye up to a wonderful domed skylight. People might say that the design for Bascom Hall "didn't go" with the old building, but in time they would come to accept it. Such was the case with I. M. Pei's glass pyramid, which was installed in the courtyard of the Louvre. In any event, I had already made up my mind that the design was beautiful.

"I'll be damned. He knew what he was talking about," said Toby, referring to Arp. "These are remarkable." Toby carefully laid the drawings on the dining room table.

"Are they ours to keep?" I asked.

"It's tempting to think so, but they belong to the scholarly world. The usual place for the originals would be the Frank Lloyd Wright Trust, but I think these drawings should go to the university. They have the greatest stake in this. Why don't we turn them over to Diane? I'll have copies made for us to keep, as well as for Arp, as I promised. It's really something, though, to hold the originals in your hands. I can hardly believe we've found them."

I searched a moment for the right word to express my feelings, then found it. "It's thrilling," I said.

I held class that morning in the old wing of the Chazen, as I did from time to time, to encourage students to see the art we were studying in person and in its natural habitat. We spent the hour looking at and commenting on various nineteenth-century paintings in the collection. One work was impossible to ignore because of its size. Corot's *Orpheus Greeting the Dawn*, at 78″ × 54″, dominates an entire room. The class formed a semicircle around me in front of the painting while we discussed some of its features that were of particular interest to us. Corot is usually grouped with the Barbizon artists, who were noted for painting realistic landscapes outdoors. Following Corot, they made the transition from the Salon's academic style to impressionism. I pointed out to the class that both schools were represented in the painting. The left side of the canvas pays homage to Greek mythology, a subject prized by the Salon, with the figure of Orpheus raising his lyre to the morning sun. The right side of the painting dwarfs the figure, placing him in the natural world beside a huge tree whose leaves are rendered with the feathery brushstrokes that made Corot famous. What the impressionists learned from Corot was his touch, which gave them a new way to apply paint to canvas.

As I finished my remarks, two men who had been standing at the back of the group advanced to say hello. One was an older man with beautifully coiffed white hair and kind eyes. He wore an expensive-looking sports jacket and crisp, pressed slacks. The other man I had recognized while giving my talk. He was Doug Harrison, the chair of the art history department. He looked inelegant by comparison, dressed in a summer-weight seersucker suit with ornamental patches on the elbows. "Mr. Meredith, this is Professor Barnes," he said, making the introduction. "She's visiting us this summer on a teaching exchange." To me he said, "This is Peter Meredith, an alumnus of our department and its most generous donor. We've been looking at some of the museum's recent acquisitions."

We shook hands and the generous donor proffered a business card. It read simply, "Dr. Peter Meredith, President, Meredith Pharmaceuticals," with a Milwaukee address. His card gave me a clue where his money came from. It wasn't art history. Meredith must have switched fields when he went to graduate school. The soft-spoken alumnus complimented me on my docent talk, and we strolled around the room conversing about other paintings. Harrison was uncharacteristically gracious toward me in the presence of his benefactor. However, he hustled Meredith away as soon as he could. This encounter with the chair of art history reminded me of the unresolved question of a job offer and what I would do if one were made.

I ran into Harrison again as I was leaving the building. This time he was alone. "You made quite an impression on Meredith," he said, following me outside. "He was greatly taken with you—even asked if we were planning to make you an offer. Said you'd be a catch."

I was flustered and didn't know what to say.

"When our biggest donor takes an interest in a faculty hire, so does the department," he said. "Come see me again before you leave."

I said I would, but I didn't know if I would follow through.

Diane was out when we called at her office after lunch. We were told she was attending a workshop at UW–Milwaukee and would be gone for the rest of the day. I left her a note about our discovery of the pendant and made an appointment to see her the next day. Then Toby and I considered how to spend the remainder of the afternoon. Arp had ignited our interest in seeing Monona Terrace by his description of Wright's grand urban design plan for Madison. We decided on the spur of the moment to visit the building. Toby thought we could even fit in a boat ride to view the structure from the vantage point of the lake. That clinched it for me. The prospect of being out on the water on a hot summer afternoon had an appeal all on its own. On the way, we stopped at the house to pick up Angie, who was happy to join us for the visit.

The story of Monona Terrace has many twists. Wright devoted more years to this project than to any other. The enormous structure he envisaged as a civic center in 1938 was meant to house a courthouse, a city hall, an auditorium, a marina, a railroad depot, and a jail. The site he chose was a bluff two blocks behind the Capitol building and sixty feet above the waters of Lake Monona. From the start, the project was embroiled in controversy. To meet objections and lower costs, Wright himself redesigned the building eight times, yet it still hadn't been realized by the time he died in 1959. Monona Terrace finally opened in 1997, nearly sixty years after Wright first proposed it. By then the building had been redesigned again, this time by other hands, to another purpose. A civic center had already been built downtown while the city dithered over Wright's proposal. Therefore, a team of architects reworked his plans so that the building could function as a convention center. The hybrid effort that saw Monona Terrace through to completion has led some to question its authenticity as a legitimate Frank Lloyd Wright design. All the same, it's an imposing building.

We began our visit at the street-level entrance to the pedestrian esplanade on the roof. According to Arp's account, Wright's plans for this space were never realized—a major glass dome and a suite of smaller domes and fountains, which would use water recycled from the lake. Without the domes and fountains, the completed esplanade is rather plain. However, it provided us a sweeping view of the whole of Lake Monona.

We pressed the call button for the elevator, and when it came, we took it down to the main level and got off at the lobby. The circle is the geometric form repeated throughout the building. It appears everywhere, starting with the vast, semicircular Grand Terrace. The form is echoed in the scalloped window trim both inside and out. Two cylindrical structures border the Grand Terrace. At both ends of the building, whirligig parking garages anticipate the spiral design of the Guggenheim.

The Grand Terrace is cavernous, with acres of carpeting and floor-to-ceiling windows that offer a curved panorama of the lake. Angie was impressed with the size of the building's public spaces—the meeting rooms, the lecture hall, the auditorium. Truly, they are huge. Yet to me, the interior seemed rather barren. It lacked the architect's final touch.

"Are you disappointed?" asked Toby. "Don't be. Wait till you see this building from the lake."

"How do you know what that will look like?" asked Angie.

"I'm guessing from aerial photographs of the city with Monona Terrace in the foreground. I have a theory I'd like to test out."

"All right, Captain Toby, lead on," I said.

"The proper nautical language is, 'Aye aye, sir!'"

Eve had granted us the use of all the conveyances in her garage. That included the oddest little vessel ever to sail in Madison's waters. Unfortunately, there was room in it for only two, so Angie volunteered to wait for us at home while we took it out. Toby promised he would take her sailing on another day while she was here.

Eve called her little craft the Kool Boat and related how an uncle had acquired it in the early 1970s by clipping the box top from a carton of Kool cigarettes and sending it in with two hundred dollars. In a few weeks, the complete boat arrived by mail truck in a big cardboard box. The sailboat was the product of an advertising campaign devised by the cigarette company. The brand name was emblazoned on the sail in big capital letters, so that whenever the boat was on the water, the cigarettes received publicity. In return for his willingness to be seen in it, Eve's uncle became the proud owner of a boat.

The doughty craft rested athwart the rafters in the garage, and though it hadn't been used in years, Eve thought it was still seaworthy (well, at least lake-worthy). Yet how much of a boat could it be, I wondered, if that's all it cost? We would soon find out. We changed into swimsuits, and I helped Toby lower the craft from its storage perch, marveling at how light it was. The shell was all one piece, made entirely of Styrofoam, the same material used for coffee cups in vending machines. In fact, the Kool Boat looked just like a floating coffee cup. It was light in weight, easy to maintain, and cheap. The captain sat in back at the helm, and the passenger sat in the front. The equipment was simple: a tube-like aluminum mast, a sail made of nylon, a wooden rudder-and-tiller combination that hooked onto the stern, and a small wooden center-board that slipped into a slot behind the mast for ballast. The whole thing couldn't have weighed more than forty pounds, and it looked un-sinkable. Its only real flaw was that it made its passengers look ridiculous. The sail said, "Kool," but sailing in a cigarette ad was decidedly uncool.

Nevertheless, we agreed to give the boat a try. For safety, we donned the two moldy orange life jackets that were in the shell. Next came the portage. We carried the Styrofoam boat upside down on our shoulders for the two blocks that separated Rutledge Street from Lake Monona. We launched from a little park along the lake by wading into the water. There was no need for a dock. Strange as it may have looked, we were afloat, with Toby at the tiller.

"I guess I should have asked you this before," I said. "Do you know how to drive this thing?"

"It's not complicated," said Toby, fumbling with a line. "Whoops. Coming about!" he shouted too late, as the wind shifted and sent the boom swinging across the shell, grazing my head.

"Ouch!"

"Sorry. I'll get the hang of it in a minute."

After a few more minutes of uncontrolled maneuvers, he did seem to get the hang of it, and before long we were heading out away from the shore on a more or less even course. "If you need to warn me again," I said, "try to do it in plain English. What's with this 'coming about' jargon? I'm not an old salt."

"Sorry again," said Toby. "It means the boat is changing direction to pick up the wind, and the boom is going to swing around to the opposite side, so watch your head."

"Okay, then, just say 'duck.'" But he didn't have to, as we were sailing smoothly now with the wind behind us filling the sail, which billowed out over the side. I began to relax, enjoying the motion of the boat skimming over the water.

"Don't look behind you until I say so," said Toby.

I thought of Lot's wife, who couldn't contain her curiosity and was punished for disobeying a similar command. "Why? Will I turn into a pillar of salt?"

"No, but it will spoil the surprise," said Toby. "I want to get the boat into position first."

I was agreeable. I sat back and let the sun warm my face, with my arm over the side and a finger trailing in the water, leaving miniature eddies. We rocked along dreamily. I found myself thinking over the events of the night before, and that train of thought led to a question.

"Toby, do you think much about dying?"

"Only on a daily basis." He saw the disturbed expression on my face. "That was a joke. Seriously, no, I try not to. Where did this come from all of a sudden?"

"Just daydreaming, I suppose. I was wondering if anyone will ever think about us or remember anything we accomplished after we're gone, a few centuries from now."

"Didn't we have that discussion recently?"

"Yes, but I'm not talking about the great artists now, or any other famous people. I'm thinking of what you said to Arp last night about making a contribution to his field. It got me thinking about my own small contributions. Will anyone know about them or care in a few hundred years? Is the work enough to give meaning to an existence?"

Toby considered, keeping his eye on the position toward which we were heading. After a moment, he said, "I think it's enough for people to live their lives and care for one another. And we've done that. It isn't a matter of contributions or being remembered."

"Just living? Is that really enough?" I said.

"It is for me."

I thought about his answer as the Kool Boat skipped along on the choppy surface of Lake Monona. I recalled that in *Waiting for Godot*, the two characters have a similar conversation. "I can't quote the lines exactly," I said to Toby, "but one of them says that it isn't enough to have lived, and the other one says they have to talk about it."

"That's Beckett speaking for himself," said Toby. "Writers have to talk about it. That's why they're writers. For the rest of us, living a life—a full life, if possible, with time to grow old and reflect—is an accomplishment in itself."

"Aren't you setting the bar a little low?"

"I'm not setting any bar." With his forearm resting on the tiller, Toby looked at the sky. "You know, astronomers say there are billions of habitable planets out there and that the universe must be teeming with life. But so far, the only life we know for sure is right here on this little blue speck. We may very well be alone. And if we are, then human beings are the highest life form in the cosmos, and the universe has a stake in our existence. That's why every life is a milestone." He thought of something and laughed. "And that's the answer to Hamlet's question of 'To be, or not to be.' The universe wants us to be."

The wind changed direction a little, and he pulled the sail in, angling the boat against it. We traveled over the water like that, not saying anything, for about twenty minutes.

"Okay, we're almost there," he announced. "No, don't look quite yet. What this is about is how Frank Lloyd Wright outwitted his detractors. He had to redesign Monona Terrace eight times, and still no one was satisfied. Each time he had to whittle down his vision. The city didn't want to pay the cost, the politicians were against him, the jealous cranks called him a scofflaw and a deadbeat who didn't pay his bills, an egotist who had to be taken down a peg. And those domes that he kept redesigning and trying to preserve—they had to go, because whatever else they symbolized, they reminded his detractors of his pride."

We had reached the point on the lake that Toby had been aiming for. "You can turn around now. What do you see?"

I took in the view as the little boat jostled me. "I think I get it. It looks like the State Capitol is sitting in the middle of the Monona Terrace esplanade. And it's framed by the spiral parking garages on each side."

"It's a trick of perspective, of course. The Capitol building is directly behind Monona Terrace. From the middle of the lake, the eye erases the short distance between them, and it looks like the Capitol dome is part of Wright's design."

"Do you think Wright could have planned it that way?" I asked.

"That's what I'm wondering. It's a stretch. But it's how Monona Terrace gets a dome. It's as if he appropriated the State Capitol."

I felt an uncanny rush, sharing Wright's secret. Toby remarked as we came about and headed back toward shore, "I still say that life can be an accomplishment in itself. But living a life like his must have been grand!"

18

DIANE'S DOOR WAS OPEN when we went to see her the next afternoon. She was at her desk reading what looked like a report. She took off her reading glasses and rubbed the bridge of her nose in a gesture of fatigue. "Have a seat, you two, and please tell me you've got some new information, because nothing's gone right for me today." She began to recount her frustrations but stopped mid-complaint when Toby asked her to extend her hand, dropped the peace pendant into it, and closed her fist over it, while briefing her on its significance.

"Wait a minute. You mean to tell me that Professor Arp broke into your house and you didn't call the police? You're not going to press charges?"

"He won't bother us again," said Toby, "and consider the upside. We discovered four drawings made by Frank Lloyd Wright, and without realizing its significance, Arp discovered a physical item that links someone we know to the scene of the crime. This peace pendant bears his initials, 'A. K.' Alan Knight."

Diane was now at full attention.

Toby continued. "You'll remember the name. He's one of the alumni taking a class here this summer. His contemporaries recall him wearing a pendant just like it when they were students. It's pretty distinctive, real gold with a real gold chain. Arp says he found it in the Bascom attic about six months ago, long before the bones were discovered. It was buried under layers of dust, suggesting it must have lain there for years." Toby lifted the pendant by its chain and gently pulled in opposite directions. "See, the clasp is loose, which is why the chain came off during the scuffle at our house." Toby pulled the wings of the chain until the clasp gave. "Alan could have lost it the same way all those years ago."

Diane took the pendant back and worried the clasp with her finger. "I still think Arp should be charged for the break-in, but that's up to you. I'll certainly bring him in for questioning. Alan Knight too. Let's see if he can explain how his peace symbol ended up where it did. You do realize, don't you," she added, "that just because it was found in the attic doesn't prove he lost it there at a particular time."

"True," said Toby, undeterred. "That's to find out. But this is the first solid lead we've had in the case."

Diane agreed. "By the way," she said, tapping the pendant with her well-manicured finger, "I don't get how this symbolizes peace. To me it looks like an upside-down letter *Y* with a vertical bar running through it."

I said, "I took the trouble to look up its history. It started out as a British symbol for nuclear disarmament using the alphabet of semaphore signal flags. The vertical line represents the letter *D*, and the downward lines on either side represent the letter *N*, giving you 'ND' for nuclear disarmament. The symbol was picked up by the antiwar movement in the US as generally advocating peace."

"That makes sense, sort of," said Diane. "Anyhow, good work."

"Shouldn't we inform Agent Whelk?" asked Toby.

"Agent Whelk is off the case and facing a disciplinary hearing," Diane answered tartly. "I had a 'woe is me' email from him yesterday."

"Even though he recovered his bag with the bone samples inside?" said Toby.

"That didn't cut it with the FBI. Losing his carry-on meant that the evidentiary chain of custody was broken. I was afraid they'd see it that way. The bureau is sending another agent to pick up fresh samples, but he hasn't arrived yet. That means a further delay in getting DNA results."

"I'm beginning to feel sorry for the poor guy," said Toby.

Diane said, "Be careful. He's looking for a shoulder to cry on. He's already tried mine. Now, what's this about Frank Lloyd Wright drawings that you wanted to tell me?"

We were discussing the sketches with Diane when Maureen burst into the office. She was out of breath and in a state of alarm. "I need your help!" she blurted. "Jimmy's missing and I'm afraid something's happened to him." Neither Maureen nor Helen had been in class that morning, and I'd suspected something was amiss.

"Slow down," Diane said in a calming voice, "and tell us what the trouble is."

Maureen sat down heavily and pressed a fist to her chest, trying to catch her breath. "Jimmy didn't come home last night. He never does that, and I'm worried sick. I called the Madison Police to file a missing person's report, but they put me off. They said it was too soon."

"They usually don't act on the basis of one night's absence," Diane confirmed. "When was the last you heard from him?"

"He called around ten to say he'd be home late. He said he was at a bar having a few beers with Alan. He'd had more than just a few, I think. They were going to try to get into the Bascom attic to see for themselves the old cistern that everyone was talking about. It was a stupid idea, and I said so."

Diane said, "The entrance to the attic is blocked off. It's a crime scene."

"But Jimmy was bragging he could find a way to get in, the back way he once used to get up to the roof during the Dow demonstrations. Alan bet him he couldn't remember it from that long ago. It was a dare."

"And that's the last time you heard from him?" Diane asked.

"Yes."

"What about Alan?"

"He didn't come home either," said Maureen. "But Helen isn't as worried as I am. She says he's done this before, stayed out all night. But Jimmy's different. He's never disappeared overnight. He hasn't answered his phone or my texts."

"What do you think happened?" Diane asked in a neutral voice.

"I don't know. But if Theo is still alive and hiding somewhere, maybe he found Jimmy and hurt him."

"Is that what you've been thinking?" asked Diane, raising her eyebrows.

"I know you don't believe me, but could you please check the attic where the water tank is to see if Jimmy's there?"

"Maureen," I interrupted, picking up the peace pendant by its chain, "this might shed some light on the situation. Do you recognize this? Have you ever seen it before?"

She stared at it for a moment. "It looks like the pendant Alan used to wear. A peace symbol. He had one just like it."

"Thanks for your help," said Diane. She looked at me.

Jimmy might well be in danger, I thought, but not from Theo. "Let's take a look at the cistern," I said to Diane, "just to allay Maureen's fears."

"We'll do that," said Diane. She placed her hand on Maureen's shoulder. "Meanwhile, I want you to go home. Jimmy may still show up there. I'll call you as soon as we have any information." To Toby and me she said, "Let's go."

We squeezed into a small campus police car, and with Diane at the wheel, we lost no time getting to Bascom. At this late hour of the day, we were able to park behind the building in the tiny lot reserved for bigwigs. "Out fast, and follow me," she commanded, jumping out and sprinting to a plain door at basement level marked Loading Dock. Inside, an electric saw screamed, and we rushed past a startled workman cutting a plywood panel. "Sorry, Charlie," Diane called, as she sped past and punched a button to call the elevator. It opened instantly and took us to the third floor. Once there, we followed Diane to a stairwell with a dingy set of steps that led to a small landing and then another dozen steps. At the top was a door to the left, but Diane skipped that one and lunged for the door on the right. It opened onto a square hallway with four office doors numbered in the four hundreds, plus one door labeled Utility Room. That room was cordoned off with police tape.

I watched Diane rip the tape off and pull out a ring of keys. The fact that the door was locked and the police tape still intact indicated that no one had broken in. Yet Jimmy had mentioned a back way into the attic. It was possible that he and Alan had found that other means of entry. The door opened. Diane switched on a light, but there were no utilities in view. The tight space seemed more like a closet than a room.

Diane pointed straight ahead, at an old wooden ladder attached to the back wall. She flicked on a weak light somewhere above us and cautioned, "One person at a time," as she put her right foot on the first step. Despite her generous figure, she was agile. She scaled the dozen rungs without pausing and was suddenly out of sight. Toby signaled for me to go next. I tried to imitate Diane, but found that the rungs were spaced unevenly, so that I had to wave each foot around to find the next one. I was relieved to find a better grip at the top. I swung my knees over onto the planks of a new level, which was a landing for yet another steep set of stairs. Everything looked makeshift—the wood unfinished and unmatched, the construction slapdash—but the structure held firm as I mounted.

Near the top of the narrow stairs, the heat hit me like a wave. The closed attic was stifling. I looked around and noticed that the interior was unfinished, exposing the latticework of the roof. Overhead were heavy beams. Straight ahead there was a gap of empty space and then the metal curve of the enormous basin. Just above me and beyond my reach, a metal ladder hooked onto the lip of the tank and ran down its side. There were a few blocks of wood scattered about, and wooden supports between the side of the tank and the top of the stairs.

Toby came up swiftly behind me. He called out, "Jimmy!" And then louder, "Jimmy! Are you here? Alan?"

"Over here!" Diane's voice reached us from deeper in the attic. I stood up, minding my head, and saw that the planking under my feet continued as a narrow walkway between the wall and a wooden barrier in front of the cistern. I tentatively pushed further in, and then the beam of Diane's flashlight revealed a body on the floor crumpled over in fetal position. "Hold my flashlight," Diane ordered. She took a knife from her belt and began cutting into fabric around the man's neck. It was a multicolored bandana, knotted like a noose. Toby pointed to a ceiling beam charred by the 1916 fire but still in place, and Diane nodded in grim agreement. A second bandana was looped over the beam and anchored by a heavy bolt. Its other end hung loose. The scene suggested a botched hanging. The knot between the two bandanas hadn't held the man's weight. Diane rolled him over. We knew it was Jimmy before we saw his face. She listened to his chest and took his pulse. "He's alive," she said. "He's still breathing." She dialed 911. "We need the EMTs."

An index card had fallen out of Jimmy's shirt pocket. I picked it up. It had one word printed on it in block capital letters. "SORRY," it said, no more than that. As a suicide note, it was woefully inadequate. The message of a single word and the formation of the letters reminded me of the postcard at Taliesin that had ordered me to "stop." The two messages appeared to have been written by the same hand.

"Help!" The voice was faint. At first, I couldn't tell where it was coming from. Again: "Help me, I'm down here." The cistern? I made my way back to the edge, where I could lean over a waist-high wooden barrier and peer into the pit. As a result of varying water levels over time, the inner circumference of the cistern was ringed, ranging from light tan at the bottom to black at the top. I panned the flashlight around the interior and aimed it at the damaged section of the tank, at the bottom of the far end, where water and bones had broken through the rusted metal and flooded the room below. Most of the bottom was gone, but not all of it, and as I trained the beam on the jagged remainder, it brought Alan Knight out of the shadows, sprawled on his back like an overturned beetle. "I can't climb up," he called in a trembling voice.

Toby, by my side, swung a leg over the rim, grabbed the top rung of the metal ladder, and scaled down. At the bottom, he kneeled over Alan, checking his injuries. "We need another ambulance!" Toby shouted. "He's badly hurt." Diane made her way over and peered down at the scene. "What the hell happened here?" she demanded to know. She dialed 911 a second time.

Toby stayed with Alan until the EMTs arrived. They raised Alan out of the tank and provided first aid. We followed the ambulances, lights flashing and sirens whining, to the UW Hospital, where both patients were admitted to the emergency room. We found seats in the adjacent waiting room, and while we waited for news, Toby relayed Alan's version of events, which he'd heard while they were waiting for the ambulance.

"According to Alan, Jimmy led him to the attic by the old back route that he remembered from their student days. Jimmy went ahead but Alan lagged behind, took a wrong turn, and lost the way. By the time he got up there, Alan was horrified to find Jimmy already hanging from a rafter. Alan says he dragged a block over and grabbed Jimmy around the waist and tried to lift him high enough to take the weight off his neck. But Jimmy went into convulsions and started kicking, and one of the blows caught Alan in the chest and knocked him backward into the cistern."

"That conforms with the scene," said Diane.

"The trouble is," said Toby, "I don't believe him."

"Why not?" she asked.

"Just a gut feeling. For one thing, every few minutes he kept asking how Jimmy was. Was he conscious? Was he able to speak?"

"Expressing concern for a friend?" said Diane. "What's suspicious about that?"

"To me it sounded more like he was probing to find out if Jimmy was in any condition to contradict him. Jimmy's version of events might be a lot different."

Jimmy had survived a near hanging and was lucky to be alive. As the head of the ER explained to us, Jimmy was fortunate in that he hadn't suffered cardiac arrest or asphyxiation or damaged cervical vertebrae, all of which are common in such cases. He concluded that Jimmy must have been suspended only for a very short time before the knot on the bandana unraveled. The patient was unconscious and wasn't breathing properly. Even so, the doctor was optimistic about his chances for recovery. Jimmy's heart was strong. To help him breathe, they had intubated him and put him on a ventilator for the night. They hoped to wean him off the machine in the morning.

Alan was lucky too in that he had survived a backward fall into the cistern. He had shattered the arm and elbow he landed on and would need complicated surgery to repair the bones with rods and pins. In addition, he had fractured an ankle and three ribs, badly sprained his back, and had several deep lacerations that required stitches. In a fall like that, he could easily have smashed his head, but the injuries he suffered could be repaired.

Jimmy was in intensive care for the night, and Alan was assigned a private room on a different floor. Maureen and Helen had been notified and were on their way to the hospital. There was nothing more that we could do until the morning, so we went home, solemnly.

19

WE VISITED ALAN IN HIS ROOM THE NEXT DAY. He was sitting up in bed, his arm in a cast and a bandage around his ear, bruises all over. Diane was with us. It was not a social call. Jimmy had been taken off the ventilator in the morning. He was breathing on his own, talking and telling a different story from Alan's. Helen had heard Jimmy's story from Maureen and didn't know what to believe, yet she had passed what she'd heard on to Alan before going home to sleep. Alan had been thinking things through since then. "I've been expecting you," he said.

Diane asked about his condition, but there was very little small talk. She said, "You may know by now that Jimmy's accused you of attempting to strangle him. I'd like you to listen to his statement and give us your reaction." She had a small device on which she had recorded Jimmy's statement. She played it, sitting close to Alan's bed. Toby gestured to me to take the other chair in the room while he stood.

The voice on the recording was whispery but clear. Jimmy claimed that his friend had attacked him from behind, without provocation, and had tried to choke and then hang him with two of his own bandanas. Jimmy said he passed out, and when he came to, Alan had knotted the bandana he was wearing into a noose and had tied it to the other one, which was looped over a beam. Alan was in the process of trying to hoist Jimmy up when Jimmy came to. He managed to kick Alan hard enough to send him backward into the cistern. But then Jimmy felt his feet dangling in the air. There was a terrible pressure on his neck, and then he lost consciousness. Jimmy repeated he had no idea why he was attacked.

Diane switched off the recording. "I'd like to know your reaction."

"My reaction is, I'm ashamed. I did something horrible in a moment of panic," said Alan in a resigned tone.

"Why did you attack Jimmy?"

He was silent, staring ahead. Diane repeated her question.

"I think I know the answer to that," I said. "If I'm right, it goes back to something that happened many years ago." I said to Alan, "I have something of yours that you haven't seen in a long time. Do you recognize it?" I held up the peace pendant by its chain and extended it toward him.

He reached for it with a look of surprise. "Where did you find this?"

"It was found where you lost it, in the Bascom attic, when you were up there many years ago, with Theo Kearn, if I'm correct."

Alan brought the pendant close to his eyes. Then he dropped his hand in his lap and, avoiding looking at me, spoke. "I've been expecting the truth to come out any day now, ever since the bones were discovered. I'm not going to fight it. It's time."

Diane interrupted. "If you're going to make a statement, this is a caution. What you say may be taken down as evidence and later used against you in a court of law."

Alan brushed aside that worry. "I'll deal with that when I have to. I was up most of the night dredging up the past and thinking how my whole life after college has been burdened by concealment and guilt, and now the time has come, finally, to tell the truth."

"Do you want a lawyer present?" Diane asked.

"A lawyer would tell me to shut up, but I don't want to shut up."

"Then, you won't mind if I record what you say?" Diane pointed to her palm-sized device.

"Do as you like," said Alan. He leaned back against his pillows. "I heard Maureen say you were expecting DNA results on the bones any day now. That's when I knew I had to do something to deflect suspicion."

"Suspicion of what?" asked Diane.

"Of being responsible for Theo's death."

Toby was angry. "You tried to stage Jimmy's suicide to make it look like he was the one who hid Theo's body in the tank and that he was hanging himself out of guilt or remorse. You wrote that note and put it in his pocket."

Alan nodded yes.

"Where did you get the bandanas?" asked Diane.

"Jimmy always wears one. The other I got out of his drawer. Look, I know what I've done is unforgivable. I'm glad Jimmy's going to be okay. What he doesn't know, and what you don't know, is that I couldn't go through with it in the end. I tried to save him. When I saw Jimmy struggling, I grabbed his legs and lifted him up to relieve the strain on his neck. I was trying to get him down. But he lashed out and kicked me."

"You tried to save him?" Toby repeated skeptically.

I looked at Diane. She wasn't buying it.

"My conscience has always done me in," said Alan. He laughed mirthlessly. "Me, a conscientious objector. Objecting to myself."

"'Thus conscience doth make cowards of us all,'" Toby quoted.

Alan finished the lines. "'And thus the native hue of resolution / Is sicklied o'er with the pale cast of thought.' I know my Shakespeare. Especially *that* speech."

"Tell us about Theo Kearn," I said.

Diane said, "From the beginning."

Alan sighed and winced with pain. He placed his good hand over his taped ribs. "It was about a month after the bombing. On a dark night. I was by myself walking home from a meeting, and he just stepped out of the bushes and called my name. I couldn't see his face very well, but right away I knew who it was. He told me he had doubled back from Canada and was hiding in Madison right under the noses of the FBI and police. It was the last place they expected him to be."

"Where was he hiding out?" Diane asked.

"There's a maze of underground tunnels that run for miles below the campus. They carry steam-heating pipes for the buildings above. He joked that he was living directly under Bascom Hill. But he needed my help. He needed someone who could bring him groceries and personal items like toothpaste and so on. Someone who would do his bidding," he added bitterly.

Diane asked, "Why you?"

Alan shrugged. "We'd been roommates at one time. I guess he had no one else to turn to. The old crowd had broken up. Maureen was living with her parents. Jimmy was in art school. Helen was living in Spring Green with Walt. He thought they would want nothing to do with him after the bombing. Same with his ex-teammates from crew. So, it was me."

Diane asked a follow-up. "What made him sure you wouldn't turn him in? And why didn't you? Why didn't you call the police?"

"Looking back, that's what I should have done," said Alan. "It would have been better for everyone in the end. But I didn't."

"Again, why?" asked Diane.

"Because I was weak." Alan hung his head. "I was afraid of being disloyal and afraid of him, but most of all, I didn't want the notoriety of being the one who turned him in. That would have meant siding with the cops and everyone who hated the demonstrators. I was against the bombing all along, but Theo had me pegged. I was the weak reed."

I broke in with the next question. "What did you mean when you said he wanted someone to do his bidding? What did he ask you to do?"

"It started with little things, like I told you. Fetching stuff. But after a week, he let me know his real reason for coming back. He was planning another bombing to protest the war. In Canada he met up with an ex-soldier in the movement who taught him how to make a smaller bomb than the truck bomb they used for Sterling Hall. My job was to assemble the materials and scout buildings with him for the best target. In reality, I was a hostage. But I played along, telling myself that when the time came, I'd try to stop him from setting off a bomb."

Alan reached for the glass of water on a tray next to his bed and took a sip through a straw. He continued. "Well, the first building on the list was Bascom Hall. It was the best-known building on campus and housed the chancellor's office. That's what we were doing up in the attic in the middle of the night, looking for a spot to place a small explosive device where it wouldn't be discovered. And there was this huge water tank. Maybe the bomb could be placed so that the tank would burst and flood the floors below. Theo was leaning over the side, peering into it, when I made my move. I hadn't planned anything in advance. There was a small crowbar hanging from a hook. I grabbed it and went at him. He half turned and reached for my neck to stop me. Maybe that's when I lost the pendant. I broke free and hit him on the side of the head, not meaning to kill him, but just to stop him. He went over the rim and into the water. I tell you, I hadn't planned anything that night. But I was thinking of the death and destruction another bombing would cause, and I had promised myself I'd prevent it."

"So, you hit him and he went over into the tank. What did you do next?" asked Diane.

He didn't answer for a moment. She repeated the question.

"I panicked," said Alan. "I ran away."

"Did you look to see if Theo was dead or alive in the water? Conscious and moving or not?"

"I should have, but I was afraid to look. I didn't hear him splashing around. I just got out of there as fast as I could and never went back. And for all these years I soothed my conscience by telling myself maybe Theo didn't die in that cistern. Maybe he came to in the water and climbed up the ladder and got out. That was something I could believe until a few weeks ago when the bones turned up. I knew then that he had died in the cistern and that the truth would have to come out. Now it has."

Alan slumped back against his pillows, as if played out, a man carrying a heavy burden who had finally put it down. I wasn't convinced. "That may be part of the truth, but it's not the whole truth and nothing but the truth, is it?" I asked. Diane looked at me with a puzzled expression. I went on: "You convinced yourself after the fact that by attacking Theo, you were trying to prevent another bombing. I'd call that a textbook example of rationalization. That wasn't the real reason you attacked him. It certainly wasn't the only reason."

"What are you talking about?" he said.

"You resented Theo. Not just because of politics. You envied him because of his relationship with Maureen."

"No! That's crazy."

"Is it?" I asked.

My accusation might be hard to prove, but it wasn't crazy. Alan's lovesick gaze during the fireworks had given him away. His relationship with Helen was a cover for his true feelings. He was fixated on Maureen, just as he'd been in his student days. He had wanted her then when she was Theo's girl and Theo was his roommate. He had wanted her when she married Jimmy, and he wanted her now as much as ever. Jealousy was the mainspring of his actions. His violent acts were spurred by passion, as most violent acts are, not by some idea of right action.

"What's more," I said, "you set up Jimmy's fake suicide not only to pin Theo's death on him and make it look like he was repenting for a crime he didn't commit—you hoped that with Jimmy out of the way, Maureen would finally fall into your arms. Jimmy was your last remaining obstacle."

"That's a lie," he said, coloring and biting his lip. I'd hit a nerve. Until now Alan had been cooperative, voluble in fact, but he stubbornly refused to answer any more questions. Instead, he asked us to leave. "I've changed my mind," he said. "I do want a lawyer." Lawyers shut you up. He realized too late that he should have asked for one sooner. He would now have to answer for his actions.

Bar Blue Violet, named for Wisconsin's state flower, was located off the south side of the Capitol Square, on a seedy street leading down to the railroad tracks. True to its violet hue, the bar welcomed the LGBTQ crowd (a rainbow sign said so) and held a drag queen contest once a month. The blue might have stood for the blues. Once a week during the summer, there was free jazz from five to seven. Ben Sidran, one of the organizers of the Madison Reunion, played piano and hosted what he billed as a "Salon for Secular Humanists, Arch Democrats, and Freethinkers." Diane suggested we repair there to debrief and unwind after our interrogation of Alan. She was a golfing partner of Ben's wife, Judy, and tried to attend the salon every week, partly out of friendship with Judy but mostly because she liked the people she met there.

I called Angie, who was shopping nearby on State Street, and invited her to meet us at the bar. Toby and I drove to a parking lot near the tracks and walked back uphill to the entrance. We were early, but the place was already crowded. We squeezed past the long, old-fashioned bar at the entrance and aimed for the large room off to the side with tables and chairs and a stage, where the band was setting up. As I entered the bustling room, I felt a cool hand on my back and heard a woman's voice. "Nora? I'm Judy Sidran. Diane had me save you seats." She guided us to a table and settled my sweater over the two extra chairs that went with it. Turning toward the bar to resume her role as hostess, she showed a profile that resembled that of Queen Nefertiti. I imagined Judy was one of Madison's strong women. Diane was another.

While we waited for Diane and Angie, we looked over the audience. It was an older crowd than we'd seen in the student bars closer to campus. Maybe it was the jazz. Milling about was a mix of midlevel professionals and academics. We noticed a contingent of government workers from the Capitol building up the street. The men had their sleeves rolled up, and the women had swapped their heels for comfortable shoes. There were shaggy graduate students and young professors, aging hippies and artistic-looking types who were stuck with mundane day jobs—a varied sampling of college town hangers-on.

Diane arrived trailing a waitress with a pitcher of beer and mugs. Toby filled them while Diane threw out an opening question—what did we make of Alan Knight's confession?

"I'll start," I said. "It was entirely self-serving."

"That's the word I was looking for," said Diane, snapping her fingers. "Self-serving. Tell me how and in what way."

I had to speak loudly. The noise level was rising. "He did everything he could to place his actions in the best possible light. First, with Theo Kearn. He admits he struck him on the head and left him to drown in the cistern. Then he tells us that he acted for the good of others to prevent a second bombing. I'm sorry, but I don't buy it. There was no imminent threat that night. Kearn wasn't setting a bomb; he was looking for a site for one. And at any point, Alan could have gone to the police. He always had a choice."

"And Jimmy?" asked Diane.

"Alan planned to stage Jimmy's suicide, but he claims he changed his mind at the last minute and tried to save him from hanging. How believable is that?"

"That's for a jury to decide," said Toby. "They'll have to weigh Alan's testimony against Jimmy's."

Diane had been jotting on a pad. "What struck me was how confident Alan seemed at the beginning. He felt totally in control. But he lost it when you put it to him that he wanted Jimmy out of the way so he could pursue the wife. Now that's a motive any jury could understand. How did you know?"

I explained the incidents and observations that led to my conclusion but had to admit that I had no concrete proof. It was guesswork.

Toby added, "Excellent guesswork. Motive is always difficult to prove because you can't get inside a defendant's head. Nora's insights have the ring of truth. But a good trial lawyer would argue that her conclusions are subjective."

Diane put down her mug. "That's not the only aspect of this case that troubles me. What do we know now for a fact after Alan's confession that we didn't know before?"

For a moment her question stumped us. Then Toby said, "We know that Alan is responsible for Kearn's death. Whether he committed first- or second-degree murder, or justifiable homicide, is up to a prosecutor. The key point is that we have a confession."

"We have a confession," Diane repeated glumly, "but we don't have a body, at least not yet, in the legal sense. We're still waiting for the remains to be identified. That makes for an awkward situation."

I said, "You don't really think the bones could belong to anyone other than Theo Kearn, do you, after what we've heard from Alan? The alternative is so improbable as to be dismissed. You would have to believe that Kearn crawled out of the cistern after his injury and that someone else was dumped in at a later date."

Diane agreed. "I don't expect the DNA will tell us that the bones belong to Jimmy Hoffa or some other missing person. What worries me, though, is that the results could come back muddled or unreadable, as they did from the State Crime Lab because of the water factor. What if the FBI can't salvage usable DNA from the bones, either?"

"Then what?" asked Toby. "What happens to Alan's confession if the DNA results are inconclusive?"

Diane made a rueful growl. "No prosecutor is going to take a case to trial based on a confession alone. There has to be corroborating evidence. The police get false confessions all the time from people with mental illness or who have all sorts of other motives. The defense attorney can always say, 'My client is delusional. He thinks he murdered Jane Smith. But we don't even know if Jane Smith is dead.' No witnesses. No physical evidence. No body. No case."

"You mean that after all this, Alan could go scot-free?" I asked.

Toby reassured me. "He won't walk away from the assault on Jimmy. That was premeditated. He swiped one of Jimmy's bandanas from his apartment and brought it to the attic. That shows intent. You've supplied a plausible motive. We have physical evidence. We're witnesses. And Jimmy can testify. So, Alan is in trouble, no matter what happens with the bones."

"That may be true, but I want him charged for both his crimes," said Diane.

Toby raised his mug. "I'll drink to that. Here's to a positive DNA result and a quick resolution." We all clinked glasses.

About this time, Angie arrived, and as she did, the music started. I introduced her to Diane and they chatted briefly before pausing to listen to the entertainment. At the piano, Sidran had a way of talking through his songs that made you want to listen. A young drummer and a jazz guitarist made up the trio.

We were enjoying the music when Angie suddenly went pale and scooted under the table. "It's him!" she said in a muffled voice. "The FBI agent!" Whelk indeed had walked in the door. Angie was terrified, afraid she would be arrested if he found her. Before I could stop her, she duck-waddled toward the restrooms, keeping her head low so she wouldn't be seen.

Whelk squinted, peering around the crowded room. Eventually he spotted Diane and made his way over to our table. "Your office told me you might be here," he said, almost apologetically.

"Hello, Daryl."

"Do you mind if I sit down?" He pointed to the empty chair. Angie's. To us he asked politely, "May I join you?" There was a new diffidence to his manner that I found disarming. He slouched so as not to tower over the rest of us. He looked different, too. His hair was cut short as if in penance. People don't change overnight, but he was working on a course correction. Having lowered his mask as extrovert, he now projected neediness.

"Yes, by all means join us," said Diane. "In fact, we were just talking about the FBI. Do you have any information as to when the new DNA results will be available?"

He avoided meeting her eyes. "I don't have any information at all about the FBI, not anymore. I'm out. They gave me a reprimand and suspended me without pay, and I resigned."

Diane frowned. "I'm sorry it came to that," she said.

Her sympathy buoyed his spirits. "Don't be." He gave a nervous little laugh. "Do you know what? I've been offered a new job and with better pay. My brother owns a very successful used-car dealership, Whelk's Auto Exchange, in Wauwatosa. He's wanted me to come work for him for a long time. I'm going to be a vice president for sales!" He managed a smile.

"Congratulations," said Toby. "Wau-wa-tosa. Where's that?"

"Right outside Milwaukee," Whelk answered. "If you're a big fan of Frank Lloyd Wright, there's a building of his in town that you should see, the Annunciation Greek Orthodox Church."

"In Wauwatosa?" Toby repeated. "Weally? I mean, really?"

"Yes," said Whelk, oblivious to the gibe. "It's one of a kind. It's got a huge dome that rests on a bed of ball bearings. You should come and see it."

"No kidding? We just might," said Toby, somewhat taken aback by the new Whelk. "Tell me, what exactly does a vice president for sales do?"

Whelk gave the matter some thought. "Sells cars, I guess," he said, obviously not sure.

"Well, then, Mr. Car Salesman, welcome to the club!" said Toby, referring to Whelk's previous disparagement of his own means of livelihood. Toby said it with a smile and without rancor, extending his hand, which Whelk shook amiably. He was in on the joke this time, rather than being the butt of it.

"What are you driving these days?" he asked Toby, pouring himself a mug of beer.

"I think you can tell Angie to come out of hiding," Diane said to me. "It looks like the war is over."

I went to get Angie and brought her back with me without recourse to the duck waddle. The men were talking cars. After the briefest of introductions, she asked Whelk baldly, "Are you going to arrest me?"

"I couldn't arrest you if I wanted to, and I don't want to," Whelk replied, getting up from the seat that was hers and fetching another chair.

While in hiding, Angie had been stoking her righteous indignation. "Do you have any idea how badly you behaved in the airport? You terrified me, you scared me half to death. You should be ashamed of yourself!"

Whelk cringed. "I'm really sorry about that. I hope you can forgive me, in time."

Surprised, Angie said, "I'll think about it," and pressing her advantage, demanded, "Where's my suitcase? I'm running out of my sister's underwear."

That remark gave rise to a general round of laughter and dissipated any remaining tension. Toby fetched another pitcher of beer, and everyone sat back and enjoyed the music. At about 7 p.m., the trio launched into a catchy jazz version of "Goodnight, Irene," after which they began to pack up. People started filing out.

"What do you say we go out for pizza?" Diane proposed. Angie was about to say sure, but I gave her a nudge. Whelk looked like an eager pet with its leash in its mouth and its eyes begging for a walk. "You too, Daryl. You're included," said Diane. She even gave him a smile. A small one.

"I'd love to," he said. You could practically see his tail wagging.

"That sounds like fun, but we have something on for tonight," I fibbed, "so we'll have to take a rain check. But why don't the two of you run along?"

Diane said, "Why not?"

For a moment Whelk looked stunned. It took him a few seconds to recover. "That would be great," he said. Then he excused himself to make a trip to the restroom to primp. I exchanged a glance of surprise with Toby.

"I decided to give him another chance," said Diane. "He seems different now that he's had a setback."

I agreed. "Didn't the ancient Greeks say that out of suffering comes wisdom?"

"Aeschylus said so. I don't know that it's a general truth," said Toby. "A lot of people suffer in this world but don't seem any the wiser for it."

"That may be," Diane replied. "Anyhow, I didn't say Daryl had earned another chance. I said I was willing to give him one. That's me."

There was no arguing with that. We said good night. I pushed back from the table and the others followed, leaving Diane waiting for the beneficiary of her bounty to return from the bathroom.

On the way out, Toby mused, "Who would have believed it? If Whelk can be redeemed, there's hope for everyone."

"Diane is an extraordinary woman," I pointed out. "You know, Toby, Madison seems to have mellowed you. For a minute there, you sounded like an optimist."

"If I did, it was a fleeting thought. I'm not any kind of ist," he replied. We started walking to the car.

"What's an ist?" asked Angie.

"An ist is someone who goes all in for a particular point of view until it dominates his thinking and ruins his conversation," said Toby. "The ists of the world are generally troublemakers, though I suppose the optimists cause less harm than most."

A few drops of rain spattered the sidewalk. We quickened our steps. Toby surveyed the sky and offered an opinion that the storm would pass over.

"That sounds like optimism to me," said Angie. We made it to the car just as it started to come down.

20

THE MORNING'S PAPER STILL HAD NOTHING about Alan's attack on Jimmy in the Bascom attic. That would make the day easier for Maureen and Helen, but I worried about them nonetheless. I wasn't surprised that they weren't in class. As I packed up my teaching things, I imagined Maureen at Jimmy's bedside, but where would Helen be? Would loyalty tie her to Alan after all he'd done? I felt a need to seek them out. The hospital would be the place to start.

When I arrived outside Jimmy's room, I took a moment to compose myself. I reminded myself that there was a weight of suffering inside. I knocked and stood in the partly open doorway, and Maureen called me in. She was leaning over Jimmy's bed, adjusting a pillow so that he could sit more upright.

"I don't want to interrupt," I said. "It's good to see you sitting up and breathing without tubes. It looks as if Maureen's care is just what you need."

"It is," said Jimmy. "She's been with me day and night. No matter when I open my eyes, the first thing I see is the woman I'm living for." He reached for his wife's hand and held it tightly. "Sit down," he said to me. "Tell me about finding me. I don't remember the rescue at all."

I went over the details again, starting when Maureen burst into Diane's office and ending with the arrival of two EMT crews, one for Alan and one for Jimmy. "Even though you were breathing, you looked awful, and we worried about whether you'd make it."

"How is Alan?" Jimmy asked, without bitterness. Maureen flushed and pressed her lips together, as if holding in smoke.

"He was a complicated case for the bone doctors, but he'll live to face his crimes."

"Is it up to me to press charges?" Jimmy raised his eyebrows and his free hand, as if to put off the question.

"No. For a serious crime like attempted homicide, it's in the district attorney's hands," I said.

Jimmy said, "Oh."

"Alan has to be tried," said Maureen. "He's not a teenager with mixed-up motives and an unformed conscience. He's not the good man we thought he was, either. What he's done is criminal. He hid murder in his heart for fifty years, and then it broke out again. Against Jimmy. For no good reason."

I couldn't let that go. "There was a reason," I said. "To save his own skin, obviously. But there may be something more to it. I've come to suspect that Alan was in love with you himself, all these years. His two victims were the men you loved, then and now. Did you ever think Alan had a thing for you?"

"Alan? No, of course not. I never really knew him that well. He was part of our circle, but I never gave him much thought. In fact, when he turned up as Helen's boyfriend this summer, I found I didn't really like him. There was something phony about him. Well, I guess that's obvious now. I must have smelled the lies on him."

I saw a look of comprehension on Jimmy's face. He said, "I saw it. Not back in college, but in these last weeks. He's been looking at you in a way no husband would like—lingering looks, like pawing. I knew he was with Helen, so I thought to myself he was one of those guys who drools over every woman he sees. I didn't take it as love—more like lust. I didn't like it, but I thought he was harmless."

"He was far from harmless," I said.

Jimmy's eyes went to the door, and there I saw Helen, looking decades older than when I'd last seen her. The muscles of her face drooped, furrowing in wrinkles. She said, "I heard that, and it's true. I am so sorry for what Alan did. I never guessed. Please forgive me. I can't forgive myself."

"Come in, Helen," Maureen said, walking to her friend and taking her in an embrace. "You're not to blame."

"Well, my eyes have been opened," Helen said. "I can't love the man that Alan is. I've washed my hands of him now that his brother has arrived from Cleveland. Out of common decency, I helped by contacting his family and urging them to put someone in charge of his welfare, but his future is not my responsibility. I'm done."

"You're free," said Maureen.

"That's right," Helen said, "and with your forgiveness, I'll be fine. My life in Chicago is still there to take up again."

Maureen looked thoughtful. She said, "I feel free too. I feel freed of the grip that Theo's crime had on my soul. I always felt like a sister tainted by her brother's misdeeds. I wanted him to return so that we could talk and I could understand his actions and free myself from any guilt that I might have stopped him. Now I'll have to accept that I will never know. What I do know is that Jimmy is my only love, and we'll finish our lives together." She turned to Jimmy for confirmation, but he'd fallen asleep.

On the following Monday, Toby and I were invited to meet the chancellor. She wanted to thank us personally for recovering Wright's plans for a dome on Bascom Hall and gifting them to the university. She also wanted to thank us for our work assisting the university police in their investigation. Diane had briefed her thoroughly on both matters.

The Office of the Chancellor occupies an entire wing on the first floor of Bascom Hall. We arrived a few minutes early for our appointment, passed through security, and waited in an antechamber presided over by a male receptionist who carried himself with assumed authority. Perhaps he was the chief of staff. Precisely on the hour, he opened the door to the inner office, and with the gesture of an upturned palm, ushered us in. We found ourselves in a spacious, airy room with a high ceiling and lovely old oak trim. On the near side of the room was a long conference table in dark wood, on which the Frank Lloyd Wright drawings were displayed. The chancellor's desk was at the far end of the room, and in the middle was a homelike sitting area furnished with a small sofa, comfortable chairs, and a floor lamp.

The chancellor, a woman in her early sixties, rose from the chair behind her desk and strode briskly across the room to greet us. She was very tall, I noticed, almost as tall as Angie. She wore large, round-framed glasses with thick lenses that gave her an owlish mien. But her size and bearing suggested a larger, regal bird of prey, perhaps a falcon. She was the model of graciousness as she welcomed us, indicating that we should seat ourselves on the sofa, while she pulled up a chair. Something about her told me she would make short work of a visitor who displeased her. An agronomist by training, she had risen through the ranks from department chair to associate dean to dean, and then from dean to provost to chancellor. Nobody makes it to the top twig without ruffling a few feathers.

Yet her smile was warm and genuine. We shook hands. "Professor Barnes, it's good to meet you. And Mr. Sandler. You know, my calendar is filled with meetings I'd rather avoid, but I've been looking forward to this one." She pulled her chair closer to the sofa. "We owe you our deepest thanks for pointing the way toward a solution to the question of the bones. And now these wonderful Frank Lloyd Wright drawings!" She gestured toward the conference table. "I want to thank you on behalf of the university for this meaningful gift. Tell me more about how you found the drawings, and then I'll share with you an idea I'm brewing about what they might do for the university."

I let Toby tell the tale of how and where he discovered the Wright drawings. True to his word, he gave Arp full credit for the role he played in their discovery. He even summarized Arp's theory of what restoring the dome may have meant for Wright. "A new dome for the building in line of sight with the Capitol could symbolize a renewed partnership between the university and the state."

"That's exactly my own conclusion," said the chancellor. "It's the opportunity I've been waiting for to reboot what we call the Wisconsin Idea: 'The boundaries of the university are the boundaries of the state.' The partnership has a proud history but it's now in tatters, and it would be prudent to repair it before we lose the little state funding we still have. Strengthening the relationship is the number one goal in my next strategic plan. And the dome may be one way to do it. The Frank Lloyd Wright connection will open a lot of doors. Yes, we're going to build that dome."

"That's great news!" said Toby.

I said so too.

"But we're not going to use state money to do it. This is a perfect project for our next fundraising drive. Earlier today I met with one of our most important donors, Peter Meredith. I think you've met him. He mentioned your name."

"Yes, he's a graduate of art history," I said.

"That's right. He's as enthusiastic about this project as I am, and in fact, he's already made a generous pledge. Now, let me tell you my idea. For cochairs of the campaign, I'm planning to appoint a representative of the business world and a representative of the faculty. What's your opinion about appointing Professor Arp for the job? After all, he's the campus expert on Frank Lloyd Wright. From the other side, I'm thinking of naming Regent Reynolds. He's been one of our sharpest critics. He's not only from the business world but has served in the state legislature. He's the regent who was speaking when the flood upstairs occurred."

How could we forget? Toby whispered in my ear, "Mister Militant Ignorance himself."

I don't think she heard or noticed. "If I could get them to agree to work together," the chancellor said, "the symbolism would speak volumes."

We remained silent. She read my eyes. "What?"

"Have you met Professor Arp?" I asked.

"Not yet. Tell me."

"He's a brilliant scholar," I said, "but he's not exactly a 'people person.'"

"He's more of an ogre person," Toby said, sotto voce.

"I heard that," said the chancellor. Toby looked abashed.

"And judging by that talk he gave on the day of the flood," I continued, "Regent Reynolds has a similar personality. Frankly, they're both rather belligerent. It's hard to picture them working together." That was an understatement. I thought to myself: they would drag each other over a cliff like Sherlock Holmes and his arch enemy, Moriarty, locked in combat at the Reichenbach Falls. Aloud, I said, "What would you think of Dr. Meredith leading the drive?"

"Marvelous idea," said the chancellor, without missing a beat. "And the other two can be honorary cochairs with their names on the letterhead and never have to be in the same room together. We do that all the time." Her eyes narrowed behind her thick lenses. I could tell that she was reassessing me. "Nora," she said, "have you ever considered administrative work? You've got the skills."

I swallowed. "I haven't."

"Well, you should. You've got the cojones, too. Do you understand Spanish? Well, never mind." She folded her hands in her lap with the tips of her thumbs touching to form a tent. "There's going to be an opening next year for the chair of art history. I'd encourage you to apply." I thought I heard the flapping wings of a falcon circling in the sky.

I replied feebly, "I didn't know Professor Harrison was stepping down."

"He may not know it, either." Out came the talons, then they retracted. "But I'm sure he does. It's the norm to have three-year rotations for department chairs, and this fall he'll be entering his third year."

Toby was curious. "I didn't know that's how it worked. What's the normal term for deans?"

"It varies. Deans serve at the pleasure of the chancellor." She smiled.

In all innocence, he asked, "Is there a normal term for chancellors too?" He didn't mean anything by it. He just wanted to know.

"Chairs rotate; chancellors ascend." She was joking, of course. Wasn't she? There was a faraway look in her eyes.

I recalled my meeting with Doug Harrison in his office. He knew to the minute that his time as chair was running out. Having enjoyed a modest elevation of status that went with the position, he looked on returning to the classroom as a backward step in his career. That's why he was scanning the ads for job offers in administration.

"Usually," continued the chancellor, "chairs are chosen from within the department, but in the case of fractious departments, the dean can appoint one from outside. I'm not without influence with the dean."

Again I heard the flapping of wings. Effortlessly she glided to a landing.

"Once you have a few years as chair under your belt, we'll see where we can fit you in. I can't promise anything that far ahead, but we can always use people like you in Bascom."

It was all so complimentary, yet it felt like I was in her beak. I couldn't suppress a desperate wriggle on my sofa cushion.

"Thank you. That's extremely flattering, Chancellor. It would be an honor to be considered for a faculty position here or a position in the administration. My college can't begin to match the resources of this institution. But I've been very happy there."

Having said so, I felt sure that I would not be applying for a position at Madison. My happiness was rooted where I was, living with Toby in Bodega Bay and teaching at Sonoma College with colleagues who were my friends and who shared my priority for undergraduate teaching. If ever I had the urge to become a department chair, I would rather it be with them.

"We can make you happier," the chancellor said, moving on to her next target. It seemed as if her outspread wings cast a shadow over the sofa. "Now, Toby, I hope you'll be open to working with the campaign committee. We could make you the focus of a human-interest angle in the story of how we acquired the drawings. I'm wondering if you'd be willing to speak at fundraising events now and then?"

Toby was at a loss for words, which doesn't happen very often. He gulped and said, "What kind of events do you have in mind?"

"The first will be a launch of the fundraising campaign in Madison this fall, and then events wherever we have large alumni organizations.

San Francisco, Los Angeles, Chicago, the eastern cities. We'll cover your expenses, of course, and provide compensation. I can picture you and Professor Arp recounting how you bid against each other for Wright's desk and then ended up working together to find its secret cache."

I cringed at the thought of Toby harnessed to Magnus Arp in an endless round of reenactments. That would surely strain the limits of his forbearance. "I'll have to give that some thought," said Toby. "But I appreciate your confidence in me."

"Naturally," said the chancellor, "you two will have to talk things over. I only wanted to plant the seeds today for a future conversation."

There was a discreet rap of knuckles on the door. The receptionist stuck his head in and announced, "The photographer is here."

"Good. Send him in. We're just going to take some publicity shots for the university news service," she explained. "They'll be used in various university publications and offered to the press."

The photographer, a youngish man with a professional manner, arranged us around the conference table, as if we were looking at and handling the Wright drawings. In one shot, Toby was posed passing a drawing to the chancellor for inspection. Then we were asked to stand for a more formal portrait, the chancellor in the middle, towering over Toby and me, one on each side. I was thinking all the while about the chancellor's offer and feeling firm in my decision to decline. I had to admit, though, it was gratifying to be recruited by the top academic officer of a major university.

The photographer said, "Smile!" And I did.

"Okay, you can stop now," Toby said, as we walked down Bascom Hill.

"Stop what?"

"You're still smiling."

That's how I knew I'd made the right decision.

Postscripts

Hi, Nora,

I've been meaning to write, but I've had my hands full here. It's been a pain in the butt starting out as chair and trying to run a department in the middle of a pandemic. Because of COVID-19, we had to cancel the entire summer session and convert all our classes to remote learning. Then one glitch followed another. The older faculty are technophobes who can't figure out how to use Zoom. Everyone expects me, the medievalist, to fix things.

Speaking of faculty, or maybe I should say speaking of fixing things, Harrison finally landed an outside offer (at one of those fly-by-night, for-profit colleges) and announced he's leaving. I won't be sorry to see him go. His departure gives us an opportunity to fill a replacement position in the 19th or 20th century. I'm asking for permission to hire at the senior level. That's why I'm writing today, Nora. I hope that you will reconsider a move to Wisconsin and apply. Having spent that summer in Bodega Bay through our exchange, I realize how hard it would be for anyone to leave. It's an enchanting place. But there would be compensations. And it would be great to have you here in Madison! I'll keep you posted on developments concerning the job listing. There's not much other department news. Magnus Arp has finished his book and comes up for full professor next semester. I suppose he's earned it. Every department gets to have its resident crackpot, so he can be ours.

As ever,
Eve

Hi, Nora! I've got the best, best news. Bobby and I are expecting! God willing, I'll give birth to a baby girl in February! We're thrilled. We've known for a while, but we waited to tell the family until the doctor said the baby is healthy and growing well. I have to apologize that Mary knew before any Barnes did. In fact, she's the one who guessed I was pregnant. She noticed when I started refusing her fried eggs and reaching for, of all things, the belVita breakfast biscuits, the blandest food known to Irishmen. I didn't believe her, but when the nausea came daily, I got a home pregnancy test, and the proof was in the two red lines. You and Toby are going to be Aunt Nora and Uncle Toby!

We'll see you both next week for our regular Skype, but I wanted to write because there's something I want to say to just you, not in front of Bobby or Mary. I want to thank you for how much you helped me two years ago. I was letting fear stall my relationship with Bobby. It was in Madison with you and Toby that I worked through it. When I returned to Ireland in August, I was sure. I'm so glad we were able to have you and the whole family here for a fall wedding, and wasn't it fun? There was no COVID then. We could go to restaurants and pubs and enjoy all that's great about Achill Island. A year later, Ireland shut down, and we're still not open. With the pubs closed, Bobby can't play with his group, and he misses his friends, but the thought of an expanded family makes sticking to home easier. We're fixing up a nursery and childproofing the house.

I hope you'll be able to come for the baby's baptism in spring or summer, but we have to wait to see what COVID does. Anyhow, whenever you come, I'll show you the garden I was dreaming of when we walked through the public gardens in Madison. When I told Mary how much it meant to me, she helped me find old-fashioned rose bushes that bloom from spring to fall and don't need deadheading. The bushes are young and short, but they're thick with red roses. Now I love the way the place looks when you turn into the driveway, and it feels more like mine. Ours, actually.

Things have turned out so differently from what I imagined. I found out that I don't have the temperament of a cheese-maker, not at all. Mary's the one who is meticulous, patient, and happy in the solitude of the cheese room. So, she runs the cheese business, which has expanded in spite of the COVID recession. Bobby and I share care of the sheep. He takes the lead on breeding, grazing, and monitoring their health. I'm in charge of milking, barn life, and lambing. We all pitch in at shearing time, and we're always consulting each other. Things could change when the baby comes, but we'll plan for that in our weekly meetings. We have a beautiful life, and we're glad to be bringing a little girl into it. Please send Toby our love. We can't wait to see you both, hopefully in spring, around the baptismal font.

Your loving sister,
Angie

Hi, Nora. Sorry it's been so long. I've been remiss in keeping up with my social correspondence. But I thought of you today, as it's the 50th anniversary of the Sterling Hall bombing. There was a story about it in the paper. Of course, hardly anyone who remembers it is here now. The campus was dead quiet. It's been a ghost town since the pandemic rules went into effect. Have you heard? Alan Knight is appealing his conviction. We'll see what happens. I don't think he's going anywhere any time soon. Hope you and Toby are masking and social distancing. You don't want to catch this thing.

    Take care,
    Diane
    P.S. Daryl says hello.

Dear Nora,

I know I promised to write, and here I've let two years slide by
without keeping my promise. Tonight I made a deal with myself that I
won't go to bed until I finish this letter. So here goes.

It's been a strange day. I think I saw Theo. I know the FBI says he's
dead and that the DNA proved it. I know that his bones are sitting
somewhere in an evidence box and that Alan is sitting in prison for
what he's done. And I know that the mind plays tricks. But, Nora, I'm
telling you that I saw him today, Theo Kearn, or else his ghost. And I
had to tell someone.

Let me back up a little. I've been in Madison since June, living
with Beth and Anne. You met them at their July 4th picnic when you
were here. Beth didn't want me living alone in Chicago with the
COVID-19 menace raging and killing seniors, who seem the most
vulnerable. Here I don't have to leave the house and hardly do. Beth
does the shopping and gets me what I need. They both go out of their
way to keep me safe. I'm very grateful.

I decided to go out today for a special reason. Today was the 50th
anniversary of the bombing of the Army Math Research Center in
Sterling Hall. I thought there would be some kind of memorial
service or ceremony, but there was nothing in the paper about one.
That didn't seem right. There's a memorial plaque now on the
building. I decided I would go there and bow my head for a minute of
silence in memory of the person who died in the bombing. It was the
least I could do.

I drove to campus, parked in Helen C. White, and started walking
up Bascom Hill. It really does get steeper every year, as people say. The
university is under lockdown, and the campus was deserted—except
for this one man who seemed as old as me, slowly making his way up
the hill ahead of me. I was wearing a face mask, and so was he. He was
also wearing a baseball cap pulled down low on his forehead, so I
couldn't see much of his face. But something about him seemed familiar.
I hung back and followed at a distance. I don't think he noticed me.

He passed Bascom Hall and turned down Charter St. at the corner, heading toward Sterling. I could tell he was walking with a purpose. At Sterling, he went directly to the side of the building where the plaque is mounted, and he stood before it motionless, reading. He must have read it several times over. You've seen it, haven't you? It gives the date and time of the bombing and memorializes the research scientist who was killed. The plaque mentions the experiment he was doing, gives his age, 33, and says that he was married and had three young children.

The stranger raised a hand to his face as if to wipe away a tear, or was that my imagination? For by now I had conjured the face of Theo Kearn under the mask and cap. I watched him turn and move away. His size, his stance, his walk—were Theo's. His pilgrimage today, which I alone witnessed, stamped my certainty. You can say he was a product of my imagination. He was that, and more than that. At the time I felt it in my bones that he was Theo. Though now as I write this, I confess I'm beginning to have doubts. I'm losing him.

I lost him at the site, too. When he was finished reading the plaque, I stepped up and read it to myself, then stood for a minute with my head bowed, as I had planned. When I went back out to the street, he was gone. I looked up and down Charter St., but he had disappeared.

Make of this what you will, Nora. It's my bedtime now. I wish you and Toby good health.

I'm enclosing a cartoon from the *New Yorker* that Anne asked me to send to Toby. She says she enjoyed talking physics with him and he might get a kick out of it.

Peace,
Helen

The cartoon: A man is sitting in the waiting room of a pet hospital, reading a magazine. A woman one seat away is holding a little dog with an anti-scratch cone on its head. The man looks up at a veterinarian, who's wearing scrubs and has a stethoscope around her neck. The caption reads: "About your cat, Mr. Schrödinger—I have good news and bad news."

Authors' Note

When we mentioned to friends that we were writing a mystery set at the university, they assumed that it would be a roman à clef, in which each character has a counterpart in real life. That isn't the case. Previously in the series we established that our narrator is an art historian, so when Nora comes to Madison on a faculty exchange, the Department of Art History is her home. But the department in the novel is a made-up place, and so are its denizens. The same holds true for university officials, who are identified by title, not by name. We generally stick to the facts when describing the larger setting and actual events, but we do take small liberties. For example, the two plays that Nora and Toby attend at the American Players Theatre were not on the schedule in 2018 but were produced in earlier seasons.

Ironically, some of the factual aspects of the novel may seem fictitious to the reader. For instance, there really is a cistern in the attic of Bascom Hall. It has been there since the nineteenth century, and it saved the building from burning down when its wooden dome caught fire in 1916. Frank Lloyd Wright was a student at the university in 1886 and knew the building when it still had its dome, but he never designed a replacement for it. However, in his original plan for Monona Terrace, he designed a glass dome for the rooftop esplanade. Had the building been constructed using that design, its dome would have echoed the dome of the State Capitol two blocks away. That possibility was the springboard for a fanciful subplot involving Frank Lloyd Wright and domes.

When we first learned of the cistern in the Bascom attic, we immediately thought it would make a good place to hide a body. The plot idea was reinforced by the actual case of a skeleton found in a chimney in a store in downtown Madison in 1989. It took better than three decades to identify the remains. On May 13, 2024, as we were proofreading this text, the news broke that Lindsey Ludden, a Madison police detective, working with the DNA Doe Project, had given a name and face to the victim. Whoever killed him is still at large.

The Thai Pavilion, which Nora and Angie visit, has become a popular local landmark. It arrived in Madison in 2001 as a gift to the university from its alumni club in Thailand. The campus had no safe place to put it, but a suitable site was found at the Olbrich Botanical Gardens, where the pavilion stands today.

The Madison Reunion, a homecoming party and a conference on Madison in the 1960s, was held at the Memorial Union in the summer of 2018. The reunion, which drew a thousand participants, is the occasion that brings our alumni characters back to campus. Betsy attended the conference and was deeply moved by the eyewitness accounts of former students who had been anguished by the Vietnam War and by the violence of the infamous protest against it, the bombing of Sterling Hall on August 24, 1970.

The bombing was a traumatic event for the city and the campus. Michael was teaching in the summer session at the time, completing his first year as an instructor in the Department of English. An argument broke out in his class the next day between students who condemned the attack and those who defended it. The most ardent defender was a young woman with frizzy blond hair. She stood up to make a point and left a lasting impression. He can still recall her name and the dress she wore.

Soon after the bombing, the FBI identified four suspects. One by one, three of them were caught, tried, convicted, and sent to prison. The fourth has never been found. He appears here as a fictional character based in part on information available in the public record. We have changed his name.

Acknowledgments

The following individuals generously gave their time and provided information that was indispensable for the writing of this book. We thank Daniel Einstein, historic and cultural resources manager at the UW–Madison Division of Facilities Planning and Management, for leading Betsy on a safari to the Bascom attic to inspect the cistern described in the novel; Aaron Elkins (our favorite mystery writer) for fielding questions related to forensic anthropology and for his support throughout this series; David Hinden, former lawyer and teacher of biology and chemistry, for information on DNA and points of law, as well as for brotherly encouragement; Marc Lovicott, executive director of communications for the UW–Madison Police Department, for information on the workings of the university police; Carla Moore, RN, former coordinator for bone marrow transplants, UW Hospital, for information on transporting human tissue on commercial airline flights; Ben and Judy Sidran, for creating and hosting the Madison Reunion and for sharing documents about it; Julie Laundrie, public records custodian at the City of Madison Police Department, for communications on "the skeleton in the chimney case"; Sue Riseling, former chief of UW–Madison Police, for details about her workplace and for modeling an ethical, humane university police officer with a sense of humor; and Anne Rhyme, for information about Madison gardens that arose from her work as a master gardener and volunteer for Olbrich Gardens.

Conversations with friends who were at UW–Madison in the turbulent years, 1965 to 1970, anchored our story in lived experience. For their vivid memories and candor, we wish to thank the following, who were then at the beginning of their careers at UW–Madison: Ed Friedman of political science; Joe and the late Jo Elder of sociology; Lee Pondrom of physics; Richard Knowles, Cyrena Pondrom, Joseph Wiesenfarth, and the late Charles Scott of English; and David Ward, from geography, later provost and chancellor. Friends who were students either at Madison or elsewhere during the era also contributed distinct memories: Richard Begam, Kathy Dauck, Thomas Schaub, Ron Wallace, Elizabeth Whalley, and the late Susan Friedman (all later faculty or staff in the English department); Judith Leavitt, Mariamne Whatley, and Nancy Worcester of gender and women's studies; and Judith Ward of the Waisman Center.

We also wish to thank supportive groups. The Feel Good Golfers, who have played weekly for thirty years on the city's Glenway Golf Course, have always discussed our writing projects, and many could speak of their Vietnam era memories. In addition to friends previously mentioned, we thank Colleen Cleary, Marilyn Graves, Sharon James, Janet Laube, Linda Maraniss, Linda Baldwin O'Hern, Susan Pigorsch, Clare Radtke, Francine Tompkins, Julie Underwood, and Jan Wheaton.

Members of Betsy's walking group and reading group recalled the years of protest. Thanks to walkers Barb Bryce, Susan Cambria, Carol Cantwell, Nancy Daly, Genevieve Murtaugh, Kim Vergeront, Nan Youngerman, Janet Laube, and, again, Judy, Colleen, and Anne. Sincere thanks to the reading group for their encouragement and ideas: Jane Camerini, Ellen Henningsen, Margot Kennard, Peg Larabell, Charlotte Meyer, Giovanna Miceli Jeffries, Susan Murray, Mary Pinkerton, Melissa Reed, Carol Rubin, JoAnn Skloot, and Sylvia Stalker.

There's a Gourmet Group, too. For nearly five decades, we've met bimonthly with a small group of friends to cook, talk food, and eat our concoctions. Playful conversations in the kitchen and at table have given us everything from fictional menus to plot ideas. Hats (or toques) off to Ken Robbins, Louise Root-Robbins, Buck and Anne Rhyme, and Ben and Judy. Pam Gardiner introduced us to the group before leaving Madison to become managing director of the Miami City Ballet. She maintains ties with her classmates from the War years at UW–Madison and shared with us her recollections of anti-war activities.

Our dear friend Helen Aarli passed away before we began this book, but we're glad that we discussed politics, nonviolence, and protest with her in her last months. She inspired our character Helen Foreman. The real-life Helen had none of the character's brashness, but her quick affection, joie de vivre, and passion for social justice flowed into our imagining of Helen Foreman. We thank her daughters, Lisa and Marta Aarli, for sharing Helen with us in life and in memory.

There are friends you tell everything to (except your plot twists) and who give you the support to get through stretches of enforced solitude. Sometimes they offer tips on writing or life that you incorporate so thoroughly that you forget their origin. In Madison, this group includes Bertie Donovan, Aleen Grabow, JoAnn and Bob Skloot, Lewis and Judy Leavitt, Carla Moore, Sylvia Stalker, Tom Schaub and Jan Beaver, Peg and Ron Wallace, and the loyal members of the breakfast club, who wish to remain anonymous. Howard and Jean Gelman are in the network, though in Australia now. From Switzerland, Kim Hays, a close friend and fellow mystery writer, provided valuable coaching on the crafts of writing and publication. From the East and West Coasts and from Belgium and Bali, our siblings, nieces and nephews, cousins, in-laws, and the next generation shared love and laughter and kept us light-hearted.

In bringing this book to fruition, we wish to thank Dennis Lloyd, director of the University of Wisconsin Press, for advice that helped us shape the narrative; Lynn Miller, author of *Death of a Department Chair*, for useful suggestions on how to revise the manuscript; copyeditor Michelle Wing, whose research was as careful as her ear for a strong sentence; Adam Mehring, design and production manager, and Jennifer Conn, art director, for giving the book and the series a distinctive look; Alison Shay, publicity manager, for getting the word out; and most of all, Sheila McMahon, managing editor, who shepherded the entire project with sensitivity, clear communication, and attention to detail.

Finally, we owe thanks to those authors who provided background information. We found the following books on Frank Lloyd Wright particularly useful: Paul E. Sprague, ed., *Frank Lloyd Wright and Madison: Eight Decades of Artistic and Social Interaction* (Madison: Elvehjem Museum of Art, 1990); David Mollenhoff and Mary Jane Hamilton, eds., *Frank Lloyd Wright's Monona Terrace: The Enduring Power of a Civic Vision* (Madison: The University of Wisconsin Press, 1999); and Alberto Izzo and Camillo Gubitosi, eds., *Frank Lloyd Wright: Three-quarters of a Century of Drawings* (New York: Horizon Press, 1981).

Among the many fine books and articles on the protest years at UW–Madison and the bombing of Sterling Hall, we relied most on: David Maraniss, *They Marched into Sunlight: War and Peace, Vietnam and America, October 1967* (New York: Simon & Schuster, 2003); Tom Bates, *Rads: The 1970 Bombing of the Army Math Research Center at the University of Wisconsin and Its Aftermath* (New York: HarperCollins, 1992); and Matthew Levin, *Cold War University: Madison and the New Left in the Sixties* (Madison: University of Wisconsin Press, 2013). The film documentary *The War at Home* (1979) brought the protest years in Madison to life.

The cartoon described by Nora at the end of the novel is by Benjamin Schwartz, published in the *New Yorker*, March 30, 2015.

Any errors of fact are solely our responsibility and are not attributable to our sources or informants.

Books by Betsy Draine and Michael Hinden

A NORA BARNES AND TOBY SANDLER MYSTERY

Murder in Lascaux
The Body in Bodega Bay
Death on a Starry Night
The Dead of Achill Island

A Castle in the Backyard: The Dream of a House in France
The Walnut Cookbook by Jean-Luc Toussaint (translators and editors)

BETSY DRAINE AND MICHAEL HINDEN are emeritus professors of English at the University of Wisconsin–Madison and the co-authors of the Nora Barnes and Toby Sandler mystery series. Their first collaboration was a memoir, *A Castle in the Backyard: The Dream of a House in France* (2002), inspired by their twenty summers in the Dordogne in southwest France.

MICHAEL HINDEN won a Kiekhofer Award for Excellence in Teaching in 1972 and was named Bascom Professor of Integrated Liberal Studies in 2004. At the University of Wisconsin–Madison, he taught modern drama in the Department of English and literature and the arts in the Integrated Liberal Studies Program. He chaired the ILS Program from 1981 to 1984 and served as Associate Dean of International Studies from 1991 to 2003. His publications include *Long Day's Journey into Night: Native Eloquence* (1990).

BETSY DRAINE served as Chair of Women's Studies (1989–92) and Vice Provost for Academic Affairs (1992–99) at the University of Wisconsin–Madison. The focus of her administrative work was on gender equity and work climate. She taught courses in women's literature, literary theory, and modern British and American fiction and is the author of *Substance under Pressure: Artistic Coherence and Evolving Form in the Novels of Doris Lessing* (1983). She won the 1990 Chancellor's Award for Excellence in Teaching and the 2002 Phi Beta Kappa Teaching Award.